ADVANCE PRAISE FOR

Portraits at an Exhibition

"Patrick E. Horrigan's *Portraits at an Exhibition* explores the power of portraiture to transport us into distant worlds of imagination and desire. The celebrated paintings featured in the book are far from static images to be dissected and tamed by art historical analysis. Instead, they function as shimmering mirrors and portals, leading Horrigan's characters and readers into deeply felt journeys of the mind, senses, and spirit. Like the Renaissance painters whose works the novel so acutely reproduces, Horrigan's subjects are men and women who struggle to shape their own destinies even as they confront the vagaries of chance, the haunting shadows of loss and doubt, and the relentless pull of their own desires. *Portraits at an Exhibition* speaks to the strange magic—the wonderfully unpredictable and far-reaching adventure—of the aesthetic encounter."

—MARIO DIGANGI, PROFESSOR OF ENGLISH AND LESBIAN/GAY STUDIES AT LEHMAN COLLEGE AND THE GRADUATE CENTER, CUNY

"A masterful debut novel that calls into question the barriers between artist, subject and admirer. *Portraits at an Exhibition* is one of those rare novels that makes the reader both think and feel simultaneously, a vibrant and intellectually challenging exploration of love, family, illness, loss and art, told through five of the world's most celebrated paintings."

—JACOB M. APPEL, AUTHOR OF *THE BIOLOGY OF LUCK*

"*Portraits at an Exhibition* is a poignant rumination on the potential of antiquated paintings to speak to the conundrums of modern existence. Evocatively weaving fiction into history, Horrigan sketches the infinitely ambiguous boundaries between self and other, art and life, hope and despair, love and loathing, as reflected in and refracted through his rich cast of characters and the old master portraits upon which they gaze. A refreshing balm to our vainglorious era of selfies, *Portraits at an Exhibition* demonstrates, as Proust proffered, that 'museums are dwellings that house only thoughts.'"

—PAUL B. FRANKLIN, ART HISTORIAN AND SPECIALIST ON MARCEL DUCHAMP

Portraits at an Exhibition

a novel

Patrick E. Horrigan

LETHE PRESS
MAPLE SHADE, NEW JERSEY

Published by LETHE PRESS
118 Heritage Ave, Maple Shade, NJ 08052
lethepressbooks.com

Copyright © 2015 PATRICK E. HORRIGAN

ISBN 978-1-59021-4770

No part of this work may be reproduced or utilized in any form or by any means, electronic or mechanical, including photocopying, microfilm, and recording, or by any information storage and retrieval system, without permission in writing from the Author or Publisher.

Cover and interior design
by MATT CRESSWELL (INKSPIRAL DESIGN)

LIBRARY OF CONGRESS CIP DATA

Horrigan, Patrick E.
 Portraits at an exhibition : a novel / Patrick E. Horrigan.
        pages ; cm
 ISBN 978-1-59021-477-0 (softcover : acid-free paper)
 1. Young men--Fiction. 2. Art--Exhibitions--Fiction.
      3. Self-realization--Fiction.
  4. Self-actualization (Psychology)--Fiction.
     5. Psychological fiction. I.
            Title.
      PS3608.O7685P67 2015
          813'.6--dc23
                           2015002521

for Eduardo

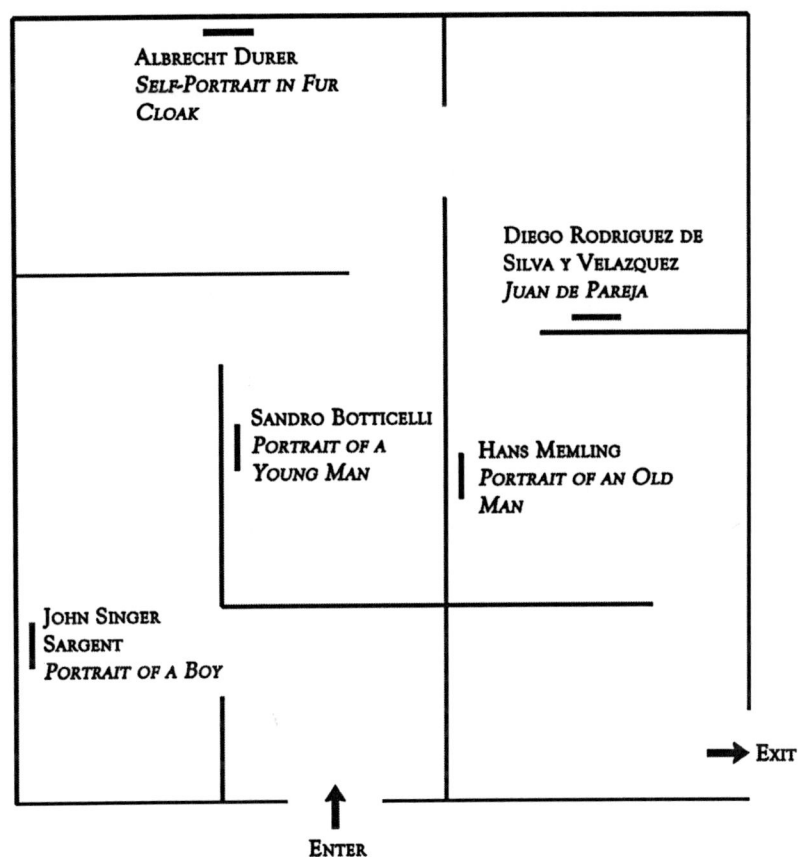

FLOOR PLAN

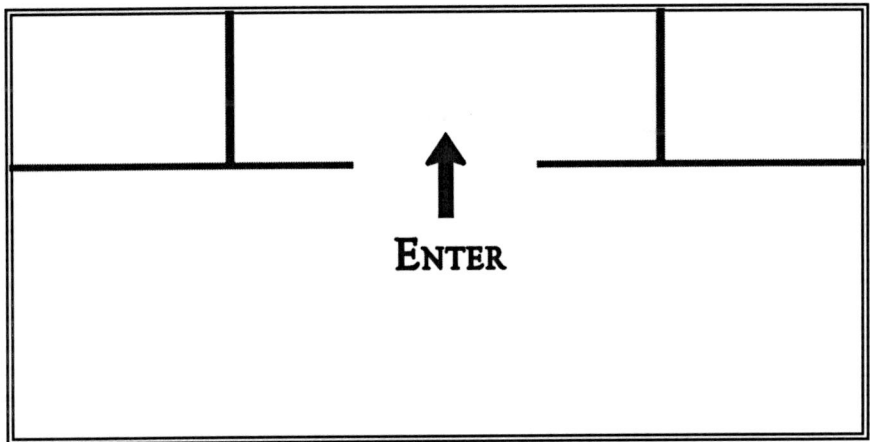

MOTIONS OF THE MIND
The Renaissance Portrait and Its Legacy

During the Renaissance in Europe, the portrait as we know it—the head-and-shoulders likeness of an individual human being—came of age. The demand for portraiture, starting in the fifteenth century, was made possible by several technical developments, including the dis A guy and a girl sauntered up, arm in arm, and planted themselves right in front of Robin, blocking his view of the text on the wall just inside the entrance to the exhibition. Pushy straight couples, he thought, they act like they rule the world. He stepped a few feet to the left. including the discovery of unified perspective and the use of oil-based paint, both of which permitted ever more lifelike depictions of the human form. (Though he had to admit the guy was kind of cute.) Renaissance writers, furthermore, championed the idea of human worth, lending philosophical justification to the depiction of "ordinary" people. He could still see them out of the corner of his eye. In his

1486 TREATISE ON THE DIGNITY OF MAN, Now they were kissing! Had they come to see the exhibition or to force other people to look at them? **PICO DELLA MIRANDOLA IMAGINES GOD ADDRESSING ADAM AS FOLLOWS:** Maybe he should have stayed home. **"I HAVE PLACED YOU AT THE VERY CENTER OF THE WORLD,** But if he'd stayed home, he would have just spent the day freaking out. He thought of the blood oozing from his penis last night. **SO THAT FROM THAT VANTAGE POINT YOU MAY WITH GREATER EASE GLANCE ROUND ABOUT YOU ON ALL THAT THE WORLD CONTAINS.** He was afraid he'd done it this time. He was afraid his luck had run out. **WE HAVE MADE YOU A CREATURE NEITHER OF HEAVEN NOR OF EARTH, NEITHER MORTAL NOR IMMORTAL,** After years of having unsafe sex and narrowly escaping catastrophe again and again, he was afraid his long-delayed but seemingly inevitable rendezvous with HIV had finally arrived. **IN ORDER THAT YOU MAY, AS THE FREE AND PROUD SHAPER OF YOUR OWN BEING, FASHION YOURSELF IN THE FORM YOU MAY PREFER."** He stepped a few feet further to his left, hoping to put the amorous couple out of sight and mind. **THIS NOTION OF HUMANS AS THE CENTER OF GOD'S CREATION WITH A FREE WILL OF THEIR OWN** But why begrudge the pleasure they take in being together? he wondered. It's not their fault I might be a walking time-bomb. **HELPED JUSTIFY THE APPETITES OF A NASCENT MIDDLE CLASS** It's not their fault my love life sucks. **WHOSE SELF-REGARD WAS FURTHER BOOSTED BY STEADILY EXPANDING COLONIAL ADVENTURES IN THE NEW WORLD AND INCREASING SOCIAL MOBILITY AT HOME.**

Still, he resented their nonchalance.

PORTRAITS SERVED VARIOUS FUNCTIONS IN THE EARLY MODERN PERIOD. THEY REINFORCED A SITTER'S SOCIAL STATUS, RECORDED WORLDLY ACCOMPLISHMENTS, ASSERTED THE PECULIARITIES AND PERFECTIONS OF FACE AND BODY, AND HINTED AT THE VAGARIES OF CHARACTER. DESPITE CHANGING SOCIAL CONDITIONS AND AESTHETIC TRENDS, PORTRAITS HAVE CONTINUED TO SERVE MUCH THE SAME FUNCTIONS EVER SINCE. Oh brother, he said to himself, the slickness of blockbuster exhibitions! He could raise plenty of objections to that last sentence if he allowed himself—he had a gut resistance to the whole "Family of Man" approach to art history—but there was also something obscurely comforting, he felt, in the narrative's embrace. **TODAY, PORTRAITURE IS UBIQUITOUS: PEOPLE STARE OUT AT US FROM NEWSPAPERS, MAGAZINES, AND WEBSITES; MOVIES AND TV SHOWS CONTAIN COUNTLESS "CLOSE-UPS"; OUR OWN FACES ADORN ID CARDS, PASSPORTS, DRIVER'S LICENSES, AND ONLINE NETWORKING SITES; SNAPSHOTS FILL OUR WALLETS AND PHOTO ALBUMS; PICTURES OF FAMILY AND FRIENDS COVER OUR WALLS AT HOME AND OUR DESKS AT WORK.** He thought of his desk at work. He had finally put away the picture of Brian after weeks of pretending it wasn't really over. Now there was just the one of Stephen and himself when they were seven years old, dressed for Halloween as Batman and Robin (he always came second—"Little Squirt" Stephen used to call him), and the photo of the two of them, arm in arm, on the day of their high school graduation. **THE VAST MAJORITY OF THESE PORTRAITS ARE PHOTOGRAPHIC.** "Bookends," Leonore remarked upon seeing it the other day, and he pictured a row of books falling over at one end like dominoes. **THE CAMERA'S ABILITY TO PRODUCE AN ACCURATE MIRROR REFLECTION OF WHATEVER IT SEES IN THE WORLD IS PERHAPS THE MOST VITAL LEGACY OF THE RENAISSANCE PORTRAIT.**

But he was getting impatient. He wanted to stop reading and start looking. He wasn't in the mood for grand narratives and windy theoretical pronouncements. He wanted to be distracted, taken out of himself. He wanted images and stories of other people. Faces and bodies. Flesh and blood. Oil on canvas.

ONE OF THE GENRE'S GREATEST PRACTITIONERS, LEONARDO DA VINCI, NOTED HOW THE "MOTIONS OF THE MIND," THOUGH INVISIBLE, COULD NEVERTHELESS BE SUGGESTED BY THE NUANCED RENDERING OF FACIAL EXPRESSION AND POSTURE. ACCORDINGLY, HIS MOST FAMOUS PORTRAIT, THE *MONA LISA*, WITH HER NOTORIOUSLY ENIGMATIC SMILE,

HAS PROVOKED A STAGGERING RANGE OF INTERPRETATIONS. THE UNCANNY ABILITY OF A PORTRAIT TO PERSUADE US OF THE REAL PRESENCE HERE AND NOW OF SOMEONE LONG DEAD OR DISTANT IN TIME AND SPACE CONTINUES TO FASCINATE US, Maybe that's what I need, he thought—not just a temporary distraction, but the ultimate escape! **PERHAPS ESPECIALLY WHEN KNOWLEDGE OF THE SITTER'S IDENTITY AND OF THE PAINTING'S ORIGINAL PURPOSE HAVE BEEN LOST.** But where would I go? **WE FEEL THE ALLURE OF THE PERSON IN THE PAINTING** How would I get there? **AND CONJURE UP IN OUR MINDS A PERSONALITY AND A LIFE BASED ON THE PRECIOUS BUT FEW SHARDS OF INFORMATION LEFT TO US.** And would I have to go it alone? **IN SO DOING, WE ENGAGE WITH PORTRAITURE AT ITS DEEPEST, MOST HUMAN LEVEL.**

Robin turned from the wall text and headed toward the first room of the exhibition, devoted (counterintuitively, he thought) to portraiture *after* the Renaissance. He stopped at the threshold. His eyes fell upon a large, dark portrait of a little boy and a woman reading, hung directly opposite the entrance. Feeling a mysterious and instantaneous kinship with the child in the picture (Little Squirt, he thought; I will always come last), he made his advance.

JOHN SINGER SARGENT (1856-1925)
PORTRAIT OF A BOY, 1890
OIL ON CANVAS

JOHN SINGER SARGENT
PORTRAIT OF A BOY

Capt. Hull was pacing the quarter-deck with short, quick steps, trying to look cool, but inwardly on fire with excitement. This might calm him down, she thought. *But the shot of the enemy began to take effect, and the impatience of the gunners grew more intense.* It wasn't her idea of an improving book for a boy, but he had no patience for Little Lord Fauntleroy. *Lieut. Morris, the second in command, asked leave to respond with a broadside.* She had prevailed in getting him to put on his black velvet suit, though he complained mightily when she tied the bow around his neck. John agreed he looked splendid. "Like a fairy prince," he said. But she preferred him with long hair. Augustus merely made fun of her, saying something about the infant Jesus having His hair cut. Well I suppose it had to be done, she thought wistfully, if he's going to sit for his portrait. *"Not yet," responded Capt. Hull, with cool decision.* He was listening. He was still. Thank Heaven she had got his attention. "Difficult but never quite impossible," she always said of him. He had Gus' spunk, no denying that, but she hoped he would grow up to be a finer man than her husband. After all, he was closer to her than to anyone else. She had given him her maiden name, Homer, in honor of her father. Poor Papa. That awful Christmas. Homer was an infant. She was right to have taken him with her to Roxbury to share her mother's grief, she couldn't be faulted for that, but she had to admit it was a relief to be separated from Gus. And in spite of her own deep sorrow, she believed her health had actually improved that year. In a week they would sail to Europe, she and Homer and her mother. Another six months apart from Gus.

Then the smothered excitement in Hull's breast broke out. She knew what he and his friends said about her behind her back: "disagreeable," "sharp-tongued," "an animated clothes rack," "a hotel sofa." Oh they could be cruel! They said Gus did better work when she was not there. Well, if she was such an impediment to his work, why didn't he leave her? She sometimes felt he was as childish as Homer. Night after night, at the beer parlor on Broadway, he and his friends would carry on: singing songs, calling each other names, laughing like zanies. When she complained he would shoot back, "The pursuit of happiness is an inalienable right, God-given, one and indivisible," getting up on his haunches (he must have been drunk), "and I'm damned if I don't think I have the right to be!" "And what rights do I have?" was on the tip of her tongue, but she pursued the argument no further. Instead of sympathy and patience, her condition—the problems with her hearing, the anemia, the constant fatigue—only inspired ridicule. She overheard Augustus tell Stanford that marriage would be the beginning of his troubles. They laughed and patted each other on the back and went out into the garden for a smoke. His "troubles"! Men didn't know the meaning of the word! She'd had two miscarriages since Homer was born, and none of them had any idea how she suffered. The operation during her first one lasted more than an hour, and it was sheer, blind torture. The bleeding was much greater than she expected. In her delirium she felt death would be a relief. Afterward, all reminders of the ordeal were removed. No one showed her the baby.

Conversation was restricted to happier subjects. "You had better decide to chase away the little blue devils," the doctor scolded her. "You'll have another," he said; "it was an accident." But to her it felt more like a failure than an accident—*her failure* to do what a woman is expected to do. And Augustus was hard at work the next day, his spirits as bright as ever.

She knew he had other women. It was the Frenchman in him. They posed for him naked, flirted with him, and he succumbed to their charms. He spent evenings and sometimes whole nights at the studio. He even dared to joke in her presence about converting to Mormonism! Davida was his favorite. He praised her high forehead, her handsome Greek nose, her veil-like eyelids, her lithe Amazonian body—qualities she herself possessed. But he'd grown tired of her. She was 42. The truth is she'd never been dead in love with him. Still, she tried to fill her place as wife. She would carry on the maintenance of their home, though it wasn't easy, especially now that they were in the midst of moving. "I beg of you not to come down from the high place you hold in my heart," he crooned the other night, when she wanted to start a row. "If I hold such a prominent place in your heart, then why—" she started, but she dared not burden him with her discontent. She saw the futility of that early on in their marriage, even though it was *her* money that supported them in those days, *her* parents' generosity, before his success with the Farragut monument. After that, the cone of silence fell over everything. Never could she speak her mind. "Don't mouth me!" he would shout, and she had no choice but to withdraw. There were now so few people she could let it out upon; she kept everything bottled up. Except Rosie. She could share her feelings with Rosie, for she had lost her son the same year Homer was born. Her loving, sympathetic presence was a comfort. And Homer. He was a great comfort and pleasure, when he minded her. He was listening with intent.

"Hull her, boys! Hull her!" he shouted; and the crew, catching up the cry, made the decks ring with shouts of "Hull her!" as they rapidly loaded and let fly again.

"Augusta, I'm putting you into it. Stay as you are; just keep on reading. You're perfect like that. Homer, you have a fine head."

Deep down in the cock-pit of the "Guerriere," Capt. Orne, who had been listening to the muffled thunder of the cannonade at long range, suddenly heard a tremendous explosion from the opposing frigate.

mister sargent walked backward and then forward and jabbed his paintbrush at the picture like a sword and the carpet underneath his feet was red and brown with leaves and flowers and cups and he was big and fat and he got angry when he punched him and rammed his head into his big fat belly and mama said homer shame on you mister sargent is a friend of your father visiting from london five thousand miles across the sea and he jumped up and down and ran in circles and said are we sailing to london and mister sargent asked mama what music did you bring and she said foray he said wonderful a very good friend of mine and he didnt like foray he wanted the maple leaf rag and mister sargent made him sit in the chair and he kicked his legs and flapped his arms like a goose and he said mama im a goose and mama said homer you are not a goose and mister sargent said if the goose dont sit still im going to sit on top of the goose and he flapped his wings and mister sargent grabbed his arms and squeezed his legs and said homer thats enough and then he turned around and said alright now im going to flatten the goose and sat on top of him and he screamed and mama said homer im taking you home if you cant behave and he wanted to go outside and tie his scooter to the back step of the bus and ride down fifth avenue but mama said you will do no such thing you could get yourself killed and mister sargent said augusta why dont you read him a story and mama said i brought blue jackets of 1812 and he said read the constitution and the gurrair and she read the story of the ships and all the fighting and the fire and explosions and blood and dead men

he was having his picture painted today

"*I heard a tremendous shock on deck, and was told that the mizzen-mast was shot away.*"

There was something heavy about her, Sargent thought. Amazonian. Handsome. Eyes almost black, eyebrows dark and thick, nose straight and large, jaw square. Her clothes were heavy and drab, though the flower at her bosom gave a touch of fine femininity. When she smiled, a much lighter attractiveness took over her face. Poor woman, to be saddled with a child like that. Immature for his age. Startlingly self-possessed. Now, after making that awful scene, the boy was still. He resented a little the way they strode into the studio this afternoon, which immediately threw him off balance. Abruptly she said how sorry she was to hear the news about his father, and he froze. She carried on as if they shared some sort of intimate understanding, saying she still remembered so vividly the day her *own* dear father had died ten years ago. "It was Christmas Day," she said; "such an awful Christmas." She made him feel things he had no use for this afternoon. He thought of the little portrait drawing he made of his father when he was five, which had dropped out of his mother's letter last night. He remembered how his father depended on his letters, and how infrequently he had written in the last five years. His achievements had been the subject dearest to his father's heart. A surprising intimacy had grown up between them. Every night during his last months, he would lead the old man from the dinner table, sit alone with him, and smoke until it was time to put him to bed. Proudly he would say to the servants, "I am going to sit and smoke with my son John." But he was away in Paris doing portrait commissions when the end came. He hated to think of it, much less make an attempt to share his feelings with acquaintances. He never looked outside his family for emotional comfort. He had his sisters and sometimes his mother for that. And frankly, he was not menaced by this urge for confession, this rage for introspection. He distrusted any direct statement of feeling. Women tended to go in for that sort of thing, especially women like Augusta—the sick, forever suffering, frustrated kind. He thought of his own mother's unending, indefinable illnesses—headaches and sore throat, fatigue and chills that kept them chasing over half the globe in search of mild climates, never settling in one place long enough to become familiar, much less intimate, with the people who lived there. His father suffered more than any of them perhaps, putting aside his medical career, his writing, and his drawing, all because she insisted they keep moving. But it wasn't only *her* fault. His father let it happen. He had never been sprightly, and with age he became even less so. Eventually self-denial overwhelmed all his ambition and curiosity—except for his interest in art. Sargent derived his own restraint, he knew, from his father. He thanked Augusta for her condolences, but what else was there to say?

There she sat, stolidly behind Homer, her head bent toward the page, reading aloud. He could accomplish her quickly. All of it, in fact, would work nicely as a kind of sketch, except for Homer's head and hands, which he would put in last. Otherwise nothing too finished, nothing too fussy or polished. That seemed, somehow, in keeping with the boy himself—manic, aggressive, demanding—though he was very pretty indeed. His beauty almost made it possible to overlook his personality. Almost. He had a way with children, but this was hardly what he wanted to be doing with his gifts. And all because Gus was keen on doing a bas relief of Violet—or was it that Violet wanted Gus to sculpt her? Gus and his ladies! But he needn't worry about Violet. He knew Gus well enough to know she was in good hands with him. Anyway, it was *Davida* Gus was mad for. Augusta must know. How could he hide a thing like that from her? He seemed downright proud of it. He refused to give Davida up, no matter the cost to his family if it should ever come out. But everyone had secrets.

He began to whistle. He thought of his manservant Nicola. Tonight he would sketch him as the nude Christ of Cellini's *Crucifix*.

and fell, throwing the topmen far out into the sea. She envied John's work. He worked with enormous concentration, like Gus. She saw how the joys of work could make up for every other kind of unhappiness. Nothing, it seemed, gave Gus more pure, sensual pleasure than marble, travertine, alabaster, granite. When he worked, he bawled the *andante* from Beethoven's Seventh at the top of his lungs, and though it was the most tragic music in the world, he seemed completely content. Now John was whistling. She herself was happiest painting old chairs and tables. She could do it for hours. When she was painting, it didn't matter that she was hard of hearing. She was grateful for any opportunity to work for Gus in the studio. It wasn't the management of the business she enjoyed: supervising assistants, making appointments, keeping the ledger—though it was gratifying to think he depended on her for those things. What she liked most were the times when she actually got to use her hands. She could justly claim the braid on Farragut's tunic as her own. And she would never forget those feverish nights helping to finish the St. Thomas altar screen. It was dawn to dusk, seven days a week, for three weeks straight! They completed an angel every two and a half days. She didn't even mind being the only woman in the studio. It made her feel part of a team.

"Augusta, keep your left hand underneath the book. And your right hand at the bottom center, as you had before."

She didn't want to be in the portrait. She would much prefer to sit outside his line of sight and watch him paint. Sometimes watching was all she wanted. She knew she would never be a serious artist, though she enjoyed painting interiors of the places they lived, and the view of Mt. Ascutney from the porch up at Aspet. Perhaps she might paint the mountain in each of the four seasons. It would make a nice series for the stairwell. That is, if she ever found time to do it. She was afraid she had become dilettantish. She hadn't always been so. When her parents couldn't find an academy that admitted women, she taught herself by copying the old masters at the Palazzo Barberini. She still thought her copy of Guido Reni's *Beatrice Cenci* the best thing she ever did (it hung over the sideboard in the dining room at Aspet), though Augustus called it "workmanlike." She used to think his criticisms splendid when he was interested in her progress, but he had given up on her long ago. "No one ever succeeded in art unless born with an uncontrollable instinct toward it" was his motto. But one needed more than talent or instinct. One needed instruction, support, friends, colleagues, even students. Gus had them by the dozen. Now he was preoccupied with the Shaw monument, and the statue for Clover Adams' grave. She thought of Clover's final moments. Potassium cyanide, the chemical used for developing photographs. She must have died instantly. Somehow it seemed a rebuke to her husband, Henry. It was the camera's honesty that attracted Clover to photography (it "had not yet learned to flatter," she used to say), as opposed to painting (she looked up at John, whistling as he jabbed the canvas). After her death, Henry declared his hatred of photographs. Stunted little man. Even Henry James thought Clover had a touch of genius, but her husband—were all married men alike?—her husband thought her mind a thin, wiry, one-stringed instrument. Poor thing. She remembered the words of Clover's last letter: "I'm not real—oh, make me real—you are all of you real!" She tried to fathom the meaning of those words. Frustration, unhappiness she could understand. But not feeling real? What did it mean?

"That's fine, Homer. Try to keep still. Just a few more minutes."

Would it have made a difference if Clover had had children? "All women want children," she once said, though she and Henry had none. But maybe a child wouldn't have been the answer. Augusta found it strange that, as the years passed, her death became more and more incomprehensible. People said she fell into a despair beyond grief over the death of her father. She didn't doubt it, if what Clover felt was anything like what *she* felt when *her* father died. Still, the wish to take one's own life—... But it was even harder to grasp than that: it was the power to kill, to kill oneself—*that* she would never understand. (Maybe killing oneself became possible once you felt unreal...) Violence of any kind made her cringe. Somehow, miraculously, Gus did her justice. Henry wanted the figure for her grave to suggest an acceptance of the inevitable. On an impulse, Gus told the Italian boy who mixed the clay to strike some poses. Immediately Henry saw what he envisioned, and an agreement was made. But it was Gus's shaping hand, she thought, for all his insensitivity to a woman's plight, which made the difference. The more you looked at her, the more you felt her gravity. There she sat, in the corner of the studio, behind the curtain, massive and strange, shrouded in her heavy cowl, her eyes lowered in contemplation, her right hand raised enigmatically to her cheek, so still she seemed almost to move. She has achieved self-mastery and serenity. She has extinguished all passions. She has lived through the ages and will go on meditating for eternity. She is large. Withdrawn. Both male and female. Free from desire and pain.

Instantly, from the deck of each ship rang out

"I think that's enough for now," Sargent said suddenly, relaxing his posture and laying his palette and brushes on the table next to the easel. "Shall we have a rest?"

Homer leapt up from the chair, jumped off the platform, darted to the other side of the canvas, and, without stopping to look, ran in circles around the studio.

"Homer!" Augusta cried.

"Let him be," Sargent replied generously. "He won't do any harm. Let's take a look at that song by Mr. Faure." He went to the piano and quickly read through the music, at the same time glancing at the lyrics ("'hum, mum mum mum, *o ma farouche*,' yes, lovely"), then spread the music before him and began to play.

The song was pretty without being sweet. She was amazed by his facility at the keyboard. To be able to play such music at first sight! He made her feel what an amateur she was (but her hardness of hearing was to blame). He skated over the difficult passages but managed to convey the sense of them nonetheless. Already he seemed to be committing the song to memory. The music made him more extroverted, more pleasant somehow. Intermittently he sang the words, but mostly he just hummed the melody. It was refreshing after the tedium of reading while Homer sat. She leaned against the side of the piano, half listening to the music, half observing Homer as he amused himself with a deck of playing cards on the floor. She was afraid she had misspoken when they arrived (she feared John was already angry because they were late—he was so scrupulous about his appointments). She had expressed her sorrow over the death of his father and then mentioned the death of her own father. He seemed puzzled and uncomfortable. "Thank you for your kind words," he said awkwardly, but he made her feel it was a mistake to have mentioned death. Then Homer butted his head into his stomach and started gamboling about the studio, and the two of them got into a tussle. What a relief it was now to see him playing quietly on the floor, keeping still.

"... *Mon enfer et mon paradis!*... "

She straightened herself and walked over to the window. There was a building under construction across the way. Their house at 45th Street was still such a mess—dust and plaster and pipes everywhere, the plumbers and masons still in the house, and nothing to show for it but the mantelpieces from Washington Place instead of the hideous marble ones. This morning, looking at the fireplace stripped of its woodwork, an ungainly, open wound in her parlor, she had suddenly burst into tears. She hadn't wanted to leave Washington Place, but it was sold over their heads, and suddenly it was *adieu* to their home of nearly eleven years. Would she ever find a home that suited her entirely? The house in New Hampshire was in a perpetual state of disrepair, and it was so far from New York. She looked down at the traffic on 23rd Street. A stagecoach trundled past. A delivery wagon. Two men on white horses. A girl and a boy holding hands, crossing the street. A woman in black carrying a box. She found it comforting to speak of the dead, but apparently John did not. She recalled the words from Washington Irving's *Sketch Book*: "The sorrow for the dead is the only sorrow from which we refuse to be divorced. Every other wound we seek to heal, every other affliction to forget; but this wound we consider it a duty to keep open; this affliction we cherish and brood over in solitude."

"...*Ou mes baisers s'epuiseront.*" The song was finished. Sargent lingered at the keyboard after the sound melted away, staring at his fingers, still pressed into the keys. After another minute, he turned on his stool to look at Homer. "He *is* one of the handsomest little fellows I ever saw," he said but thought how tired he was of painting portraits. Augusta was heavy and silent, which made him uneasy. Another twenty minutes was all he wanted. He might not need to ask them back for another session. His schedule was alarmingly full with sittings straight through the next eight weeks. By the end of the summer, he would have done a hundred! It was fatiguing, sometimes, how portraiture resisted experimentation. He wished he were out of doors right now, painting mountains, boats, seascapes, buildings—anything except people. But this was New York, Violet had insisted on staying the summer, and he was on a mission to make money and establish contacts.

Boston, on the other hand, would be a haven for new ideas. He luxuriated in the thought of Boston. He envisioned the third-floor gallery of the Boston Public Library. He estimated its size compared with the studio—about three times the length. What a fine thing it would be to have some big work on hand that called for continued labor and all of his ability! Decoration, he thought, is so much better than portraiture. It is truly an artist's work. You can study on and on and crowd your life into it, while the portrait means an attack that lasts a week or a month and then is over. The library murals would be his *magnum opus*. The idea had come to him in a flash at the Player's Club: a history of Spanish literature. (Homer was preoccupied with the playing cards, at the moment trying to hold as many as he could fanwise in one hand, but cards kept dropping to the floor.) At one end of the gallery, images from *El Poema de Mio Cid*, he decided; at the other, *Don Quixote*. The scheme should be simple and bold, and it should make a statement. Between these two works of literature, one marking the birth of the vernacular, the other the glittering representative of its Golden Age, was contained all of Spain's genius, all of her pomp and violence and wisdom and hilarity. He might surround them with characters from the great Spanish dramatists—Calderon and Lope de Vega—or perhaps with figures from the popular arts: gypsies and laborers, horsemen and beggars, flamenco dancers and bullfighters. For therein lay the genius of Spain. She wasn't made for European ways, probably because of her proximity to Africa and the Moorish blood in her veins. An ancient, dark, musical people. He thought of his own *El Jaleo* and its rough, unfinished quality. But with this commission he wanted to go beyond surfaces, beyond the quick impression of the moment, to turn the common stuff of paint into intellectual gold. To *say* something. But how to say something in paint?

"Mama, look." Homer was building a house of cards.

"Yes, dear."

He would begin with *El Cid*. The harsh crusader should be the first thing you encounter when you come up the stair. He pictured the Cid in his grandest attire— white linen shirt, gold and silver cufflinks, silk gown in gold brocade, red coat lined in fur, savage spear and bulging shield—mounted upon Babieca, his muscular steed. Opposite the Cid, Don Quixote—tall body, long, wrinkled neck, thin, sallow face, tapering fingers, decrepit armor, broken staff—sitting erect and dignified upon the tremulous, long-suffering Rocinante. He could easily make the Cid look impressive, in the same way he made the most unlovely matron look attractive or the most unruly child angelic, but how could he make Don Quixote, the toothless beggar, the crazed holy man—how could he show that Don Quixote de la Mancha was the Cid's superior? For it was his idea that the Cid's grandeur was merely a matter of brute military prowess, whereas the wonder of Don Quixote was moral, psychological, intellectual. He thought of the Don's many flights of eloquence, his speech while dining in the company of shepherds, scooping up a handful of acorns and singing the praises of that Golden Age when the human race "did not know those two words *thine* and *mine*"—

Homer screamed! John and Augusta started. The house of cards had fallen.

"Try it again," she said gently.

Where was he? Don Quixote surrounded by a company of shepherds. The "Golden Age" speech, yes. He might design a triptych with the Don in the central panel surrounded by shepherds like Jesus among his disciples, flanked on either side by his mad pursuits—charging a squadron of sheep, attacking a troop of puppets, thrusting his lance into the sail of a windmill. It would make a wonderful contrast, he thought, with the violent, blood-soaked, medieval crusader, El Cid. He looked at Homer kneeling before his little house of cards. He had raised it to two fragile stories. Perfect silence and concentration reigned in the studio. He took a long, luxurious drag of his cigarette. A horse whinnied in the street. The clock struck three. A moment passed.

Then the house fell. Homer screamed and pounded his fists on the pile of cards.

John rose from the piano stool and, pulling a piece of toffee from his pocket, said, "Here Homer, have one of these. Let's finish your portrait." Taking up his palette and brushes, "Augusta?" he said.

They resumed their positions.

"Augusta, the book."

She picked up the story where she had left off.

Instantly, from the deck of each ship rang out the short, sharp blare of the bugle, John worked now with total concentration, backing away from the canvas with slow but deliberate steps, his brush in one hand, his palette gripped by the other, his cigarette smoldering in his mouth. Augusta marveled at the sheer physicality with which he worked (Gus said he probably walked four miles a day in the studio), stepping back then lunging forward, stepping back, puffing his cigarette, lunging forward, humming the tune by Faure, smoking, muttering to himself. Then he stopped, and she glanced up from the book and saw him standing before the canvas, looking neither at her nor at Homer but past them, not moving, not making a sound, but standing silent, like a statue. She wondered what he was thinking.

"Mama, keep going."

Flames were seen coming from the windows of the cabin,

Sargent's mind, eye, and hand worked together in a complete circuit as he built up the head with one quick circular stroke after another. A dark line ran across Homer's brow. He seemed to be listening with fresh attention, as if he were hearing the story for the first time. He looked as if all the horrors of the scene were now before him. It was an interesting expression; it made his close-set eyes—his one facial flaw—look even more so, though it wasn't the expression he wanted for the portrait. But he mustn't disturb the child's concentration. He suspended his brush. Don Quixote, he thought. The most important figure in Spanish literature (fixing his eyes, now, neither on Homer, Augusta, nor the canvas, but on a mark upon the wall behind them), important not simply for the beauty of his speeches or the endlessly surprising alternation of his madness with flashes of lucidity, but because... He saw Don Quixote preaching to the shepherds ("people of those days did not know those two words *thine* and *mine*") and thought of Jesus preaching to the disciples. Sancho dubbed him "The Knight of the Sad Countenance" because hunger and loss of teeth had given him such a dismal face. In payment for his freeing of the galley slaves, they pummeled him, flung pebbles at him, stripped him of his jacket, divided the rest of the spoils, and fled, leaving him a dirty, miserable wretch. The scenes of his misfortune were the Passion of Christ transported to Renaissance Spain. And yet he persisted in his quest, "stumbling here, falling there, flung down in one place and rising up in another... to revive the now extinct order of knight errantry." He thought of the Sermon on the Mount. "Blest are you when they insult you and persecute you and utter every kind of slander against you because of me." He thought of Sancho's touching declaration of love for his master: "His soul is as clean as a pitcher. He can do no harm to anyone, only good to everybody. There's no malice in him. A child might make him believe it's night at noonday. And for that simplicity I love him as dearly as my heartstrings... " He looked at the woman and child before him. The sharp line that had darkened Homer's eyes now disappeared (*"J'aime tes yeaux, j'aime ton front,* I love your eyes, I love your face," he began singing), for the little boy was wholly absorbed in the story his mother was reading *Flames were seen coming from the windows of the cabin* and his eyes turned softly vacant *Oh my rebel, oh my wild one* and his lips regained their fullness *I love your eyes, I love your mouth* as if in another moment they would part *Where my kisses will exhaust themselves* and out of the face with one, two, three quick strokes, Homer's mouth bloomed.

"*At about half-past seven o'clock, I went on deck, and there beheld a scene which it would be difficult to describe."*

He would choose a different theme for the murals at the Boston Public Library than the one he had promised McKim, Meade, and White. Its centerpiece would be the Sermon on the Mount. "How blest are the poor in spirit; the reign of God is theirs." Not Don Quixote preaching to the shepherds, but Jesus preaching to the people, a child close by his side, his hand on the child's head (he thought of the eldest child in Van Dyck's *Children of Charles I*, the one with his hand on the head of that enormous dog). "Blest too are the sorrowing; they shall be consoled." Not the history of Spanish literature, but the history of religion, from the pagan to the Christian era (he would insist on the use of all four walls of the gallery, for he would need more space to realize this grander conception). "Blest are the lowly; they shall inherit the land." The triumph not of the institutional Christian church but of Jesus' teaching. "Blest are they who hunger and thirst for holiness; they shall have their fill." The triumph of the democratic, earth-shattering ideals set forth in the Sermon on the Mount! "Blest are those persecuted for holiness' sake; the reign of God is theirs." It would surprise his audience, who thought of him only as a latter-day Van Dyck, a living descendant of the Renaissance court portraitist, the flatterer of elegant society.

"The decks were covered with blood, and had the appearance of a ship's slaughter-house. The gun-tackles were not made fast; and several of the guns got loose, and were surging from one side to the other. Some of the petty officers and seamen got liquor, and were intoxicated; and what with the groans of the wounded, the noise and confusion of the enraged survivors on board of the ill-fated ship, rendered the whole scene a perfect hell."

Now for the hands. He advanced toward Homer, cupped his knees, and spread his legs apart, gently, so as not to disturb his absorption in the sound of his mother's voice. He shook Homer's hands one at a time to make them limp and placed them, one on top of the other, over his privates. As he painted the soft, latticed fingers and the tiny bones of the wrists, he thought, the most charming thing about you, little boy, is that your arms have outgrown your sleeves.

ॐ

"Little Boy," Robin thought. It was the nickname for the atomic bomb the Americans dropped on Hiroshima. A pre-pubescent bombshell in a Fauntleroy suit. Something about the boy possessed him. As soon as he entered the gallery, almost without thinking, he walked straight over to the portrait, ignoring everything else in the room. His usual method of looking at paintings at an exhibition was nothing if not methodical. He would start at the beginning and try to see everything in the order in which it was presented, and if certain paintings interested him more than others, they would have to wait their turn. After all, an exhibition was like an essay, and to grasp the argument you had to read it straight through. There were huge gaps in his knowledge of art history, and when going to an exhibition his first hope was always that he might learn something. He also found that, by approaching an exhibition this way, the payoff was the unique if sober pleasure of delayed gratification. He sometimes wondered if the six years he'd spent in graduate school had spoiled the almost physical pleasure he used to take in looking at paintings when he was a college student. In that case, it was just as well that he never finished his PhD. Better to still be able to *feel something* in the presence of a work of art, he told himself, than to become one of those heartless academics who, when they see a beautiful painting, can only think how it confirms some theory in their heads, eventually to be put down in writing and published in an academic journal that no one reads or set forth in a classroom full of distractible undergraduates who would no more choose to spend time losing themselves in front of a painting than choose vinyl over iTunes! No, it was a good thing he threw in the towel on graduate school when he did. On the other hand, if he *had* finished his PhD, he might have outgrown his starchy schoolboy habits. He might have acquired a sense of mastery (he'd seen it in his favorite professors at Harvard), allowing him to walk confidently through any collection, choose a painting that happened to catch his eye, and appreciate it without the help of wall texts or labels or headsets, assured that his response, whatever it might be, was appropriate, well-informed, and meaningful. That, he supposed, would be a higher form of pleasure.

But today he didn't care to be a worshipful student of art or a master art historian. He just needed to take the day off, get out of his apartment, rest his eyes on some paintings, and forget about last night. His body still felt drained. He couldn't go on abusing himself like this, staying out until four in the morning and then suffering from lack of sleep all the next day. He was afraid Leonore could tell he was lying when he called in sick this morning. Oh well, what's done is done. He looked at his watch. Already past 3:30pm and he was only just getting started.

Maybe it was the boy's hands. They stood out as the whitest things in the painting, along with his face and the big fluffy bow at his neck. But it was more than their whiteness that affected him. They were fragile. He liked the way one was placed delicately on top of the other, making a kind of latticework of the fingers. They were the fingers of a child, not fully articulated. He looked at the boy's face. Tender, white. It reminded him of the clown by Watteau at the Louvre. He stood there alone, awkwardly offering himself to the viewer, his sweet adolescent face atop an enormous white collar, his hat forming a halo around his head. Meanwhile a group of jesters huddled behind him, making fun. He looked sad, embarrassed, exposed from head to toe as if naked, even though his body was completely swallowed up inside the baggy white costume (he remembered standing on stage as the Tin Man in the eighth grade talent show, wrapped in silver foil from head to toe, singing "If I Only Had a Heart"—never had he wanted anything so much as to be the Tin Man and to sing that song for the contest!—when Pat Hoberman, at the back of the auditorium, held up a sign that said "FAGGOT"). There was a similar sadness, he felt, in this boy's face.

Or was it fatigue? His eyes seemed inwardly focused, distant. He looked sleepy, a little flush, a bit red around the eyes. His lips were thick. The lower lip looked moist, as if at any moment the mouth might drop open and drool. His head was bent slightly toward the woman reading, as if he were listening to the sound of her voice (she might be reading him a fairy tale, he fancied, or *Little Lord Fauntleroy*, dressed as he was like a little prince). As he bent his head, the baby flesh beneath his chin puckered. Maybe it wasn't so much melancholy or fatigue he saw in the face as... He searched for the word. Pliancy? His tiny body seemed pliant. His little shoulders slouched. And, sweetest of all, his black patent leather shoes—more like ballet slippers—didn't quite touch the ground. Or did they? He stepped closer to the painting. No, the boy was pressing his left heel on the rung of the chair, and both feet were angled so the toes just touched the carpet. But that meant he wasn't so relaxed after all. Was he fidgeting? There didn't seem to be any restlessness in his face.

Robin stepped back a little. If anything, the boy seemed to float in a mildly narcotic state of bliss. He thought of Marilyn Monroe. His eyes looked as if they were falling shut. His lips were full and red. He seemed available somehow, available for other people's attraction to him, maybe because of the way he spread his legs like a kind of welcome. (Was he "attracted" to the boy?) But then his hands were placed right over his crotch, as if to put a stop to whatever approach the viewer might make. Or was that just another sort of come-on? He noticed it was the only painting in the gallery with a rope in front of it (was that the reason he was automatically drawn to it?).

He moved a few feet to the right. He had to keep changing position in order to see different parts of the canvas. He couldn't find a single spot that allowed him to see all of it at once, and he wondered if the problem was the way the painting had been lit, or was it something about the painting itself, the somber colors, the varnish perhaps? Now when he looked into the dark area between the boy's legs, all he could see was his own eye reflected in the lens of his glasses, as in a mirror. He thought how difficult it was to look at a thing, anything, and it occurred to him that, whenever he looked at a painting, he was never really looking directly at the painting itself. There was always some barrier between him and the paint—varnish, glass, rope. His own eyeglasses. He never saw paint with the naked eye. But even if he could, his vision would remain in some sense partial, at an angle. Filtered through some idea in his head. What would it mean, he wondered, if I could close the distance between me and a painting? He took off his glasses, but of course now everything was a blur—because of his "lazy eye," an expression that always made him think of a person hauling garbage or a sack of dirty laundry, or a pair of Siamese twins, one of whom was sick or sleeping, and his brother had to carry him around everywhere he went. Stephen never wore glasses; his vision was always 20/20. Robin usually thought of *himself* as the "lazy" one, the "weak" one, the one being carted around by his older brother (born twenty minutes after Stephen, but it went way beyond that). He put his glasses back on. Now all of that had changed, for he was alive and Stephen was dead. He looked into the murkiness between the boy's legs. There was the reflection of his eye again.

Last night at the sex club he had been thinking about the impossibility of seeing. The five hours he paid for were nearly over and still he hadn't found anyone who really interested him. He'd had sex with a couple of guys, but each of them was disappointing for one reason or another. Part of his bad luck, he figured, was that he literally couldn't see very well. The hallway outside his room was so dark (must have been a burned-out bulb) that he couldn't clearly see the men who came to his door. One guy looked pretty good in shadow, but when he came into the room where the light was better, instantly the creases in his skin and the blemishes on his cheeks became visible. Out of politeness Robin let him suck his cock for a minute, but as soon as the guy made a move to kiss his lips he said he "needed to take a break," though he said it with a pleasant smile to conceal the mild revulsion he was feeling and to avoid seeming unkind. After that he tried taking off his glasses, thinking he would seem more attractive without them, and so more likely to attract better-looking guys. But without his glasses he couldn't see anything at all. Obviously it wasn't his night.

As he was coming back from the men's room, thinking he might just as well cut his losses and go home (the clock on the wall read 3:15am), he noticed a guy standing down the hall in the doorway of his room, looking at him. Robin stopped and looked in return. "Do I know you?" he murmured to himself. That was always the sign of the "right" person in cruising situations: the sense that he already knew the stranger, that he recognized him at first sight. His feeling in such moments was always, "Yes, I know you." The question presupposed the answer. It wasn't a matter of thinking they had actually met somewhere before, or that the stranger bore a literal, physical resemblance to someone he knew. It was a spiritual resemblance, if anything. More and more he had the uncanny experience of being struck by someone in passing who reminded him of a person he knew, not because of their physical appearance but for qualities intangible, though interfused somehow with the body. Sometimes, when it happened, he felt as though he'd had a real if momentary encounter with some important person in his life, usually someone from his past.

This had happened, in fact, one morning last week on the L train on his way to work. He found himself staring at a young guy leaning against the subway doors—tall, pale skin, short dark hair that stood straight up, wearing a loose-fitting white dress shirt not tucked in. He wasn't wearing a backpack, wasn't holding a book or a magazine. He was completely unencumbered. "Free" in some sense. But he also looked bereft. There were circles under his dark, deep-set eyes, as if he hadn't slept in days. Suddenly he was reminded of his friend Timothy from Columbia—Tim, who died of leukemia two months after graduation. It was his first experience of the death of someone his own age, someone he was close to (great preparation for Stephen's death, he thought bitterly). It had felt like his own death, compounded by the fact that he had just graduated and still had no idea what he was going to do with the rest of his life (Stephen was already set for his MBA at Berkeley). Tim had escaped the problem of what to do with the rest of his life. The guy on the subway didn't look anything like Tim, except maybe something about his casual dress (Tim never cared about looking well-groomed) and his dark eyes (near the end, what stood out most about Tim's face were the huge dark circles around eyes that seemed to recede into his skull, as if at some point they would just disappear, leaving two dark holes). Looking at the guy on the subway, Robin felt a surge of warmth throughout his body. He could have stayed on the L train looking at him until the end of the line.

But there were other times, as with the guy last night at the sex club, where his sense of knowing the stranger wasn't even based on so tenuous a "resemblance." It came, instead, from the immediate sensation that he knew who the person was, that he knew what was most essential to his life—what he wanted, what obstacles he faced, what inner weakness he battled, what frightened him, embarrassed him, drove him mad, drove him to ecstasy. It was the sense, finally, that this person's life was somehow already intimately entwined with his own, that in Reality (and

Robin believed that Reality had very little to do with anything directly available to the senses) he and this person were one.

Do I know you? he silently asked the guy standing at the end of the hallway, before his open door. Yes, I know you, he answered, and started walking toward him.

With that, the guy turned his head away from Robin and stared into his room, otherwise not moving. The closer Robin got, the more he liked what he saw. He was about the same height as Robin. Young, maybe in his early 20s, and slim, almost delicate, with smooth yet well-defined muscles. His brown hair was long and wavy. His eyes were dark and narrow. He looked Brazilian.

"What's your name?"

"Joe."

"I'm Stephen," Robin said (for ever since Brian had broken up with him, he'd been assuming his brother's name in situations like this).

Without another word, Joe took his hand, led him inside the room, and shut the door. He pulled the towel down from around Robin's waist and dropped his own towel to the floor. Robin pressed against him, cupped his hands around his ass—it was already wet with lube—and started kissing him. His kisses were heavenly. Abruptly Joe backed off and lay down on the bed. Propping his head against the pillow, he reached behind the pillow and withdrew a small bottle of lube. He flicked it open, put some on his fingers, and rubbed it on Robin's dick. Reluctantly going along with Joe's rhythm (he was so beautiful; Robin wished they could have kissed and kissed for an hour before fucking), he settled on top of him and pushed his dick up Joe's ass. His ass was tight, and for a moment Robin felt something inside that he couldn't identify—it didn't seem like shit because it felt sharp. Joe turned his head to the side, as if he knew something was wrong and didn't dare make eye contact. For some reason Robin wasn't deterred. He kept fucking him, harder and harder, and the harder he fucked, the more Joe's hair fell across his face. Robin brushed it aside because he wanted to see his face, but it didn't matter because he just looked away. In less than a minute Robin could feel he was about to come, and he said "I'm gonna come," but Joe didn't tell him to pull out. Instead he tightened his ass and said, "Yeah?" like he was daring him to come inside, only he said it with his head still turned away. Then Robin came, the feeling of extreme pleasure mixed with alienation (why isn't he looking at me? This is so weird) and the thought, I shouldn't be doing this, it isn't safe, for all he knows I'm HIV positive, or what if *he's* got HIV?

Then it was all over. Robin pulled his dick out (Joe hadn't come and suddenly seemed uninterested in coming) and reached for his towel on the floor. It was then he noticed blood on the sheet. Then he saw blood coming out of his penis.

Saying nothing to Joe, he put his towel back on and left the room (no parting kiss or hug, no further eye contact, not even a muttered "thanks" from either of them). He ran to the men's room, his heart pounding. In the shower he squeezed his dick and blood came out of it. He squeezed it again and more blood came out. He stopped squeezing and just let the water wash over him. Maybe that was the last of it. The water washed his dick clean. He stepped away from the shower. He squeezed his dick. A drop of blood formed at the tip.

He tried not to think about it.

HOMER SAINT-GAUDENS (1880-1953), SON OF THE CELEBRATED AMERICAN SCULPTOR AUGUSTUS SAINT-GAUDENS (1848-1907), IS SHOWN HERE WITH HIS MOTHER, AUGUSTA (1848-1926). He figured her for a nurse, or maybe an older sister. She looked subservient, sitting behind him, her head bent dutifully over the book, her clothes plain, her hair pulled back as if she were a working woman rather than the boy's mother. She looked almost too young to be his mother. Born in 1848–so she was 42. She didn't look 42 (he remembered his mother, the other day when someone said with surprise, "you don't *look* 53," snapping back, "what's 53 supposed to look like?"—she was so touchy about her age). Her face seemed coarse. He might have pegged her for a husky German girl. Perhaps it was her mouth, heavy-lipped, clumsy, open in the act of reading aloud, turned down slightly at the corners. Or her brow: severe, knit. She didn't look happy. Dutiful, perhaps; dogged even. Half of her skirt and part of the book were cut off by the left edge of the canvas, which seemed to demote her in rank. Shouldn't the boy's mother be given a more imposing place in the picture? (His mother always said she was irrelevant in his life compared to Stephen; other twins he'd known said the same thing: no one, not even a parent, not even a spouse, was as important as their twin.) Her upper body merged with the enveloping darkness, making her head appear to float bodiless above the boy's ear. And her skin: olive, ruddy, smudged. It looked like she'd been sketched in rapidly, almost as an afterthought.

IN APRIL 1890, SAINT-GAUDENS EXPRESSED A DESIRE TO SCULPT A PORTRAIT OF SARGENT'S TWENTY-YEAR-OLD SISTER, VIOLET, IN EXCHANGE FOR ONE BY SARGENT OF SAINT-GAUDENS'S TEN-YEAR-OLD SON, HOMER. Augusta, Homer, Violet: mere items of exchange between two successful, fully-entitled men, the kind of stuff he'd read in graduate school (Levi-Strauss plus Sedgwick). He'd learned to perceive and to disapprove of injustice, perhaps, but more and more he felt that grad school hadn't taught him to *see*, at least not to see in the way he wanted to see now. **SARGENT POSITIONS THE BOY ASTRIDE A LARGE CHAIR WHOSE ELABORATELY CARVED FORMS ECHO THE LINES OF HIS RESTLESS BODY AND, BY SUBTLE IMPLICATION, THE MOTIONS OF HIS AGITATED MIND.** He wasn't convinced the boy was restless. Or rather, he thought, on some level Sargent hasn't made up his mind about the boy, and maybe that's what makes this an interesting painting. But there was also something appealing in the idea that the personality of the sitter might be conveyed by elements adjacent to the sitter, not simply by the way the sitter himself is represented. The chair was regal, ornate, like a throne. But if it echoed anything about the boy, he thought, it was his beauty. He looked at Homer, and Homer appeared to look back at him sympathetically, almost pityingly (his expression kept changing every time Robin looked at him), as if to say: I know but I cannot tell.

HOMER SAINT-GAUDENS LATER RECALLED THAT HE AND SARGENT DID NOT GET ALONG. He was almost sorry to read this. He looked into Homer's eyes. What had seemed the distant, dreamy expression of a child falling asleep now seemed distant for another reason. His eyes bespoke the coldness of contempt. His beauty became a gift he would not bestow (I know but cannot, will not, tell). **HE GREW IMPATIENT IN THE STUDIO, AND TO SETTLE HIM DOWN HIS MOTHER READ OVER AND OVER THE STORY OF THE SEA BATTLE BETWEEN THE *CONSTITUTION* AND THE *GUERRIERE* FROM *BLUE JACKETS OF 1812* (1887) BY WILLIS J. ABBOT.** That, too, altered his perception of the painting. Here was a child whose imagination was fired not by fairy tales or stories about lucky little boys, but by the hard, cold facts of war. Again he looked into Homer's eyes, fixed, apparently, upon the bloody scenes of battle, gunfire, explosions, ships tossing, and men falling into the sea.

AN AMERICAN EXPATRIATE WHO RESIDED IN EUROPE, SARGENT MADE TWO PORTRAIT-PAINTING VISITS TO THE UNITED STATES IN 1887-88 AND 1890. HE DEVELOPED HIS CLOSEST AMERICAN TIES IN BOSTON, WHERE HE WON COMMISSIONS FOR A NUMBER OF MONUMENTAL UNDERTAKINGS, He heard voices and turned his head. Two of the guards were chatting. One of them said something about Blue Cross Blue Shield. **THE CHIEF OF WHICH WAS A SERIES OF MURALS (1890-1919) FOR THE NEWLY BUILT BOSTON PUBLIC LIBRARY. ORIGINALLY CONCEIVED BY SARGENT AS A HISTORY OF SPANISH LITERATURE, THE FOCUS OF THE MURAL PROJECT SOON SHIFTED TO A HISTORY OF RELIGION. SARGENT ESTIMATED "THE TRIUMPH OF RELIGION," AS HE TITLED THE MURALS, HIS MOST**

IMPORTANT WORK.

Surfeited with information for the moment, Robin turned on his heel and looked around. The guards' conversation had ceased. The gallery was now empty except for himself and one of the guards who had been chatting, a short, middle-aged black woman with slicked hair pulled back tightly into a bun. She sat on a stool at the threshold between this room and the next, reading a book (he wondered what it was). She wore a large purple flower on her lapel. He turned back to the label.

WIDELY CONSIDERED THE LIVING EMBODIMENT OF THE RENAISSANCE-MASTER TRADITION, SARGENT WAS ONE OF THE MOST PROLIFIC PAINTERS OF HIS TIME, EXECUTING OVER EIGHT HUNDRED PORTRAITS IN HIS CAREER. He noticed that Augusta, like the guard, wore a kind of purplish pin or flower at her breast. *Blue Jackets of 1812*—he wondered what passage she was reading. He wanted to see the page. He looked at Homer's eyes. Maybe he wasn't so much excited as enervated by the war story, as if the narrative of suffering and death had sunken into his face (making him look sad), gripped his body (making him slouch), and penetrated his very soul. He thought again of the melancholy clown by Watteau. When he got home he would Google *Blue Jackets of 1812*, maybe buy a used copy. He thought if he could find the exact passage Augusta was reading to Homer when they sat for the portrait, he might know better how to interpret it, might learn from the words filtering into the boy's ear what accounted for his enigmatic expression. He pulled a small notebook and pen from his back pocket (he always took them with him to museums) and wrote the words "Blue Jackets of 1812."

BORN IN ROXBURY, MASSACHUSETTS, HOMER SAINT-GAUDENS SPENT MUCH OF HIS YOUTH IN EUROPE. HE GRADUATED HARVARD UNIVERSITY IN 1903. Even the mere mention of Harvard made Robin wince. (But he'd done the right thing by dropping out of graduate school. Still, he hated to be reminded of it.) **AS AN ADULT**

HE WORKED AS AN ART CRITIC, STAGE DIRECTOR, DESIGNER, JOURNALIST, AND MUSEUM ADMINISTRATOR, SERVING AS THE DIRECTOR OF FINE ARTS AT THE CARNEGIE INSTITUTE FROM 1922 UNTIL HIS RETIREMENT IN 1950. There was something vaguely unsettling, he felt, about seeing the child's future pass before him. Or rather, it didn't help him to understand the thing that most concerned him now. "THE PURPOSE OF A PAINTING," SAINT-GAUDENS WROTE IN *THE AMERICAN ARTIST AND HIS TIMES* (1941), "IS TO AROUSE AN EMOTIONAL RESPONSE BY SUBLIMATING THE LOCAL AND PASSING TASTE OF ADORNMENT. BUT THE PAINTING PROFITS GREATLY BY ITS FRAME, AND THE REAL FRAME OF A PAINTING IS MORE THAN JUST SOMETHING OF WOOD AND PLASTER; IT IS FORMED BY THE FEELINGS OF THE GROUP RESPONSIBLE FOR THE PAINTING." He liked the idea that a painting was made by more than just one person; it was made by the people near to the artist, for example, and by those he emulated, alive or dead. By the sitter, of course, if it were a portrait. Even, in some sense, by the person looking at the painting a hundred years later. He jotted the words "American Artist and His Times, Homer Saint-Gaudens," thinking it might be fun to write a story about a person looking at a portrait, wanting to climb into the portrait and to see the person in it from every possible angle.

If only the painting had been hung a foot lower, he thought, he could examine Homer's face more closely. He leaned a few inches over the rope.

"And I'm leaving Rome," he added. "I must bid you good-bye." Dora could read her book and keep her eye on him at the same time. *Isabel, inconsequently enough, was now sorry to hear it.* The young man with glasses had been staring for a long time at the big portrait of the little boy with the rope in front of it. *She was on the point of naming her regret,* Now he was leaning over the rope. *but she checked herself and simply wished* Too close! He was too close to the painting. She shut the book on her finger to keep her place, got up from the stool, and took a few steps toward him.

"Not too close to the painting please," she warned in the voice she only used when making announcements in the gallery. She liked speaking in that voice. It was lower than her normal speaking voice, like she was someone else, a man even. He backed away.

She returned to the stool and opened her book. But what had she just read? Warburton announcing that he was leaving Rome. Isabel was letting him go. What more did she want? He was rich, kind, he would do anything for her. Would his castles and his millions and his love have been such a terrible burden? Apparently she wanted something different.

They shook hands, and he left her alone in the glorious room, among the shining antique marbles. Was that it? Did she just want to be left alone? Did she not like men? *Isabel sat there a long time, under the charm of their motionless grace,* Or did it have something to do with the "antique marbles," with art itself? She looked again to make sure the young man was keeping his distance. *wondering to what, of their experience, their absent eyes were open* She saw him back away from the painting as if to take in the whole after examining some tiny detail up close. *and how, to our ears, their alien lips would sound.* Then he turned and walked hurriedly past her and into the next room (she would have to read that last sentence over again), as if the little boy were the one he had come to see, to talk to, and once he'd done that he had no further business here.

Now she was alone. Like Isabel, she thought with a sudden, strange satisfaction. The gallery was empty of visitors. Had she scared the young man with glasses away? So what if she had? *Isabel sat there a long time, under the charm of their motionless grace, wondering to what, of their experience, their absent eyes were open, and how, to our ears, their alien lips would sound.*

She closed the book. She was enjoying it, but it was the kind of book she didn't want to read too fast, even though it was due for Thursday and she was only half way through. She wanted to stop every couple of sentences and think. She wouldn't be prepared for class. One of the privileges of being an adult student, she thought, was that you were doing it for yourself. If the teacher didn't like it, too bad. She was old enough to be Professor Scott's mother! She guessed he was around 30, Marion's age. He must have gone straight from college to graduate school and finished his degree in less than six years. Talk about privilege! Even if he had received a scholarship or financial aid, he was free to make the choice to continue his education. What choice did *she* have at that age? At 30 she had an 11-year-old daughter, and she was alone. She didn't have her old aunts or her mother to help out like so many women she knew.

But that was a long time ago. Today she turned 50. It was hard to believe she was half a century old. She was trying not to make a big deal out of it, even though everyone said it was a milestone and she would be sorry if she didn't celebrate. But she wanted to remain calm, quiet. She decided not to take the day off from the museum. She was happy to be working today. The only sign that today was special was the periwinkle flower she wore on her lapel. Only she knew what it meant; it was no one else's business. She liked the idea of keeping a secret with herself. She might be similar to Isabel Archer in that sense. Then it occurred to her that Gilbert Osmond was the same way, and that might be why Isabel found him more appealing than all the other eligible bachelors in the book. She remembered Isabel's conversation with him where he told her he was acting on a plan he'd made years ago "to be as quiet as possible." "The events of my life," he told her—and Dora knew as soon as she'd read the words that they should be emblazoned somewhere she could always see them (she had copied them onto a slip of paper and put it in her wallet)—"the events of my life have been absolutely unperceived by any one save myself."

She looked at the cover of the book. Henry James. *The Portrait of a Lady*. Underneath the title was a picture of a pensive white woman with a topknot of red hair in a white silk dress, resting her chin in her loosely-clasped hands, leaning her elbows comfortably on a silky white cushion. Lazy, privileged, white girl, she thought. But then, no, those would be Marion's words. Your privilege is only a scandal when there is so much poverty in the world, but your comforts and your freedoms by themselves are the dream of humanity. They are not at all contemptible. She turned the book over and read the picture credit: "'Reverie' by Edmund C. Tarbell, reproduced by courtesy of the Boston Museum of Fine Arts." Reverie, yes. She opened the book. *She sat down in the centre of the circle of these presences, regarding them vaguely, resting her eyes on their beautiful blank faces; listening, as it were, to their eternal silence.* Their beautiful blank faces, their eternal silence. The words spread in her mind like drops of ink in a glass of water, first mushrooming, a soft purple explosion, then suffusing the glass all one dark color. Silence was becoming more and more a thing she craved. Even the museum wasn't quiet enough for her these days. Whoever thought a museum was a place to get away from other people? She looked around at the walls lined with portraits. A dozen faces kept silent vigil. She thought of Isabel sitting alone among the statues in the Capitoline Museum. She imagined the lips of a statue subtly moving, or the eyes of a painted face shedding tears, and only the person who looked longest and hardest would catch the motion. It was the same with reading. Sometimes the words on the page throbbed with life in such a way that they seemed destined for her ear, for her eye only, as if all the other surrounding words had vanished, and one sentence or one phrase stood alone, framed like a painting, upon a vast expanse of white, and it was a message addressed privately to her: *The events of my life have been absolutely unperceived by any one save myself.*

No one seemed to understand what went on inside her when she read a book.

Marion would call and ask, "Mommy, what did you do today?" She would say, "I've been reading," but she knew it sounded like she'd been doing nothing, and then Marion would start talking about everything *she* did that day, how she took Louis to day care and didn't get to work until 10:30 and how her boss called her into his office as soon as she arrived and told her something had to be done because she couldn't keep coming to work late, it was unacceptable, and she was outraged because she couldn't help the fact that she didn't have a husband to share the responsibility with—what else was she supposed to do? And she hated him because he didn't have children of his own, which is why he came to work at 8am and didn't leave until 7 at night, and what kind of a life was that? He must be gay, she said. Dora would listen and try to feel what Marion felt, but more and more she only felt detached. She had done the best she could to raise her daughter, but for the first time in her life she had begun to tell herself, she may be your daughter but she's a grown woman and will have to take care of herself. Her problems are not your problems. You have your own life to live now. But she wasn't sure she believed it. She would, of course, always be Marion's mother. Marion would always be her daughter. They would always have a connection. It's just that she wasn't enjoying her daughter's company these days. She loved her, but she didn't *like* her, was that it?

A man came trooping through the gallery carrying an easel and a small suitcase. "How ya doin'?" he said as he passed her.

"Hello," she said in her cool, low, public voice.

In the next room he stopped in front of a portrait of a woman with a curiously high forehead and a large white veil. She watched him as he set up his easel, still thinking of Marion. "What are you gonna do with a Master's degree in English?" she would say with an edge of contempt in her voice. "You're only working part time now; you should relax and enjoy your grandson. What do you want to go back to school for?" The first time she told Marion she wasn't planning to spend the weekend in Jersey City as usual because she needed to study (she had to say she "needed" to study, she couldn't say she "wanted" to), Marion thought she was kidding. Then she got angry and said Dora was selfish. (The artist spread out a drip cloth on the floor.) Marion felt it her duty to remind her mother every chance she got what a "real life" consisted of, and Dora would sit and listen while Marion told her every detail of her battles with her boss and Louis' ADD and the racism of the teachers and social workers at the day care center and the traffic at the Holland Tunnel and the problems with her car and what kind of car she planned on buying next and how she wanted to trade in the old one, as if nothing *Dora* did, none of the things *Dora* spent her days doing and thinking, could possibly matter as much as Marion's crazy, hectic daily life. (He unfolded a small table and carefully laid out his paints and brushes.) Her decision to go to graduate school at the age of 49 had driven a wedge between them. It was unpleasant, but the more estranged she felt from her daughter, the more she began to think that this was the most important decision she had ever made. It put a frame around Marion's life, which was really a latter-day version of the life she herself had led for thirty years, and it allowed her to see it as something separate from herself. Marion was embattled; she could see that now more clearly than ever. Conflict with other people was what gave meaning to Marion's life. It made her feel righteous, better than everyone else. What gave meaning to her own life, she realized, was something else.

 She opened her book. *The dark red walls of the room threw them into relief; the polished marble floor reflected their beauty. She had seen them all before, but her enjoyment repeated itself, and it was all the greater because she was glad again, for the time, to be alone.* She felt the strangest sympathy for this young white woman in a book written over a hundred years ago! She would never be able to explain it to anyone, least of all

Marion. She remembered telling Marion she was thinking of writing her Master's thesis on *Portrait of a Lady*. Marion, who had an opinion about everything and who hardly ever read a book but knew enough to know that Henry James wasn't black, said, "Why aren't you reading books by black folks?"

"I am," Dora defended herself, "it's just that I think this one is challenging for me right now. What's so bad about that?"

"You're interested in feminism," Marion countered, "so why don't you write about Zora Neale Hurston? Write about *Their Eyes Was Watchin' God* if you want to write about a woman with her own mind."

"It's *Their Eyes* Were Watching God," Dora corrected her, adding, "and just because I'm a black woman, why do I have to read and write only about other black women?"

But arguing about race with Marion was always a dead end. Unless the final word was that white folks were racists and black folks were saints, Marion would have no peace. And it wasn't that she thought Marion entirely wrong about white folks, but she believed there was a difference between knowing something and acting upon that knowledge. Sometimes you had to go on faith in spite of what you knew, and then maybe you could change the reality of things. *At last, however, her attention lapsed, drawn off by a deeper tide of life. An occasional tourist came in, stopped and stared a moment at the Dying Gladiator, and then passed out of the other door, creaking over the smooth pavement.*

She closed the book once more and saw that a few people had come into the gallery. The young man with glasses was in the next room, where the artist had finished setting up his things and was now working. "Portrait of a lady." So many portraits went by that name, she thought, the identities of the sitters lost and forgotten. She wondered if Henry James had a particular one in mind. The woman the artist was copying didn't look like her idea of Isabel Archer, though her mournful, heavy-lidded eyes did seem to illustrate the passage she had just read. She watched as he rapidly sketched the silhouette of her veil in a crude black line and then proceeded to blacken the space around it. The result was an oddly menacing white shape that rose up and leaned uncomfortably off-center. She wondered, as he paused in front of his canvas, if he might leave it at that. She got up from her stool and approached him. She felt as though she were going to the rescue of this delicate, veiled woman whose downcast gaze, as he copied her, now seemed more an expression of embarrassment than of deep introspection. Just then she wished for a camera. She thought it would make an interesting picture.

Sandro Botticelli (c. 1445-1510)
Portrait of a Young Man, c. 1480-85
Tempera and oil on wood

Sandro Botticelli
Portrait of a Young Man

In life it is sometimes perilous, thought Yukio Yashiro as he climbed the stairs at the entrance of the National Gallery, to return to an old love. Disillusionment follows young enthusiasm. He stood for a moment by the railing of the portico and looked out over Trafalgar Square, at the great column with the statue of Admiral Nelson and the bronze lions and the motorcars and omnibuses circling the square and slowing down in front of the museum. He had delayed this trip to London as long as he could. He felt oppressed by a sort of fear. What if Botticelli looked different than the cherished image he held in his memory? He recalled his first encounter here with Botticelli, ten years ago. How he had loved the *Mystic Nativity*, with its band of angels dancing in midair above the manger, the pairs of men and angels embracing like long-separated brothers below, the little hairy devils scurrying for refuge in between the rocks at their feet, and, at the center of everything, the Virgin bending over the Child, with the sweet, dumb donkey to her right, lowering its muzzle in the direction of her gaze. As if answering the call of a distant friend, he hurried on to Florence and the Uffizi Gallery. There he saw the *Primavera* and the *Birth of Venus*. He was reading

Walter Pater for the first time. It was Pater who put into words his vague intuition about Botticelli, Pater who identified that "peculiar sentiment with which he infuses his profane and sacred persons, comely, and in a certain sense like angels, but with a sense of displacement or loss about them—the wistfulness of exiles, conscious of a passion and energy greater than any known issue of them explains, which runs through all his varied work with a sentiment of ineffable melancholy." He regretted that professional critics now treated Pater's interpretations as fancies. But he knew what it meant to be an exile (during the early '20s, when he was living in Europe, he always suspected that his research was approved or disapproved not on account of its merits, but because of who he was), and he believed that Pater's impression of spiritual "exiles" did in fact derive from the pictures themselves. Unless it took a man somehow in exile himself to see that same quality in Botticelli. Indeed, an artist may wait hundreds of years, he thought, for a friend from a faraway country to appear (a steady stream of people were coming up the stairs) and show him his own true reflection at last. In a way, Pater had done that for him. It was he who gave dignity to the peculiar intellectual pleasure Yashiro experienced when looking at paintings, for in his art criticism Pater indulged in the free play of the imagination, the surprising juxtaposition of one thing with another no matter how disparate. The bringing together of incongruous things, Yashiro thought, like a strange alchemical experiment, yielded genuine insight.

But now he felt an obscure discomfort, and not, he suspected, seeing a dozen or so Japanese tourists coming up the stairs, simply because of his nervous anticipation of encountering Botticelli again after the lapse of years. He was ready to move, but he waited until the tourists went ahead of him. Not that he wouldn't be seen in the company of other Japanese (a few of them nodded as they passed). It was simply, he told himself, that he didn't like to be mistaken for a tourist. He waited another minute to ensure that they were well inside. For he was an art historian and proud of his profession. He had come to reexamine Botticelli and to begin preparations for the revised edition of his book. Yes, that was the last of them.

To be sure (resuming his earlier train of thought as he entered the museum), the object of art changed along with its beholder. That was only the logical extension of Pater's theory of impressions: "Experience... is ringed round for each one of us by that thick wall of personality through which no real voice has ever pierced on its way to us, or from us to that which we can only conjecture to be without." What a surprisingly Oriental idea that was—the world outside oneself, no more than a conjecture! It implied that the self, too, was a mere conjecture, prone to melting away from day to day, changing shape moment by moment. Certainly Yashiro himself wasn't the same man he was four years ago. Could Pater have had any knowledge of Buddhism?

The grand staircase inside the museum was thronged with people walking in every direction. He liked to think that in all the Western writers and painters who most appealed to him was an Oriental unconscious, a blending of Eastern and Western sensibilities. It had been, he could see now four years after the publication of his book, his most original contribution to the scholarship on Botticelli. Of course Botticelli wasn't likely to have known anything of the Orient—he had to swerve to the right to avoid a little boy bounding down the stairs—though if anyone wanted to argue with him on historical grounds (his old defensiveness on the question flaring up) he would point out, as he had done so many times before in conversation with his Western colleagues (his defensiveness now shading into anger), that the mystic element of Indian art seemed to have arrived in Italy through the complicated intermediary of the Byzantine. Alternatively—here another child came chasing after the first—Indian mysticism could well have come west through the Persians, who were excellent designers, so that Oriental mysticism appeared in Italian art as an adaptation from Persian influences. But why feel defensive? Wasn't it his mentor in Italy, the famous Bernard Berenson himself, who wrote that Botticelli's real place among draughtsmen was scarcely with the great Europeans, but with the great Chinese and Japanese?

He took a seat on the landing in order to delay his reunion with Botticelli a few minutes longer. He opened his satchel and withdrew a copy of Boccaccio's *Decameron* (a story or two a day calmed his nerves and lightened his mood). In any case, Botticelli clasped hands with his Chinese and Japanese brothers in a place beyond history. Berenson said that Botticelli's line had a swiftness and purity that found their analogy only in some few ecstatic notes of the violin, or in the crystalline timbre of the soprano voice. The world of sensation, the realm of aesthetics—only in such places did Botticelli truly become one with his Eastern brethren. He looked up at the ceiling. He had forgotten how ornate it was. "Altamura" (high tower) was the name Berenson and Logan Pearsall Smith had given to their imagined monastery where the love of art and the aesthetic appreciation of life were practiced in perfect peace all the year round. Perhaps Berenson's villa outside Florence was meant to be the earthly embodiment of Altamura, but with its international set of hangers-on and the gradual dissolution of Berenson's genius in the soul-killing business of attribution, it was only a shadow of its theoretical counterpart. "Freed from the love of the world and the fear of death"—in 1898, perhaps, Berenson and Smith could write such things in earnest, but not now, not in 1928, after world war and natural disaster (the image of his house in Tokyo, its smashed roof where the garden used to be, flashed in his brain)—"its inhabitants... see spread before them all ages and epochs, and the echo of contemporary trouble comes but faintly to their ears." He had seen a world of trouble since his last visit to London.

He read a page from his *Decameron*...

Now it was time. He stood up and headed toward the Italian wing. He decided to test his memory of the plan of the museum by finding his way to the Botticelli room without a guide. So far he knew where he was going, and he felt, in spite of the crowds, a soothing pleasure in the familiarity of his surroundings. Even more pleasing, strangely enough, was the smell. He remembered this peculiar smell like glue. A sort of cleaning fluid? An adhesive for hanging wall fabric? Passing the gallery of the Italian *trecento*, he recognized the little Duccio triptych across the room and remembered Berenson's method of looking at paintings. He would walk rapidly through a collection to get a quick sense of what was there, as if he were leafing through the pages of a book before settling down to read it. Then he would choose a particular painting. Without saying a word, he would stare and stare at it, sometimes for half an hour, until he had, as he said, fused as much of himself into the painting, and as much of the painting into himself, as possible. Once he had looked at a painting in this way, he had seen it for all time. Years later he could conjure up the painting in his mind in all of its detail just with the aid of a photograph, no matter how poor the quality. And he could remember the room, and the corner of the room, in which he had seen it.

Through the entrance to the next gallery he could see the stunning *Baptism of Christ* by Piero. A little distasteful it was to be thinking so much of Bernard Berenson this morning. He remembered the rumor that had gotten around I Tatti and back to him: Berenson would have settled for an American if he couldn't find a European to help him revise his big book on Florentine drawings—"anyone," he had said, "but a Jap." And *this* coming from an American, and a Jew! But Yashiro didn't like to dwell on slights and insults. After all, Berenson and his wife had given him complete access to their excellent art library, without which he could never have finished his book. The perfectly foreshortened dove of peace hovered mysteriously over Christ's head in the Piero *Baptism*. In any case, misunderstandings were inevitable between people of different cultures. Westerners especially could not be counted upon to treat their Eastern counterparts with full respect. The red and yellow garments of the bystanders in the background were neatly reflected in the still waters at Jesus' feet. With Piero, he thought, you were always aware of his purely intellectual interest in geometry and optical phenomena. Could there be a Georges Seurat, he wondered, turning away from the painting, or a Pablo Picasso without Piero? And if the past could go on living in the present, wasn't it possible that two people, distant in space, might share the same thoughts, think, in some mysterious way, as one? But instead of continuing straight ahead he walked toward the room on his right, where he caught a sliver of the *Adoration of the Kings*. It was the Botticelli room.

Crossing the threshold and taking in all at once the *Mystic Nativity*, the *Adoration*, the *Portrait of a Young Man*, and the *Venus and Mars*, he felt in some sense that his critics had been right. He *had* overstated Botticelli's sentimental side. It had been his purpose to counteract the *aria virile* theory ("his works have a virile air," a contemporary observer famously remarked, "and are executed with the greatest judgment and perfect proportion"), a theory which, by the twentieth century, Yashiro believed, had gone too far and had almost banished, as unworthy of scholars, the enjoyment of Botticelli's sentimental beauty. But simply by standing and looking at the paintings as a group from this distance, he was astonished to find what a sound artist Botticelli was. "Virile" might in fact be the best word to describe him. There was no fundamental vacillation, no collapse. You can trust him, he thought, you can safely live in his world. He saw himself standing with his old mother amid throngs of people outside the still-unfinished Earthquake Memorial Hall. All of Tokyo had come to a halt. Silence reigned in the streets and shops. The trolleys and automobiles, the bustle of stalls and street sellers—all of it had ceased. The smoke on the dais billowed heavenward as they prayed in silence for the victims of September 1923, and though he had lost so many friends, it was his father he remembered in his prayer. To show him the result of his work and to see his glad face had been his greatest ambition.

He turned to the *Adoration of the Kings*. After the austerity and relative flatness of the *Mystic Nativity*, fascinating as it still was, the teeming crowd of the *tondo*, the distances shooting like arrows away toward the horizon, the grandeur of the decaying classical architecture jutting out at the viewer and seeming to soar over his head, and the almost boyish interest in nature—in all these things Botticelli took tremendous delight. He marveled at the pair of disproportionately tiny stags leaping into a wood in the middle distance on the right. He stepped forward to get a closer look.

"Sir, not so close to the painting," came the voice of one of the guards. He knew he was the culprit. He looked at the peacock perched on the stump of the right-hand pillar, presiding regally over the scene. The gentle curve of its back echoed the lovely rondure of the canvas itself. That one arabesque, he felt, gave such sinewy beauty to the steel geometry of the temple. But the peacock fascinated him even more than that, and suddenly he knew why: he was a creature flown in from the world of Chinese painting. It was difficult to believe that he *wasn't* painted by, say, a great Chinese artist of the Sung dynasty, or by the Emperor Hui Tsung himself, who once painted a dove on the branch of a peach tree, and it ruled the whole universe more surely than the Emperor himself ruled the whole vast country of the East. The true artist's eye looked at a mere bird, but his soul spoke with the Soul of the World. Botticelli's peacock, he thought, is the Soul of the World.

He could hear the sound of his own breathing. He had mentioned the peacock only briefly in the first edition; he might revisit that passage and expand upon it. Did he dare to make the comparison with Hui Tsung? But it was ideas like this that had gotten him into trouble. He remembered the stinging words of Roger Fry's review in *The Burlington Magazine*: "He fails more or less to apprehend what Florence really stands for in the history of the European spiritual drama." Of all the reviews he had gotten—and the majority, he was proud to say, were favorable—it was Fry's that rankled the most. "He undoubtedly has experienced many acute emotions in front of Botticelli's works, and he is able to communicate these with a certain flowery Oriental rhetoric, which may be stimulating to certain temperaments"—even Fry's compliments sounded as insults!—"but his experiences are of so subjective and often of so capricious a nature that they cannot be taken as a guide to anything like a temperate and objective critical estimate of Botticelli's art."

He retreated from the *Adoration* and sat down on the sofa in the center of the room. He opened his satchel and returned his *Decameron*, which had begun sticking to his sweaty palm. He thought with bitterness of his meeting with Fry in the winter of 1924. He had longed to make Fry's acquaintance ever since reading his essay on Oriental art in *The Living Age*. He was most impressed with Fry's thoughtful discrimination between Eastern expressiveness and Western verisimilitude as well as his sensitive remarks about Chinese landscape painting. Their mutual friend Arthur Waley arranged their introduction, and soon after Fry invited him down to Guilford for an afternoon's visit. Durbins, as the house was called, with its hulking gambrel roof, outsized windows, fat shutters, and jazzy, vertical stripes of red brick, boldly stood out from among its peers. "Gentlemanly residences," Fry jokingly called the other houses in the neighborhood, as they walked from the station to Durbins, and told how the neighbors complained of the eyesore in their midst, which he had designed himself. The interior was equally eccentric: letters and magazines overflowed from the table in the hall, tools and piles of photographs lay jumbled on shelves in the upstairs workroom, and in the drawing room, with its high ceiling and the light pouring in, Italian pictures, children's drawings, painted screens, African statues, Chippendale chairs, and Persian plates all mingled promiscuously and freely. As a workman dragged the square pond in the garden, they sat inside drinking tea and discussing art. Fry's range of interests was thrilling. They discovered a shared passion for Pater, but then Fry confessed that, compared with Pater, he felt himself an amateur, struggling with a medium (he meant the English language) for which he had no real gift. How to translate into words his response to a work of art, he declared, was the most difficult thing in the world. He said he loathed art criticism more and more and longed to create, but there too, he confessed, he ran into obstacles, for sometimes his instincts as a critic stood in the way of his painting. Some said his canvases suffered from too much thinking, not enough feeling. But at the age of 58 he found himself where most people found themselves thirty years earlier—at the beginning of life, not in the middle, and nowhere within sight of the end. What kept him going, he said, was the aesthetic emotion.

"What do you mean by that?"

"I'm afraid, Yukio, if I try to explain I'll sink into the depths of mysticism."

"But—"

"All I can say is that, to me, it has a peculiar quality of reality that makes it as important as anything I have ever felt."

Fry turned to a painting leaning against the bookcase by the window and asked him what he thought of it. It was a painting of his daughter, Pamela, done many years ago before the war by his friend Duncan Grant. She was nine years old at the time of the painting. She sat in profile on a colorfully patterned cushion by the garden pond. On the waters of the pond—short, vertical gray and white strokes—floated orange and green leaves, careless oval shapes, Fry observed, that seemed to push into the foreground, as if they hovered in the air about her head instead of in the water behind her. Yashiro pointed out that she sat not unlike the Buddha in prayer, with her legs crossed in the lotus position and her hands held palm-upward in front of her. The figure seemed on the verge of dissolving, they agreed, the more the brush strokes were distinguishable one from another, as if they would pull apart. She seemed to be made up, they agreed, entirely of crushed stained glass.

When the tea and conversation were finished, they parted like old friends and promised to meet again.

How, then, Yashiro wondered, could Fry have betrayed him by writing so unjust and unkind a review of his book? "The typical attitude of Orientals to art has become one which dwells in the world of associated ideas. For them the value of the work of art always resides largely in its suggestions and references, in what it calls up rather than in what it expresses directly." More and more with critics inspired chiefly by modern art, he thought, this issue of plasticity was given priority—the main relations of solid volumes, as opposed, say, to the individual, detailed forms of flowers, birds, and animals. It was true that his book had commanded attention chiefly because of the large photographs of details and the textual divisions devoted to minute studies of hands and feet, hair and drapery. But such tiny hidden beauties were too grossly neglected in modern criticism, preoccupied as it was (in the wake no doubt of Fry's influence) with rough-hewn problems of plastic construction. He knew many readers who *liked* the novelty of his detailed descriptions and comparisons. Unfortunately, those same readers often neglected his main discussion altogether. But he never imagined that a critic so discerning as Roger Fry should follow their example. It was, of course, quite possible that his want of confidence as a writer of English had accounted for Fry's failure to grasp his meaning, though if that were the case it would be ironic, even comical, he thought, given Fry's own weaknesses as a writer, and he remembered with satisfaction the reviewer for the *Times Literary Supplement* who declared his writing "more exact and sensitive" than that of "many English historians of art."

No, he had committed some other offense. Fry had objected to his chronology—was that it?—bemoaning what he called the "absence of any scholarly or clear statement of what exactly are his conclusions about the arrangement of Botticelli's oeuvre," complaining further of "his frequent inversions of the sequence of the pictures which Horne had worked out with such thoroughness that he was able to follow Botticelli's activity almost month by month throughout his career." An admirable picture of what a miserable figure he cut as a scholar! But how absurd. Did Fry really believe that the works of a painter buried in oblivion for more than four hundred years, of whose earthly existence so few documents were preserved as to be neatly put into less than twenty-nine pages of the appendix of Herbert Horne's book—did he really believe such works could possibly be arranged in monthly sequence and with objective truth? *He*, certainly, did not. Oh, there were problems with his chronology, he saw them sooner than anyone else. Living in Japan, he couldn't possibly correct the printer's proofs, and the chronology was printed without his supervision. A name printed a few lines too high or too low made a vast difference in the calculation of a period. But he would see to fixing those errors in the revised edition. In the meantime, careful students of Botticelli would know that, in spite of its defects, his chronology had been the most serious attempt of its kind until 1925. (The gallery had temporarily emptied out, leaving Yashiro alone with the paintings. But the paintings had disappeared, and his argument with Fry was all he could see. He sat in fury on the couch in the middle of the Botticelli room.) At the same time he *knew* he was terribly subjective. Who was *not* subjective in art criticism? Far be it for me, he thought, to acclaim myself an expert on Botticelli, when he has been so artistically appreciated by Walter Pater and so scrupulously studied by Herbert Horne. All I did was to love Botticelli and study his works. I only claim to be a friend, whereas Pater and Horne...

But that was it—he had criticized Horne, and Horne had been a personal friend of Fry's. *That was it!* His real offense must have been his remark that Horne's book "leaves me cold, and I doubt if Horne did not take more genuine interest in documentary research among archives than in the aesthetic contemplation of Botticelli's works." Fry rather smugly pointed out, as "one who knew him," that Horne was "a poet who, out of a kind of Quixotic bravado, posed as dryasdust. He even, I think, gained a fresh secret pleasure from seeing how many people were taken in by the pose," and he pitied Yashiro as "the latest and most evident victim of Horne's mystification." But he was quite right in being a victim of Horne's mystification, if there was any such thing, for Horne's personality, as remembered by Fry, had little to do with him.

He sighed, trying to steady his nerves, and withdrew *The Decameron* again from his satchel. He read a page before reaching into his pocket and discreetly taking out a mirror the size of a calling card. He looked around and noticed that the gallery was empty except for the guard sitting on a chair by one of the entrances. He held the mirror up to his face. In the square of the mirror he saw his eyes, his nose, his mouth. He lowered his head slightly and brought the mirror closer in order to see his bushy eyebrows. Raising his head slightly, he saw the large mole on his left cheek. He aligned the center of his face once more with the mirror. He was ashamed to see not himself but another man.

He put the mirror back in his pocket and read another page of Boccaccio. Then, still clutching the volume in his hand, he walked up to the *Portrait of a Young Man*. He felt the strange sensation of having seen him before, but not because he knew the portrait well. It was as if the face loomed out of the dark, dear to every child of man, a face that he seemed to have seen everywhere and nowhere. Who was he? No one knew. Some *discepolo* of Botticelli's, perhaps. Only a specialist would ask the question. If the figure bore a strong resemblance to its model, that resemblance died with the person. What remained, he thought, was art. Botticelli had obviously studied the face with all his energy, but his own softness intervened. He had traced the minute details, but the grand construction of masculine feature—happily!—escaped him. He was capable of representing a real person, but he invested the portrait with a beauty belonging to his own vision rather than to his subject. In realism, as always, Botticelli went halfway.

And yet there was something still deeper and more remote about the boy that attracted him. If there was a law of Western art, he hypothesized, it was energy and expressiveness. But this boy's face was negative, immobile, expressionless, or expressive only of a timeless tranquility. In some profound sense, he felt, it was an Eastern face. He looked at the glints of white in the eyes. He thought of the antic world of Boccaccio. Great pictures, he thought, are really portals through which you pass to another world. Modern critics, in their endeavor to see pictures and to know them, made an effort not to admit the existence of this other world. They clung to what they could pinpoint and measure. But the other world comes into being when what is known is penetrated by what can only be imagined. One picture contains two. A painter makes a picture with some definite intention; must we, spectators of other generations, therefore be circumscribed by that intention? Each of us may see something unique in it and be happy. What is this young man to me, he asked, and what is his intended expression *to me*? That is the question. For if he has an indefinable "something" in him which allows each of us to indulge in the free wandering of his own soul (and the eyes, he thought, still looking at the white flecks, are only important as passageways to the soul), all the better for the picture as art. This is the very infinity to which all works of art aspire. One picture contains two.

Just then, a door in the face of the young man slid open... As if in a trance, Yashiro passed through to another world...

Not so very long ago, in the noble city of Florence, which, for its great beauty, excels all others in Italy, a comely youth named Ricciardo wandered through the marketplace in search of adventure. Passing beneath the balcony of a handsome palace, he looked up and saw a miraculous young lady dressed in purest white. She lowered her eyes to where he stood and greeted him with such indescribable grace that he seemed at that moment to behold the entire range of possible bliss.

"What is your name, fair girl, and what brings you to your balcony this morning?"

"I am Francesca," she said, speaking in a low voice so that only he could hear, "and I long for something to lighten my spirits."

"But why are you sad?"

"I am betrothed to the Marquis of Saluzzo. He is old and ugly, but very rich, and my parents insist that I marry him."

"And whom does your heart desire?"

"No one at present, but if he existed, I would do everything in my power to defy my parents and run away with him."

Wishing he himself might be the lucky man to win her heart, he stretched out his arms to her, calling, "Well, then, may I introduce myself? I am Ricciardo. I come from Ravenna, where—"

Just then, a stranger approached and seized him by the collar, shouting, "There you are, you rascal! So this is how you repay my generosity!" Dragging him around the corner and down a narrow street, the stranger continued his harangue: "And where is the lapis lazuli I sent you to purchase? You've been gone three days, and now I find you flirting in the marketplace! From now on I'm confining you to the studio, and if you disobey me again so help me, Ricciardo, I'll throw you back out on the street."

Hearing the stranger call him by name, Ricciardo was amazed. "But sir, how do you know my name?"

"How do I what? I can think of worse names, you little cheat!"

"But–"

"Not another word, scamp!"

They arrived at a modest house with a shallow porch and tall windows. Still yanking Ricciardo by the collar, the stranger entered the house, hurried up the stairs, flung open the door, and pushed him through. Ricciardo found himself inside a bright, airy artist's studio. A boy some years younger than Ricciardo greeted them.

"You found him, Master! Welcome home, Ricciardo, old boy! No more special errands for you, eh?"

What on Earth is happening, Ricciardo asked himself, and why does everyone know my name?

"Will you finish the portrait today, then, Senor Botticelli?" With a flourish, the boy tore away the cloth from a painting on an easel in the middle of the room. Ricciardo nearly fainted with surprise, for there he beheld, as if in a mirror, his very own face. It was a half-finished portrait of himself!

"No, Biagio, I think we'll work on the Mars and Venus. Ricciardo, take off your clothes."

Not knowing whether he was awake or dreaming, but never shrinking from an adventure, Ricciardo did as he was told. Here, at least, was a comfortable place to eat and sleep, and the work, no doubt, would be interesting.

Now Ricciardo was a clever young man, and he quickly adapted to the routines of Botticelli's studio. During the day he crushed stones, mixed pigments, prepared panels, swept the floor, and posed for paintings (sometimes in the nude, sometimes with his clothes on). At night, he shared his master's bed, for in spite of Botticelli's low opinion of his character, he was the artist's favorite. Weeks went by, and Ricciardo became more or less content with his strange new life. Except for one thing: he longed to see again the girl from the marketplace, Francesca. But how to arrange it?

One sleepless night, pacing the floor of the studio, his eyes fell upon the now-finished portrait. "What can I do to win her heart?" he asked the young man in the picture, and the young man stared back at him with a look of Oriental tranquility. Then an answer came to him: a portrait of me by a famous artist will surely impress her—better yet, a self-portrait by me will do the trick, for a woman cannot resist a man with artistic talent. Anyway, she'll never know the difference. With this portrait, I will declare my love for her!

And so, persuading Biagio to show him where Botticelli kept the key (for he locked the studio at night), Ricciardo absconded with the portrait at daybreak while the master was still sleeping and hastened to the palace where he had first seen Francesca. He climbed up to the balcony—not an easy feat with the portrait under his arm—and, just as he was about to leave it where she would find it when she awoke, it occurred to him that the portrait should be supplemented with a text. He composed a hasty sonnet on the back of it:

None other than Ricciardo painted me,

The mirror image of a heart that bleeds.

And I am he, and he is me, the two

Of us identical in everything.

But most of all in this: our love for you,

Francesca, ruler of the Earth and sky.

Disobey your parents, dump the Marquis

Of Saluzzo, and follow your desires.

Be not afraid, sweet lady. When tonight

The moon has risen to its height, you shall
See the original of me appear
Beneath your balcony. Welcome him with
Kisses and caresses. Flee with him to
Some far country. (And take me with you.)

His heart nearly bursting with anticipation, Ricciardo jumped from the balcony and made his way toward the river, where he planned to spend the rest of the day strolling lazily and thinking of his love. Come nightfall, he would return to the palace and claim the prize he felt certain awaited him.

Several hours later, Francesca rose to greet the morning. She stepped out onto her balcony and, with a start, found the portrait with the sonnet hastily written on the back. She swooned over the charming face in the picture and thrilled to the eloquent sentiments expressed in the poem. Just then a comely youth remarkably similar in appearance to Ricciardo was hurrying through the marketplace. Francesca caught sight of him and, waiting until he passed beneath her balcony, called to him, "Ricciardo! Ricciardo!"—but in a low voice so that only he could hear. The young man stopped in his tracks and gazed up at her. He seemed at that moment to behold the entire range of possible bliss.

"How do you know my name?"

"Silly boy, I am Francesca, and you are Ricciardo. We exchanged names when first we met many weeks ago, don't you remember? And see here, you've signed your self-portrait with a precious sonnet that includes your name. Has lovesickness made your mind go soft? I hope not, for I intend to run away with you tonight, just as you proposed. I love you, dear Ricciardo. I am yours. I will wait for you tonight." With that, she turned, portrait in hand, and went back inside the palace.

The young man was dumbfounded. Who is this ravishing girl? he wondered. How does she know my name? Since when did Senor Botticelli finish my portrait? And how did she obtain it? She says she loves me and will run away with me tonight. This must be madness. And yet, I love her. More surely than I have ever felt anything else in my entire life, I love her! But he didn't stop to dream another moment, late as he was in returning to his master's studio with the coveted lapis lazuli.

For now it must be told that this young man who looked so much like Ricciardo was none other than Ricciardo's twin brother, Rinaldo. Torn apart in a shipwreck on the Adriatic Sea when they were children—a disaster, sadly, that claimed the lives of both their parents—the boys grew up separately: Ricciardo in Ravenna, Rinaldo in Florence, each believing the other one dead. When he came of age, Rinaldo, being the more sentimental of the pair, assumed the name Ricciardo in homage to his long-lost brother. Hence it was as "Ricciardo" that Rinaldo presented himself one day to the artist Botticelli on a street in Florence. The painter saw at once the boy's transcendent beauty and persuaded him to come work in his studio and share his bed. Relations between them, however, were inharmonious, and Rinaldo (whom, of course, Botticelli knew as "Ricciardo") was always, poor boy, getting into trouble for one reason or another. All his life he seemed to be following an unlucky star. To take only the most recent example, Rinaldo had been sent to purchase a handful of lapis lazuli when, on his way to the stone merchant, he was attacked by a couple of street urchins who ran off with his money. Knowing that Botticelli would punish him severely if he returned empty-handed, and being at heart a decent and honest fellow, he went to work for several weeks as a fruit seller in order to earn back the money he had lost and, so, to purchase the stones and return at last to his master.

As soon as he entered the studio, Botticelli flew into a rage. "Ricciardo, I told you if you disobeyed me one more time I would throw you back out on the street! Where did you go last night? And what have you done with the portrait?"

"Signore, I–I–"

"Well?"

"I–"

"Speak, you rodent!"

"Signore, I brought the lapis lazuli you ordered. But the portrait? Why, just a moment ago—"

Not wanting to hear any more, Botticelli knocked the stones out of his hand, pummeled him over the head, pushed him out the door, and told him never to return.

Meanwhile, Ricciardo was walking toward the river when he passed the open door of the Church of San Marco and recognized the voice of Savonarola, who at that moment was preaching a fiery sermon. Curious to hear this raving priest about whom there was so much talk in the town (for Ricciardo, as we have seen, was a nascent poet and was interested in all manner of rhetoric), he entered the church and sat down to listen:

"... were not born among Christians; behold those who were not baptized nor instructed in the law of the Gospel; behold those who never received the numerous sacraments of the Church nor heard the voices of preachers. Behold, I say, the Wise Men of the East. From the midst of perverse and evil nations, they made a great journey, only to worship the footprints of the Babe. 'We have forsaken our country,' they cried, 'our families, our friends, our kingdoms, solely to worship Him.'

"How cursed are you, then, citizens of Florence, you who were born among Christians, baptized, instructed in the law of the Gospel; you who receive the Sacraments and hear the voices of preachers. Cursed are you, for still you turn your backs upon the Lord. And yet you say in your hearts, 'God lives far off; His word is a parchment written by dead men.' But I say to you, God is near. I see a mighty hand holding a sword bearing the inscription, 'Behold, the sword of the Lord will descend suddenly and quickly upon the earth.' Unless you repent, the sky will darken, and flaming swords will rain down upon you. The sword is hanging from the sky. It is quivering. It is about to fall.

"But wait! There is a pause. There is a stillness before the storm. Lo, the winds are stayed, and the voice of God's warning may be heard. Hear it now, O Florence, chosen city in the chosen land. Repent and forsake evil. Give up your trinkets, harps, mirrors, masks, cosmetics, dice, games of chance, drawings of naked figures, portraits of comely young men and beautiful women, for it is sinful to use the hands in painting which ought to be folded continually in prayer. Give up your obscene books, your Ovid and Boccaccio, and all other items of luxury. Pile them up in a pyramid 60 feet high and 240 feet around the base. Set fire to the pile, then join hands and dance around it, singing songs of praise.

"People of Florence, the time of pagan art and frivolous living, of corrupt youths and immoral clergy, of wicked princes and clever courtiers, of all your vainglorious pleasure-seeking, has come to an end. Now is the time to shed floods of tears for your sins. Take Communion daily. Attend Mass. Do as I say, or else the Lord will smite you with swords of fire, the Earth will tremble, cities will crumble, mountains will fall, rivers and oceans will burst into flame, snakes and frogs... "

But Ricciardo, convinced that Doomsday was upon him, could endure not another word. He fled the Church of San Marco and ran like a madman for the embankment, ready to throw himself into the river. But just as he started to jump, he thought it better to make amends in the here and now for his many sins. He would start with Signore Botticelli. He had stolen the portrait and, with it, made impious love to Francesca. He resolved to return to her as promised and make his confession.

When the marketplace emptied out at nightfall, Ricciardo called up to Francesca's balcony. She appeared, holding the portrait, and he leapt impetuously into her arms.

"Ricciardo, you've come!" she cried. "Let us make our plans to leave tonight, for the Marquis of Saluzzo–"

"But wait, my dearest," he interrupted, "I have something to tell you. I have committed a terrible sin. This portrait I left for you, which I said I painted myself–I lied. It is the handiwork of the famous artist Sandro Botticelli."

"Impossible!"

"I kid you not."

"And the sonnet?"

"Well..."

"No, don't tell me. Petrarch?"

"Actually, I wrote that one myself."

"Huzzah! What a poem!"

"Grazie, Francesca!" he cried, sweeping her up in his arms, momentarily overcome by her words of praise. "But let me finish. I stole the portrait from Signore Botticelli, and I did so with the sole intention of seducing you. I can no longer aid you in disobeying your father and mother. You must marry the Marquis of Saluzzo as planned. It was dishonest and immoral of me to think you might do otherwise on my account. In addition, I must ask you to please let me have the portrait back so I can return it to Signore Botticelli."

"No, no, I won't let you. We must leave tonight, together—you, me, and the portrait! For the Marquis of Saluzzo—"

Just then, Rinaldo came dashing across the square, calling, "Francesca! Francesca! There is something I must know!" In a single bound, he leapt onto the balcony and landed in the arms of Ricciardo.

"Hey, who do you think you—?" Ricciardo began to protest. "Brother? Can it be? Are you my brother Rinaldo?"

"Brother?" Rinaldo echoed. "Can it be? Are you my long-lost, dearly beloved brother Ricciardo?"

"Brother!"

"Brother!"

Weeping, the twins embraced at the sight of each other after so many long, lonely years.

At first Francesca was frightened. Then, seeing not one but two comely youths on her balcony, she was filled with desire. Then, remembering they both answered to the name "Ricciardo," she was puzzled.

"But which one of you is Ricciardo?" she asked.

"He is," Rinaldo replied. "I only assumed his name when I came of age" (turning to Ricciardo) "in homage to the brother I remembered so fondly from childhood but lost so cruelly many years ago on the Adriatic Sea, along with our dear parents. And now I couldn't possibly be happier, for I have found my brother" (turning to Francesca) "as well as the girl of my dreams! For I love you, Francesca, though it's true we hardly know each other."

"You? You love her?" Ricciardo erupted with sudden anger.

"Yes, I saw her for the first time standing here this morning, and she declared her love to me. It was as if at that moment I beheld the entire range of–"

"But I love her, and she loves me! Don't you, Francesca?"

"Well," Francesca stammered. "I–you look so much alike."

"She belongs to me," Ricciardo insisted. "I've come tonight to defy her parents and take her away, along with this portrait, for the Marquis of Saluzzo–"

Francesca, however, only became more perplexed. "But you just told me you were going to return the portrait to Signore Botticelli."

"And that's another thing," Rinaldo said. "How did you get that portrait? What's been going on in the studio since I was away?" He picked up the portrait and clutched it to his breast. Ricciardo reached for it. A tug of war ensued, and both young men went tumbling over the balcony, portrait and all, to the pavement below.

"That's a portrait of me!"

"No it isn't, it's a portrait of me!"

The bickering continued for several minutes until, lo and behold, the Earth began to tremble, lightning flashed, and thunder cracked. All of a sudden, an enormous flaming sword came whizzing out of the sky and gouged the pavement at the boys' feet. They looked up in terror.

"What the____!" they said in unison.

Then another flaming sword came tearing out of the sky, heading their way. They pulled apart just in time for the sword to land between them.

"Holy Mary, Mother of–!" Francesca shrieked and darted inside the palace, locking the door behind her. With that, Ricciardo and Rinaldo looked at each other for an instant, then ran for their lives, as one, then another, then ten, then a hundred, then a thousand flaming swords came shooting down from the sky. Just as they were rounding a corner, a flaming sword struck Rinaldo from behind, piercing him through the heart. The portrait flew out of his hands, but Ricciardo caught it and kept on running until he came to Botticelli's studio, where he took cover under the porch and watched in disbelief as the sky rained down swords of fire. Seeing the carnage, he resolved once more to make amends with the master and to go back to work in the studio, crushing stones, mixing pigments, preparing panels, sweeping the floor, posing for paintings (sometimes in the nude, sometimes with his clothes on), and at night, obediently sharing the great artist's bed.

... His mind had drawn a blank.

"He looks impassive, don't you think? Rather foreign and disagreeable."

Yashiro glanced around. A man and a woman stood next to him in front of the portrait.

"No sign of feeling," the man said. "Inscrutable somehow."

The woman said nothing for what seemed a very long time. Then, "I think he's rather nice. Sort of quiet and tranquil. Almost angelic."

After another minute, they moved on together in silence. One picture, he thought, contains two.

He felt the volume of Boccaccio sticking to his sweaty palm again, so he returned it to his satchel. He checked his watch. He had been looking at the Botticellis for nearly half an hour. He thought he might like to wander through the museum for a change of scenery. He wasn't tired. In fact, he felt a surge of new energy. The portrait—with the help of Boccaccio—had awoken something in him.

He made his way toward the north wing. Perhaps he had been too timid, he thought, in his comparisons between Botticelli and the artists of the East. The reviewer for the *TLS* warmly appreciated his frequent references to Utamaro ("his comparison of the treatment of the hair by these two painters is delightful and full of insight") and was persuaded by his suggestion of the fundamental identity of all the arts, Eastern and Western. But he might have gone further with the idea. Rather than assuming some knowledge on the reader's part of *ukiyo-e* prints, for example, he might have entered into a fuller discussion of them, and he might have included some illustrations of them as well. Then the reader could have made the comparison with his own eyes. The problem, he surmised, was that Westerners had so little opportunity to see first-rate examples of Japanese art. When they thought about it at all, they usually thought of *ukiyo-e*, but Japanese art was so much more than woodblock prints.

He found himself in the Rembrandt room. Instinctively he walked over to the *Self-Portrait at the Age of 34*. He thought of Takanobu's portrait of Yoritomo. What Rembrandt and Takanobu had in common, it occurred to him, was an unmistakable grasp of character. Rembrandt's luxurious, almost foppish Renaissance-style costume reminded him of Yoritomo's ceremonial dress, and he thought how Takanobu combined realism with a crisp formalism (his *sokutai* was almost pure geometrical abstraction) to convey the authority and dignity of the haughty statesman and warrior. Japanese art, he thought, can hold its own against any of the great masterpieces of the West; Japanese art, he thought, is not a whit inferior. By comparing Botticelli with Utamaro and other Asian artists so casually in the first edition of his book, he had, in a sense, only assumed this proposition. But now, in the second edition, he might make the argument more explicit, more forceful. At the very least he would use the new preface to answer directly, point for point, Roger Fry's slanderous criticism—a reckless idea, but he would do it!

Wending his way from the north wing back toward the main entrance, he imagined a great international exhibition of art traveling the capitals of Europe and the United States, bringing together masterpieces from East and West, side by side, so they could be seen and appreciated together. Some day he might organize it! One would be able to turn, say, from Greek and Egyptian sculpture to the sculpture of the Asuka Period; from Rembrandt's or Frans Hals's portraits to those of the thirteenth-century Kamakura Period; from the frescoes of the Italian *trecento* and *quattrocento* to the religious paintings of the Buddhist sects. (Almost unconsciously he reached into his pocket and took out his mirror. Without turning to see if anyone observed, he looked into the mirror and saw himself without shame.) Then Japanese art would be seen and valued as part of the world's art heritage. All those Western misconceptions of a quaint and charming country peopled by tiny men and women, a land of fantasy with paper lanterns hanging in front of every door, of dainty lacquer ware and beautiful china—all that "Madama Butterfly," he thought with disgust—would be wiped away.

Perhaps it *was*, he thought, perilous to return to an old love; disillusionment follows young enthusiasm. But this was a love older than Botticelli. He thought of cherry blossoms blanketing the country in spring like a galaxy of white stars, relieved against the deep green of semi-tropical vegetation; of wisteria blooms a yard long hanging from the pine-trees in early summer, making the whole wood a decorative arabesque of white, violet, and green; of large, blood-red camellias looking out from shadowy foliage of the valley, more wonderful than the embroidered shawls of Spain.

Was it because Nature there takes on such decorative form that Japanese artists may be thought of as designers rather than painters? For as the fields turned yellow in autumn, the sudden burst of chrysanthemums, wildly capricious in form and color, surprised you like some mad kaleidoscope.

He thought of Japan Herself and felt the urge to step outside. That peculiar smell, like glue, so pervasive in the National Gallery, had given him a slight headache. Some fresh air, he thought, would do him good.

⚬⚬⚬

"Mind if I watch?"

"No, not at all. I actually like it when people watch."

Robin turned his head to see who was speaking. The guard had come in to talk with the artist copying van der Weyden's *Portrait of a Lady*. He turned back to the portrait of the boy in the red cap by Botticelli and breathed a sigh of satisfaction, as if he had just taken a lungful of fresh air. The streets of Florence in the fifteenth century must have been a Garden of Eden, he thought, with boys like this on the loose. He almost wished he could catapult himself there now. He remembered a conversation he'd had at Eric's dissertation party with John, Eric's boyfriend at the time. They got to talking about which cities in the world had the most beautiful men. Robin said he often saw something hard and unwelcoming in the eyes of men who lived in New York, probably the result of having to survive in such a harsh environment.

"I don't agree at all," John replied, almost belligerently. "I can never walk down the street without seeing five or six gorgeous guys. I think beautiful men are just falling from the trees in New York."

Robin held himself back from saying something like, "Yeah, and there aren't too many trees in New York," but he realized it came down to a question of one's attitude. It seemed that John simply enjoyed his attraction to men and wasn't burdened with frustration over not having this or that attractive guy. Robin envied him for that. It probably explained why John had a boyfriend and he did not. (His "neediness" scared most guys away—was that the problem?)

He looked at the Botticelli boy. Was it plain lust he felt? Or did he evaluate himself against the other, as if to say, "You are more beautiful than I, therefore I want you"? Sometimes it was hard to tell the difference between wanting to have someone and wanting to be like them. He thought of Stephen. Whenever he saw himself from behind, reflected, say, in the mirrors of a public toilet, or in the dressing room at a clothing store, for a split second he would think he'd seen Stephen in the mirror. The mistake was logical enough. When he was growing up it *was* Stephen he saw from behind, and from every other angle, every day, many times a day. He always measured himself against Stephen: how tall he was, how much he weighed, how much pubic hair he had grown, how many times a day he could jerk off, how many friends he had, how well he did in school, how far he could run and how fast—he compared himself to Stephen in everything. But that was kids' stuff, and he wasn't a kid anymore.

"When you paint just the silhouette like that, it makes a weird shape, like a ghost."

"Yeah, I kind of see what you mean."

Their conversation seemed wired directly into his ear. Resisting the temptation to turn around and look at the artist's work, he concentrated instead on the silhouette of the young man before him. He remembered overhearing someone say—probably at the Uffizi, the first time he saw the Botticellis there in college—if you trace the silhouette of Botticelli's figures with your finger, you will appreciate the "musical" quality of his line, and he followed the bouncing line of the boy's thick, wavy hair with an imaginary finger, just as, twelve years ago, he had traced the rhythmic peninsulas and inlets of the receding shore line in the *Birth of Venus*. He was taking a year off from English literature to study art history in London, though he knew very little about painting. His friend Sarah had just come back from a week in Florence and said she could have spent the whole seven days at the Uffizi and been perfectly content. She took him to the National Gallery and showed him Leonardo, Raphael, Titian, and Botticelli. She said if he was going to visit Florence (he planned on meeting Stephen and his mother there during the winter break), he had to know something about Italian art. And when he did go to the Uffizi (he separated from them as soon as they entered, not just because he was starting to feel his independence from Stephen, but also because looking at painting had become a strange new ecstasy he wanted to enjoy by himself), his homework paid off. The Botticellis, more than anything else in the museum, made him appreciate what great painting was, how it could grab hold of you like a novel you couldn't put down, or a piece of music you had to hear over and over. It had been a long time since he'd thought about Botticelli, but now, looking at the *Portrait of a Young Man* here at the Met, he remembered he had seen it at the National Gallery as a college student and fallen in love with it.

"I go around the world copying paintings. Then I create installations that replicate what you see in a gallery, only it's a gallery from the past. Last year I recreated an eighteenth-century drawing room. I made all the paintings, put up wall fabric, installed furniture, and then I dressed in period costume and appeared in the space myself. It's like performance art."

The artist had a scratchy, sexy kind of voice, Robin thought. In spite of himself, he was drawn to what he was saying. At the same time, he found the artist's breezy tone and obvious self-confidence irritating. Obviously he thought nothing of telling a perfect stranger all about himself and his work. Robin bristled in the company of extroverts. He turned to look at the artist. Tall and skinny with curly blond hair. A paint-splattered t-shirt hanging loosely on his broad frame. Well-developed biceps. Not an ounce of fat on him. Thirty-ish no doubt. The guard, by contrast, was short, compact, well put together. Pretty face, prominent cheekbones. Dressed entirely in black except for the large, purple flower at her lapel. Hard to guess how old she was. Forty? Together they made an unlikely pair. He wondered if they were attracted to each other. That might explain the unusually public nature of their conversation and the way they raised their voices, as if something primal was going on beneath the light banter and they couldn't help themselves. He wished they would leave him alone with the paintings.

MISTAKENLY IDENTIFIED FOR MUCH OF THE NINETEENTH CENTURY AS A SELF-PORTRAIT BY MASSACCIO, He wasn't surprised, somehow. It was the boy's expression. It gave nothing away. **THIS CRISP PORTRAIT OF A YOUNG MAN IS A SUPERB EXAMPLE OF BOTTICELLI'S MATURE STYLE AND ONE OF THE FINEST PORTRAITS OF THE QUATTROCENTO.** What made this portrait so great? he wondered. Could its greatness have anything to do with the fact that, for a hundred years, it was mistaken for something it was not? For to be misunderstood was a positive capacity in a work of art. It meant there was room for disagreement, that more was going on than meets the eye. He looked at the young man's eyes. At first they seemed identical to each other. He always cringed when he looked in the mirror and saw his lazy eye. Without glasses, he looked like a freak. Brian told him he thought his eyes were beautiful, the same way the eyes in a modernist portrait could be beautiful. He said his face was a work of art. He wished he could have believed him. But it didn't matter now, for there was no getting him back. It was almost two months, and Brian still hadn't answered his letter. Maybe he was on vacation or between jobs. Or maybe he'd moved and the letter never reached him. Or maybe he was just preoccupied with his artwork.

He liked the dip of the lower eyelid on the right and the short, sharp line coming down from the inside corner—the line, he thought grimly, that one day (as if the portrait were a living thing) would turn into a bag of flesh. The lower eyelid on the left didn't have quite the same curve. The left eye, it appeared, was slightly smaller than the right. The left eye's upper lid, too, was a touch flatter than the one on the right. Even perfect beauty isn't perfect. The left side of the mouth, he noticed (holding up his hand to cover the right side of the face from view) turned up slightly into a smile, whereas the right side (he switched hands, blocking the left side of the face) appeared to slide down into a grimace. The lines in the cheeks betrayed no warmth; if a smile was about to break out or fade, it showed almost no trace of itself. But in spite of these subtle tensions in the face, the overall expression appeared deadpan. The imbalances seemed to cancel themselves out so that, in the end, you were left with the feeling that here was a person who was essentially unknowable.

"Well, like I said, I love it. I invite all my friends to come, and then we film it. Everyone is eating and drinking, I hire musicians, people start dancing. It's cool, like a big party."

THE EYES, NOSE, AND MOUTH ARE DRAWN WITH SHARP PRECISION, BUT THE SOFT CONTOURS AND SHADED MODELING OF THE FACE TEND TOWARD A MORE RELAXED NATURALISM. Unless it wasn't so much that the boy was unknowable as that Robin himself was resisting what he knew about him. He began to see other kinds of asymmetry. The figure wasn't centered on the panel. The neck craned slightly to the left, and the head came forward and leaned still further to the left. The locks of hair on the right seemed more massive than those on the left. Also, those on the right, because they fell forward, interrupted the line from temple to jaw, whereas those on the left, because they were pushed back a bit, exposed that smooth, taut line. This might be Botticelli's way of suggesting, he thought, that we're catching the boy as he turns toward us (which might, in turn, explain all the other imbalances in the face). Or away from us. He noticed how he kept wanting to think positively about the boy. He wanted to imagine the smile blossoming, not fading, the boy approaching the viewer, not abandoning him. He began to think it wasn't so much that the boy was inscrutable, that his expression "gave nothing away," as that, whatever the truth of his expression, it must penetrate the thick wall of his own personality, through which, he sometimes feared, no authentic voice from the outside world could ever reach him. Safe sex was the perfect example. He knew what it was, he knew how he was supposed to protect himself, he knew what could happen if he became HIV positive. He was an intelligent, highly educated person, and still he persisted in having unsafe sex. Why hadn't the warning signals gotten through to him? Or, if they had, why wasn't he paying more attention to them? Was he trying to kill himself? He thought of Stephen's body sprawled out naked on his bed, pills and vodka on the night table, the room going dark and flashing bright from the blinking lights of the ambulance parked outside the house.

"You can see it on my website."

"What's the address?"

"Sorry I forgot to bring my business cards with me, but it's easy to remember: www.SaintLuke.com."

"Saint Luke?"

"You know, one of the four evangelists, as in 'the Gospel according to'? There's this tradition of images of Luke sitting before the Virgin and Child, sketching them with a tablet and pencil. He's the patron saint of painters."

LIKEWISE, THE HAIR FALLS IN A RICHLY ABSTRACT SCROLLING PATTERN, BUT SINGLE HAIRS OR TUFTS OF HAIR ESCAPE FROM THE GENERAL ARRANGEMENT AND PLAY ON ITS SURFACE, GIVING IT A CONVINCING DEPTH AND AN APPARENTLY UNSTUDIED LOOSENESS. He noticed the strands of hair escaping from the cap. He looked again at the eyelids. The lines were precise, as if drawn in pencil. The left eyelid was drawn almost straight across rather than arched. It made the expression seem cold. The eyebrows, too, he now noticed, were more horizontal than arched. But the forehead was smooth, so the brows conferred upon the face not severity, exactly, but rather...

"That's my name, too."

"Ah, so you're Luke."

"Yep."

Indifference. He didn't seem to care one way or the other. He wasn't happy, he wasn't sad. He wasn't coming, he wasn't going. He wasn't saying no, but he wasn't saying yes either. He wasn't going to make the first move; he would force *you* to do that. And once you did, he would say with a politeness worse than outright disdain, "No, that isn't what I meant at all." It was a type he knew well. Take Joe, last night at the club. At first he seemed ardent, really into it. His kisses were incredibly passionate. Then they started fucking, and something changed. Joe kept looking away. Once Robin came, it was all over. Joe seemed to turn off completely, to the point where Robin felt he needed to get out of the room with an urgency, he realized, that had nothing to do with the blood on the sheets and coming out of his dick. There was something inhuman about the guy. How could anyone be so detached from the act of lovemaking? He looked at the figure of the Botticelli boy as a whole instead of as a collection of isolated parts. The young man came together in his sight. His beauty seemed to contain a drop of poison.

MISTAKENLY IDENTIFIED FOR MUCH OF THE NINETEENTH CENTURY AS A SELF-PORTRAIT

BY MASSACCIO, Of course it was. Why was he attracted to guys like that? Selfish, self-absorbed, needing to be worshiped but unable to give anything in return, incapable half the time even of carrying on a genuine conversation. He had a penchant for artists and actors, even though nine times out of ten he found them insufferable, either as boyfriends or friends. Actors, in his experience, even the mediocre ones, were masters of deception in real life, and New York was full of them. He remembered that time at the club when he met the guy who was supposedly married to a graduate student at Teachers College. He said his name was Marcus and that his wife was writing her thesis on the way people receive compliments. He said he was doing some informal research for her at the club. Of the guys he had complimented that night, Marcus explained, most of them had refused the compliment. For example, if he said, "You're cute," they would say, "I don't think so" or "You're cuter." But when he told Robin, "You're adorable," Robin simply replied, "Thank you." Marcus said that was the best response he'd heard all night.

"You must have a great self-image," he said.

"I doubt it," Robin laughed.

"Whoops! You just refused a compliment." They both laughed.

"So what do you do?" Robin asked him.

"I'm a cop."

"You're kidding!" He was amazed not only to be having sex with a straight, married cop, but also that a cop should be married to a woman whose research was so intriguing. Also, he couldn't imagine a guy in Marcus' position actually going around a gay sex club conducting, as he said, "informal research" for his wife! It was all too incredible.

How could he have fallen for it? They made a date for later in the week, and over dinner Marcus confessed that he was neither a cop nor married to a woman.

He *was*, however, a graduate student at Teachers College, and he *was* doing his thesis on the way people, specifically men, received compliments. His name was Jimmy, not Marcus—Marcus was the name of his older brother who had died of AIDS. He even showed Robin the name and picture on his Teachers College ID as proof. Robin wondered if the ID was fake. Why should he believe anything the guy told him? He had never been lied to so brazenly before. But all his attempts to find out why Marcus—or, rather, why Jimmy—lied, in a strange way, led nowhere. It was a joke. It was just for fun. Jimmy said he really liked Robin and had decided to tell him the truth because he seemed like such a nice person. It was no big deal. And when it came time to pay the check and decide where to go next, or whether to say goodnight and good riddance, which of course is what he should have done, Robin inexplicably invited him to come out to his place in Williamsburg and sleep over. Later that night, in the middle of having sex, Robin looked at him and thought: I'm not enjoying this. I can't get over the fact that you lied to me. I want you to leave. He told him they had to stop and that he should leave now. Jimmy refused to go. Robin tried to be firm, but he didn't really know how—he had never been in a situation where he actually had to *throw* somebody out of his apartment. Using physical force didn't come naturally to him. Words alone, however, weren't working. He asked him again, will you please leave? Finally he threatened to call the police, and Jimmy left.

THIS CRISP PORTRAIT OF A YOUNG MAN How could he have let things go so far, and with someone he *knew* to be deceitful? He looked at the portrait of the young man. Crisp, he thought. The British word for potato chip. But that was something else he found interesting about the portrait. For all the modeling of certain areas of the face and neck, and the way the head seemed to jut forward convincingly, the figure seemed flat overall. Two-dimensional, like a cardboard cut-out you could slide in and out of a puppet theater. The black background, no doubt, contributed to that impression. It seemed to isolate the figure, to take him out of spatial and historical context. Perhaps the black suggested mystery, as if the young man came to you with a shady past, with something to hide. The flatness of the figure (like a potato chip) only added to its seeming artificiality and untrustworthiness. But it was the young man's untrustworthiness, combined with his beauty, Robin thought, that makes him so irresistible. And why, he wondered, should I be more attracted to him the more I feel I can't trust him?

THE SITTER, SHOWN BUST-LENGTH IN A STRONG LIGHT FROM THE LEFT, CONFRONTS US FULL-FACE. It was rare, he thought, ever to come full face with another person. He thought of his niece, Elizabeth. How old was she now? Almost ten. He remembered the week he spent in San Diego the summer after Stephen's death. Elizabeth was four. She understood what had happened to her daddy, yet she could still smile and play. It was as if she knew what the grieving adults around her needed most and, so, found it within herself to give comfort. She crept into his bedroom each morning, sat on top of him, and brought her face within an inch of his nose. She perched there while he pretended to sleep. He could hear her nasally breathing and had to suppress a laugh. Opening his eyes, he would feign surprise, asking in astonishment, "Where did you come from?"

She would giggle and say, "Nowhere."

"Did you come through the window?" he would ask.

"No!" she would answer, laughing even louder.

"Shh! You'll wake up Mommy."

"Shh!" she would imitate him, now unable to control her giggles. Back and forth the game would go. He was missing out on so much of her childhood. Some weekend he should fly out to San Diego for a visit.

CONFRONTS US FULL-FACE. One of the awful things about last night, he thought bitterly, was that Joe never looked him in the face while they were fucking. What he loved most about fucking was to be able to look someone in the eyes while doing it. And that was why he never wanted to wear a condom. All he wanted was to fuck someone and to look him in the eyes and to be looked at in return with nothing between them. That's why he loved having sex with Brian. Brian was always fully present when they had sex; he gave everything of himself. It was disgusting to think he might have permanently damaged his health last night from fucking someone who wouldn't even look at him. **THE EXPRESSION OF THIS UNKNOWN SITTER, PERHAPS ONE OF BOTTICELLI'S WORKSHOP ASSISTANTS, IS INTRIGUING AND ENIGMATIC.** He had clues, it now occurred to him, right from the start. Everything happened so quickly. At first it appeared as if Joe was waiting especially for him, had chosen him from all the other guys at the club. But the way he turned his head as Robin approached him, the way he ushered him into the room and onto the bed so unceremoniously, and with so little foreplay, just a couple of kisses, now made Robin think that he just wanted to get fucked by somebody, anybody, it didn't matter whom.

CRITICS HAVE VARIOUSLY DESCRIBED THE YOUNG MAN AS FRANK, IMPASSIVE, CONFIDENT, ANGELIC, DISINGENUOUS, HARD, REFINED, BRIGHT, IMPUDENT, OPEN, EAGER, AND JOYFUL. He suddenly realized the young man looked like no one so much as his old friend Ricky. The same healthy, luminous white skin; the same rich auburn hair that came down to his shoulders; the same intelligent, inscrutable look in his eyes. It was that air of inscrutability that made Ricky so seductive. Amazing, he thought, in a sixteen year old. He remembered the day they stood by the entrance to the gymnasium after play practice their junior year in high school. The entire building seemed empty except for the two of them. Ricky said they should hang out some time over the weekend, go to a movie or something. So few of the guys in Robin's class would have anything to do with him, but Ricky just seemed to rise above his peers.

And Robin needed friends. Even though Stephen had always been and still was his best friend, by the time they hit their teens and Robin began to realize he was gay, he knew he needed someone other than his brother.

"I've run out of my allowance," Robin said to Ricky, almost not wanting to believe his good fortune.

"Oh that's nothing," he replied. "I'll pay for you. What are friends for?" And he reached across the space between them and squeezed Robin's shoulder, all the while looking him straight in the eyes. He had never been shown such affection by another boy before. Only with Stephen had he felt anything like that glow of affection (although by then their little physical intimacies had stopped).

But his joy didn't last long. As he was getting ready to go out that Saturday evening, Stephen asked when Ricky was coming over to pick them up. Robin had to conceal his disappointment at realizing it wasn't going to be just the two of them, he and Ricky, but the three of them. And all evening long it seemed that Ricky ignored him and talked only to Stephen, laughing at all kinds of private jokes that excluded him. He began to wonder if something was going on between Ricky and Stephen. But if it was, why would they have invited him to go out with them?

ANGELIC, DISINGENUOUS, HARD That night he cried himself to sleep. But now, looking at the portrait of the young man, he wondered if his tears hadn't been as much about Stephen as about Ricky. For he could trace a lot of the antipathy he felt for Stephen to their friendship with Ricky and to that night in particular. It wasn't that he thought Stephen was gay. But he figured that Stephen knew *he* was, even though he had never outright admitted it, and it seemed to him that Stephen, in this very indirect way, was taunting him that night. From then on, he saw very little of Ricky, while Ricky and Stephen became inseparable, going out drinking every weekend. Stephen's problems with alcohol, and later drugs, seemed to be exacerbated by his friendship with Ricky.

But he knew it wasn't Ricky or anyone else who made Stephen an addict. **OPEN, EAGER, JOYFUL** We each had our own ways of comforting ourselves, he thought, after Dad died. Stephen's was alcohol (like father, like son). Mom's was alcohol and shopping. And mine? He remembered the long, hot summer of 1986, reading novel after novel—*Sense and Sensibility*, *Middlemarch*, *Madame Bovary*, *Anna Karenina*, *The Portrait of a Lady*, even *Little Women* (always it had to be a novel about women), running seven, sometimes ten miles a day, and realizing that jogging was somehow like reading, they had a similar effect on the brain. If anything good came of his father's death, he thought, looking at the young man (who now seemed positively attentive to his thoughts), it was this: he had broken his dependence on Stephen. He had learned how to be alone with himself.

A PARTICULARLY SUGGESTIVE INTERPRETATION COMES FROM THE ART HISTORIAN YUKIO YASHIRO, WHO, IN HIS 1925 MONOGRAPH ON BOTTICELLI, WROTE THAT "EVERYONE GREETS HIS OWN FRIEND IN THIS UNKNOWN YOUTH.... IT IS AS IF A FACE LOOMED OUT OF THE DARK, DEAR TO EVERY CHILD OF MAN, A FACE WHICH, IF YOU TRY TO RECALL, YOU SEEM TO HAVE SEEN EVERYWHERE AND NOWHERE." He was floored to discover that someone in such a faraway time and place had put words to a sensation he felt not only from looking at this picture but from looking at people—men especially—in his daily wanderings (he pulled the tiny notebook from his pocket and wrote the name "Yashiro"). To call him "friend"—he looked into the young man's eyes, which now seemed gentle, almost sorrowful—changed utterly his appearance, changed everything. He noticed a single fleck of white in each eye. Signs of life, he thought and felt tears gathering inside him.

"Does the museum charge you a fee?"

"No, but you have to apply for a permit. They have different rules, depending on whether you live locally or come from out of town."

APPRENTICED AS A CHILD TO THE WORKSHOP OF HIS GOLDSMITH BROTHER

"I'm from Austin, Texas, so I get to paint five days in a row."

AND SOON AFTER TO THE WORKSHOP OF THE PAINTER FILIPPO LIPPI,

"Texas? Oh, uh-huh."

BY 1470 BOTTICELLI WAS RECORDED AS THE PROPRIETOR OF HIS OWN WORKSHOP. IN 1481 HE WAS SUMMONED TO ROME BY POPE SIXTUS IV TO PAINT

"You sure have come a long way."

His thoughts no longer able to compete with the sound of their voices, Robin sat down on the couch in the middle of the room, facing the Botticelli boy while eavesdropping on the conversation.

"Yeah. I was staying with a friend in San Francisco, and I went to three museums there and none of them allow copying. I was pretty disappointed. So I took a Greyhound bus across the country, through Albuquerque, Oklahoma City, and St. Louis. I stopped in Cleveland to copy a Vernet. And then I thought I'd try New York City, even though I was reluctant. You know, I'm really a country boy. I find New York pretty harsh."

"Are you working on a new installation?"

"Well, actually, I went to art school, but now I'm getting my PhD. I'm interested in the influence of Chinese and Far Eastern landscape painting on European art. Today I'm taking a breather from landscape, but that's my main interest. But yeah, I still do the installations. The next one is probably going to be all landscapes."

"Doesn't it bother you to have people coming up to you all the time and looking over your shoulder?"

"No, I like painting in this setting. I mean, first of all, the architecture of museums is so incredible! It's a maze of rooms, and the rooms are large and open.

There's often natural light. It's quiet."

"You like the quiet."

"Honestly, I prefer noise. I like working in public. A dozen people talk to me on any given day. I get constant feedback, and some of it is very helpful."

"What do they say to you?"

"Oh, people like to give advice, you know? They say, 'hey, why don't you move that tree over there?' I'll stay in one spot for a couple of hours, and it's cool because even though most people just look at a painting for a few seconds, it's like I'm setting an example of how to pay attention."

"People don't really look at the paintings. I've noticed that."

"But it's fun to listen to what they say. I wish I could record their comments. Actually, you know, that'd be cool! To film the whole thing while I'm copying in the gallery. I wonder if museums allow filming. Probably not."

"It's not allowed here."

They were silent for a moment. He painted, and the guard watched.

"Well, good luck to you."

"Thanks."

The guard returned to her stool and opened the book she held in her hand. Robin stood up and approached the *Portrait of a Young Man*.

During the last twenty years of his life, Botticelli fell under the influence of the charismatic preacher Girolamo Savonarola, whose notorious "bonfires of the vanities" (public burnings of books, paintings, and other material objects thought to breed corruption), along with his fiery denunciations of immorality among Florentine citizens as well as the Catholic clergy, culminated in his excommunication and execution in 1498. During this period, Botticelli illustrated an edition of Dante's *Divine Comedy* and was twice publically

DENOUNCED FOR IMMORALITY AND SODOMY.

He looked at the boy and wondered if the sitter was one of Botticelli's lovers. DURING HIS LIFETIME, BOTTICELLI WAS CALLED THE "NEW APELLES"; COMPARED FAVORABLY WITH GIOTTO, POLLAIOLO, PERUGINO, AND GHIRLANDAIO; PRAISED FOR HIS KNOWLEDGE AND USE OF THE SCIENCE OF PERSPECTIVE; AND DESCRIBED, FAMOUSLY, AS A "MOST EXCELLENT PAINTER ON PANEL AND ON WALL. HIS WORKS HAVE A VIRILE AIR AND ARE EXECUTED WITH THE GREATEST JUDGMENT AND PERFECT PROPORTION." BUT HIS REPUTATION QUICKLY FADED WITH THE RISE AND INFLUENCE OF THE GREATER REALISM OF RAPHAEL, AND FOR NEARLY FOUR HUNDRED YEARS HE WAS LARGELY FORGOTTEN. NOT UNTIL A HANDFUL OF LATE NINETEENTH-CENTURY ARTISTS AND CRITICS, MOST NOTABLY WALTER PATER, BEGAN CELEBRATING WHAT THEY PERCEIVED AS THE APPEALING ARTIFICIALITY AND FEMININE LANGUOR IN HIS WORKS DID HE COME AGAIN TO BE SEEN (BUT NOW FOR VERY DIFFERENT REASONS) AS ONE OF THE GREAT MASTERS OF THE ITALIAN RENAISSANCE. It pained him these days whenever he came across a reference to Walter Pater, or to any of the people he planned to write about in his dissertation. The chapter on Pater would have been the first, but it was the one he got stuck on. After three years, and Stephen's death, and his big HIV scare the following year, all he had to show for his efforts were thirty inconclusive pages on *The Renaissance*. Not even the whole book, just the initial chapter on the two Medieval French stories that, according to Pater, prefigured the Renaissance, and then not even both of them, just the first of the two, *Li Amitiez de Amis et Amile*. He remembered the story of two dear friends whose looks were strangely similar, whose love for each other was epitomized by Amile's willingness to murder his own children in order to wash his friend Amis in their blood to cure him of leprosy, and whose coffins, placed in separate churches, were found one morning, miraculously, side by side, as if of their own volition or by divine intervention, thus sealing their bond of friendship for all eternity. He had thought the missing piece of the puzzle was Montaigne's essay on friendship and his argument that friendship between two men is superior to the love a man feels for his children, his wife, his brother, or any object of sexual attraction. He was particularly interested in Montaigne's comments about brotherhood: "that confusion of ownership, the dividing, and the fact that the richness of one is the poverty of the other, wonderfully softens and loosens the solder of brotherhood. Since brothers have to guide their careers along the same path and at the same rate, it is inevitable that they often jostle and clash with each other." He thought of the change in his relationship with Stephen, starting in their junior year of high school, and then their estrangement once he'd finally come out on their 20th birthday. It was hard for him to accept that their bond, which had seemed so perfect in childhood, had been broken in adolescence and for ever after.

"The richness of one is the poverty of the other." Montaigne seemed to have diagnosed the problem between him and Stephan exactly, and in 1572! But then he drowned himself in the literature on friendship, getting confused about its overlap with the literature on homosexuality and the whole question of love between men. The first time he read Pater he missed entirely that Amis and Amile were *not* twin brothers but, rather, friends who happened to look exactly alike ("Wal-ter Pa-ter was a big fat queen," he remembered and smiled to himself as he silently sang the lyrics he and Eric made up, to the tune of Mozart's *Eine kleine Nachtmusik*, one weekend at the art history conference in Detroit: "all he e-ver wore was red sateen, / plumed hats and sequined knee-socks, / and paisley bloomers / all edged with maribou"). By the end of the summer of 2002 the chapter still wasn't finished, and it became clear it never would be. It was then he decided to quit graduate school, move to New York, and look for a full-time job in a gallery.

But encountering even just this passing reference to Pater reminded him of how late nineteenth-century aestheticism (Pater, Fromentin, Wilde) had the effect of awakening thought in him, or at least his sense of humor ("and he would prance and shriek, / and wave his fan about"). He looked at the Botticelli boy. If he was kin to all those pretty, androgynous boy angels who flock about the head of the Virgin in Botticelli's religious paintings, he was a fallen angel. He had already graduated from that ethereal company and begun a more earth-bound career ("and slap the house boy, / just like the silly queen, / that he completely was"). He might be one of those non-professional actors in a Pasolini film, like the sexy young actor with the mop of curly hair in *The Decameron* (Nino or Ninetto something—what was his name?) who always seemed to be jumping into bed with the first person he met and whose attitude toward sex—it seemed to be Pasolini's universal attitude, and it was the thing that made his movies so appealing, but also at times so painful, for it was never Robin's own feeling—Pasolini's characters always seemed completely carefree about sex and romance. They often laughed for the sheer pleasure it gave them. Even when it got them into trouble, as it often did (he thought of the curly-headed actor drowning in a pool of shit in one of the episodes from *The Decameron*), somehow they always wound up skipping lightheartedly down some road toward the horizon and the next big adventure.

He thought of New York in the 1970s, before AIDS, and wondered what it must have been like to live in the city then. He began to recover his earlier sense of the young man in the portrait as something of a scamp, a rogue, a trickster, and he wondered why, according to the label, nothing was known about him (*was* Botticelli gay? he wondered; could this have been one of his young lovers?). He amused himself with the thought that he had risen from the pages of Boccaccio or was conjured up in the slutty imagination of Pier Paolo Pasolini, and he imagined the boy stealing into some pretty girl's bed one night (he pulled the notepad from his back pocket and jotted an idea for a possible story) and being surprised by her parents the next morning, the two of them standing up to be questioned, the bed clothes falling down around their knees, or perhaps having sex with a girl in one scene and a guy in the next, or better yet seducing a girl with the help of his twin brother, to whom he was as much attracted as he was to the girl. He thought of all the books he read in graduate school on homosexuality in the Renaissance and how in those days it was seen as part of just about everyone's sexuality, at least potentially so.

Of course, sex was never as easy for Pasolini as he made it seem in his films, or at least most of them. There was *Salo*, after all: young men and women treated no better than barnyard animals, forced to eat shit, their tongues cut out of their heads, made to fuck against their will any time of day or night just for sport (he remembered the time he allowed Brian to tie him up). It might have been someone like the boy in this painting, he thought, who murdered Pasolini. Images of Joe flashed in his brain, the blood coming out of his penis. But he mustn't think too much about it now.

He was beginning to feel hungry and a little faint. All he had for breakfast before coming to the museum was a cup of coffee. He felt hung over, even though he hadn't been drinking last night. (Since Stephen's death he never touched alcohol or drugs of any kind, not even cigarettes. Everyone called his death an accident, but Robin held on to the belief that there was something intentional about it. How could it have been otherwise? Stephen had been drinking and doing drugs since high school.) But he resisted the urge to get some nourishment, deciding, instead, to finish reading the label. **MODERN CRITICS, BY CONTRAST, STARTING WITH HERBERT HORNE'S 1908 STUDY, EMPHASIZED BOTTICELLI'S REALISTIC OBJECTIVITY, PLASTIC STRENGTH, MORAL RIGOR, AND "VIRILE AIR." THE TENSION BETWEEN THESE TWO APPROACHES DEFINED THE CRITICAL DISCOURSE ON BOTTICELLI FOR DECADES TO COME.** There *was* virility, he thought, in this boy—in the square jaw, the broad shoulders, the firm chin. He liked the way the skin puckered at the corners of his mouth. It signified youth but also advancing age, for those same smooth folds of skin (again, thinking of the painting as a live thing) would turn to sharp creases within ten years.

He turned at the sound of a snap and saw that the artist (what did he say his name was?) had already packed up his easel and paints and was folding his drip cloth. Heading into the next gallery, Robin walked past the *Portrait of a Lady*, at the same time catching a glimpse of the rough oil sketch the artist had made of it as he tucked it under his arm.

"How ya doin'?" the artist said to him.

"Good," Robin answered before he had time to think that what he most wanted was to avoid conversation, even the simplest greeting. The guy was obviously willing to talk with anyone. He was the type of person Robin went out of his way to avoid. The exchange, however, had already taken place, and the artist was already walking away.

"See you tomorrow, same place, same time," he said to the guard.

"OK now, have a good one."

Watching him go, with the easel propped against his shoulder, suitcase under one arm and canvas under the other, Robin thought he looked *not* carefree and self-assured but burdened and alone, stooped, as he was, by all the things he carried. He was a stranger in New York, a country boy who found the city harsh and unforgiving. In spite of himself Robin began to weave a character sketch of the guy in his head. Suddenly he felt he had been unfair, almost wanted to call him back, talk with him. Take a good look at that painting he'd just done. Find out more about his PhD thesis (the project did, after all, sound interesting). And as he crossed the threshold into the next room, spotting a row of self-portraits by Rembrandt, he wished he could remember the name of that website.

ALBRECHT DURER (1471-1528)
SELF-PORTRAIT IN FUR CLOAK, 1500
OIL ON BOARD

Albrecht Durer
Self-Portrait in Fur Cloak

Your can of Coke sits on top of *The Life and Art of Albrecht Durer* by Erwin Panofsky. The captain has turned on the seatbelt sign. You should finish it so it doesn't spill. The flight from New York to Dusseldorf has gotten bumpy. This past week in New York was nonstop work. Planning your one-man retrospective at the Metropolitan Museum of Art in 2003, deciding which pictures to include and which not, talking to journalists who want you to explain your work and your life in less than a minute—all of it has been thoroughly exhausting. You think of the mountains of work that await you when you get back to Dusseldorf. An infant screams in Economy. You feel a knot of tension in your back. You think how distressing for the people sitting nearby if *you* can hear it all the way up in Business. You try stretching to see if that will help. You sit forward and rotate your head, first clockwise, then counterclockwise. You raise your arms and feel your shoulder muscles. You lift your left foot off the floor and rotate it five times clockwise, five times counterclockwise. You do the same with your right. You sit back again. The knot of pain is still there.

You look out the window and see rain clouds. Your face is reflected faintly in the tiny portrait-sized window. Your face floats over thick dark clouds as you approach Dusseldorf. You take a sip of Coke, open the book, remove your passport (convenient as a bookmark), and pick up where you left off, hoping to distract yourself from the noise and the pain, with Panofsky's theory of the lifecycle of an artist: *The activities of artists are generally divided into three periods, early, middle and late. This scheme, however rudimentary, is not only based on an analogy to physical life, where we distinguish between youth, maturity and old age, but has some justification in history. However great an artist may be, he will normally begin by absorbing the traditions prevailing at the time of his youth.*

You think back to when you were nine years old. Your father returned home from a business trip to America with a present: *New York*, a book of photographs by Don Hunstein with captions in English, French, and German. The city came bursting to life in pictures of kids playing in the street, supermarket shelves piled with more goods than you'd ever seen in Dusseldorf, people of every conceivable color and ethnicity going about their daily lives, baseball fans at Yankee Stadium, sunbathers at Coney Island, ships in New York harbor, the Statue of Liberty, Times Square, Broadway… When you were a child, just thinking about New York was an escape to a private island of glad hearts and self-expression.

You check your watch. One hour before landing. The baby is howling.

At nineteen you enrolled in the Kunstakademie Dusseldorf and studied with Gerhard Richter, using photography, like Richter, mainly as a source of inspiration for painting. But spontaneously you began taking pictures of passersby in the street. Then the people disappeared from your pictures. You were interested in the built environment, the architecture of Dusseldorf, the urban structure of post-war German cities. You were reading Wolfgang Kohler on *gestalt* psychology, Walter Benjamin on the philosophy of history, Eugen Herrigel on zen and the art of archery. Richter suggested you take a class with the photographers Bernd and Hilla Becher.

For the *Rundgang* of 1976, you showed 49 photographs of empty Dusseldorf streets alongside ten shots of the backs of women's heads. The pictures were cool, detached, anonymous, not unlike the Bechers' photos of gas tanks and wooden houses. You realized you were more interested in working on things that resided outside of yourself, things not restricted to your own personal psychology. You realized you were fascinated by *analytical processes themselves*. You shifted your concentration at the Kunstakademie from painting to photography.

In 1977 you won the academy's first scholarship to New York. No longer a series of pictures in someone else's book, New York became *your own* book of pictures. You learned the various *gestalts* of the Financial District, Tribeca, SoHo, the Village, Chelsea, Midtown, Harlem. You were amazed how the atmosphere of one neighborhood could be so different from another. You positioned your tripod squarely in the middle of the street. You made pictures that looked more like clinical documents than personal "artistic" statements. At night you went skating at the Empire Roller Disco in Crown Heights and learned the unconscious choreography of the dance floor, a group performance and a hundred solo exhibitions at once. You made your first sale: eighteen prints for $50 each. When you returned to Dusseldorf in the fall of 1978, you made the decision to dedicate your life to photography.

You look out the window and see nothing but white. Your face is reflected in the tiny portrait-sized window, cast onto the white, flying hundreds of miles an hour through space, crossing time zones. The captain has turned off the seatbelt sign. The flight attendant asks if you'll have another drink. You nod yes (but the baby will not stop crying, and the pain in your back persists).

During his second phase, formerly often called his "best period," he will develop a style entirely his own and, if he is strong enough, create a tradition himself.

After years of photographing deserted city streets in black and white, you discovered Naples, Palermo, Rome—colorful, messy, multilayered, dense forests of signs and structures where time leaves traces, layer upon layer, everywhere you look, where nothing dies but accumulates year by year, century after century, and so the pictures of straight lines, right angles, and orderly rows, all the geometric modernity of Dusseldorf and New York, gave way to crazy buildings piled one on top of another, crumbling facades, classical pediments, lopsided cornices, ancient shutters, cracked tiles, tattered awnings, flowers bursting from windows boxes, laundry hanging out to dry, twisted railings, TV antennae, and telephone wires tangled together in the heat and dust, and so much noise! In Rome in the mid-1980s you discovered you could *see analytically.* You no longer needed the controlling device of single-point perspective. Now you could see complexity, find structure embedded in chaos, capture thousands upon thousands of details in a picture knowing that everything is interrelated, that information is created by the *dynamics among* the disparate elements, not simply the elements themselves, that the elements work together in a very precise way, but it would be impossible to explain *how* they work. You simply know by intuition.

Meanwhile, you had begun to photograph families. At first it was just your friends the Johnstons from Scotland and the Shimadas from Japan. You saw parallels to your pictures of urban streets. The family portraits depicted not only diverse individuals but the hidden dynamics that create a group identity, a cultural identity. You made a picture of your own family, but you weren't happy with it—you looked too much like a random collection of people dressed up with no idea where they were. So you made more and more pictures of families. You realized that making pictures of other people's families was a way to analyze and understand your own. (You do not have a choice when it comes to family. Growing up in Germany in the 1950s and '60s, you had questions about your family, about other people's families, what they did under fascism, whether they accepted it.)

The flight attendant brings you another Coke. The crying baby sounds like a wounded animal.

In the late '80s you made a portrait of the art historian Giles Robertson at his home in Edinburgh, sitting at a table with 17th- and 18th-century paintings on the wall behind. This suggested the potential for merging the present and the past on one photographic plane. The next year in Naples you visited the studio of Giulia Zoretti, a restorer of old paintings. Restorers get closer to paintings than anyone except the artists who originally made them. The experience brought you back in contact with the medium you'd left behind when you decided to become a photographer. At the end of your visit, you made a photograph of Giulia and three of her colleagues at the former refectory of San Lorenzo Maggiore, surrounded by dozens of Renaissance paintings in various stages of repair. This was the beginning of the Museum Photographs series. By now you were being exhibited and collected all over Europe and America. You found yourself spending more and more time in museums. You became fascinated by the way people behaved when passing through galleries and looking at pictures. You wondered what they were looking for as they stood in front of all those old pictures. You sensed that people have too much respect for the celebrity status of the works on display. They forget that paintings are made by everyday people in everyday circumstances (it is easy to forget sometimes, especially now with your upcoming retrospective, that you yourself are an everyday person). You began to photograph groups of people at the Louvre, the Rijksmuseum, the Art Institute of Chicago—ordinary, everyday people of all ages and ethnicities, men and women, standing in front of Delacroix's *Liberty Leading the People*, Gericault's *Raft of the Medusa*, Caillabotte's *Paris Street, Rainy Day*. The people in your pictures display every conceivable emotion when confronted by great painting—confusion, distraction, boredom, fear, irritation, hilarity, absorption, curiosity, fascination, enlightenment, rapture. The pictures struck a chord with art lovers and collectors worldwide and made you famous—so famous, in fact, that nowadays people approach you in museums and ask, "Are you the photographer Thomas Struth?"

The flight attendant hands you a landing card. You take a pen from your shirt pocket and begin to fill it out. You open your passport to retrieve the ID number. You are taken aback by your portrait. Your eyes are large. Your hairline recedes. You have a growth of stubble on your cheek. You look naked. Exposed. It is you, as it says there in the passport, with your name, sex, date and place of birth, date of issue and expiration. But it is not really you. Not the real you. The real you doesn't appear in pictures. The real you is to be found in the pictures you make of empty streets and the backs of women's heads and other people's families and ordinary men, women, and children looking at great paintings (you close the passport, thinking you'll fill out the landing card inside the airport).

An interviewer once asked, only half jokingly, had you ever thought to make a photograph of people looking at one of your photographs of people looking at paintings? You dismissed the question at the time, thinking, if for no other reason than inane questions like that, I may after all have taken my last museum photograph, no matter how popular and lucrative they are! But then only last month, you think, opening the passport again and seeing your portrait, while visiting the Alte Pinakothek in Munich on the last day of 1999, you spontaneously placed a 35mm camera on a bench and made a snapshot of yourself standing in front of Albrecht Durer's *Self-Portrait in Fur Cloak*. You remember that you didn't much like the photograph. The problem was, it was clearly a picture of *Thomas Struth* looking at Albrecht Durer's *Self-Portrait in Fur Cloak*. You were too much in the picture.

In the last phase, finally, he may either continue with the style of his maturity in a more or less mechanical way and thereby cease to be productive, or else—and this applies to the greatest only—he will outgrow the tradition established by himself.... He will therefore cease to have an immediate following and often forfeit his former popularity, not because he is "outmoded" but because he has overstepped the limits of contemporary understanding. The latest works of Rembrandt, Titian, Michelangelo and Beethoven are cases in point.

When applying this tripartite scheme to the evolution of Dürer we are not wholly satisfied.

You close the book and put it aside. "Not wholly satisfied." You wonder if you are still in your "middle" period, or is this the beginning of the end? You are 46 years old. The new millennium has just begun. The twenty-first century. You look out the window and see your face floating over clouds stretching away to infinity. You think of your photographs of Paradise. Starting in the early '90s, while scouting locations for pictures of cities, you began to photograph jungles and forests in Australia, China, Japan, and Brazil. The pictures were gigantic and green and densely loaded with twisting, tangling branches, vines, moss, leaves. (When you're a German, you look back and see disaster, atrocity, murder, crime of unexplainable dimensions. Then you look further back and grab for something interesting, something fascinating and playful, something that does not harm. Music. Literature. Art. Then *all the way back to the beginning. To Nature itself.*)

When you first exhibited the jungle pictures you realized that when you enter a room with these pictures, they make you very quiet. You know exactly what you are seeing. You don't have to search for an explanation. You see a structure that's immensely complicated, but you give up searching for highlights, for telling details, for clues, and so the rushing stream forever searching for explanations in your brain stops. Goes quiet. And what you have is the feeling, I am standing in an exhibition space, I am looking at pictures of jungle, I am here in this moment of time. You named the series "New Pictures from Paradise" so people would understand that the pictures are not about botany or plants, not about the jungle, not about nostalgia for some lost paradise. They are about structure, about the play of observation, about what this situation of observation does within *you*, the viewer. The way it makes you conscious in a very quiet, peaceful way. Conscious that you are here now.

You remember visiting New York in 1993, shortly after the bombing of the World Trade Center. You were walking in the Village when a young man and woman cruised by on roller skates, holding a sign between them that said, "PEACE." Further along you passed a white brick wall, and you noticed some graffiti. You stopped to read the words: "You are alive." You didn't have a camera with you at the time. Otherwise, you would have made a picture.

You are alive.

The baby has stopped crying.

You are here now.

Suddenly you have an idea: return to the Alte Pinakothek and re-stage your self-portrait with Durer, only this time take "Thomas Struth" out of the picture. The only "person" identifiable in the picture will be Albrecht Durer himself. *You* will appear only as a blur, off to one side, from the neck down, unrecognizable—a neck, a shoulder, an arm, a torso. When the viewer looks at the photograph—at Thomas Struth's "self-portrait"—all he will see clearly is Albrecht Durer's *Self-Portrait in Fur Cloak*.

You realize the tension in your back has gone away.

You look out the window and see only an expanse of blue.

⊙⊛⊙

Details were hard to make out because, unlike the other paintings in the gallery, this one was protected by a wall-mounted glass case. **FROM EARLY ADOLESCENCE UNTIL HIS**

DEATH AT THE AGE OF 57, ALBRECHT DURER (1471-1528) CREATED AN UNPRECEDENTED SERIES OF SELF-PORTRAIT DRAWINGS AND PAINTINGS. HERE IN HIS GREATEST, MOST COMPLEX SELF-PORTRAIT, HE APPEARS AT HIS PHYSICAL AND ARTISTIC PEAK IN A POSE PROVOCATIVELY SUGGESTIVE OF TRADITIONAL REPRESENTATIONS OF JESUS CHRIST. So I was right! Bernard thought, it *does* look like the face of Christ. And not just the face—the right hand as well, as if he were giving a blessing. But the left hand? Only the sleeve was visible along the bottom edge of the painting. He stepped closer to see what if anything was inside Durer's left sleeve. It looked empty, as if the left hand had been chopped off, or the fist clenched within. The invisible hand, he thought, of the psychotherapist. He remembered, early on in her treatment, how Vanessa had objected to the very premise of talk therapy according to which the patient reveals herself to the therapist but the therapist remains largely silent. "Masked" was the word she used. Interesting word choice, he said to himself, feeling the impact of the full-frontal presentation of Durer's face. In a sense the *Self-Portrait in Fur Cloak* illustrated the therapeutic relation itself: the talking patient (Durer) frankly, almost pathetically revealed; the listening therapist (the spectator in front of the painting) ever-present but at the same time invisible. He still wasn't sure Vanessa had come to accept his role as therapist, though she hadn't voiced an objection in weeks. He had felt their work together would be stymied if she continued to mistrust the process at such a basic level, but he also admired her all-pervasive skepticism. He wondered if he had ever actually said that to her. He should. He was touched to think that Vanessa might actually *want* to know things about him. And honestly, he *did* reveal more of himself to her than to any other of his patients. With Vanessa he found himself illustrating his comments with personal anecdotes. For example just this morning, when she'd been talking about wasting her time at work, and how she feared she was doomed to never finish the long, narrative poem she was writing, he responded with a story about his own writing process. He said he often finds, when writing, that the times he feels least productive are, in fact, necessary gestation periods, though he may not realize it until some later date. We just have to keep on trusting the process, he said. But still she wanted more from him.

He looked at Durer's Christ-like face. Maybe the painting revealed the therapeutic relation in the opposite sense. The patient (now he fancied *himself* in the patient's position) looked upon the therapist (the face of Durer) as if in a mirror. In the face of the therapist the patient saw whatever he wanted and needed. The therapist was at the patient's disposal, permitting him to see himself, first through the distorting light of transference, but eventually (once the transference has been called to the patient's attention) as he—or she—really is. For standing as he was before this glass box with the face of Durer inside, it did seem as if he were looking at his own reflection, as if in the mirror of a medicine chest, Bernard thought with a smile, first thing in the morning. Can you imagine, he asked himself, waking up one morning, going into the bathroom, turning on the light, looking in the mirror, and seeing not your own face but the stern, long-haired, bearded face of Albrecht Durer? And—taking the joke a step further—the way the glass case protruded from the wall *did* make it seem as if you could open it like a medicine chest, and then inside you would find (Bernard imagined himself reaching inside the glass case and opening Durer's self-portrait like the door to a medicine chest) all your HIV medications.

Suddenly the joke wasn't funny anymore. He saw his own image reflected in the glass case. He thought how portraits often concealed things in old movies—a vault, usually, containing money or jewels or deeds to a property. He had made Durer's *Self-Portrait in Fur* cough up HIV drugs. More and more he felt the need to share his HIV status with his patients, though he doubted that was the kind of disclosure Vanessa had in mind. It seemed inauthentic somehow to go on "helping" them in the guise of someone who didn't himself need help, or who was beyond help. If he had cancer, say, and needed to cancel appointments for a month because he was undergoing chemotherapy, it would be permissible, he thought, probably even a *good* idea, to inform patients of the reason. And it wouldn't be just a matter of "informing" them. Patients and colleagues might well see it as a meaningful *point of view* from which to conduct therapy. He thought of Henri Nouwen's *The Wounded Healer*, a book that had meant so much to him when he first read it in the monastery. For Nouwen, the minister's wound was loneliness—the existential loneliness that was part of the human condition, but also a professional loneliness that grew out of his sense that the minister was becoming increasingly irrelevant to modern life. He remembered the story Nouwen told about sailing on a ship when he was chaplain of the Holland-American line. A dense fog had made it near impossible to steer into port, and the captain at first rudely told him to get out of the way, then condescendingly said, "No stick around. This may be the one time I really need you." As with much of the theology he'd studied in Divinity School, the personal anecdotes stayed with him when the theoretical packaging had fallen away from memory. But he remembered this much: Nouwen believed that "no minister can offer service without a constant and vital acknowledgment of his own experiences," but you had to learn how to see and accept yourself first. Then the question became how to translate that self-acceptance into healing ministry for others. Not by the "spiritual exhibitionism," as he called it, of remarks such as, "Don't worry because I suffer from the same depression, confusion and anxiety as you do" (the kind of thing he feared he had indulged in this morning with Vanessa), and not by trying to take away the pain. Instead Nouwen advocated that the minister "deepen the pain to a level where it can be shared." The example he gave of this kind of ministry remained, for Bernard, incredibly powerful: "When a woman suffers the loss of her child, the minister is not called upon to comfort her by telling her that she still has two beautiful healthy children at home; he is challenged to help her realize that the death of her child reveals her own mortal condition, the same human condition which he and others share with her."

That passage had grown more important to Bernard since he became infected. For there was no taking HIV away, no getting it out of his body and out of his life. It had come to stay, so the only option was to treat it, of course, but then somehow to understand it, accept it, embrace it. To "deepen the pain," as Nouwen might say. To make more meaningful the experience of being HIV positive. Therein lay the embrace. How to "embrace" HIV in this way was something Bernard had now dedicated himself to finding out. He was embarked on an inward journey, and it was taking him far into himself, into parts of himself he'd never seen or touched, into other potential selves (sometimes he thought he was discovering nothing more remarkable than the unbelievably remarkable human capacity for change). It was a journey out into the world too. And that, he suspected, was why he was becoming increasingly uncomfortable with the supposedly inviolable boundary between doctor and patient. He felt that his HIV status colored every encounter he had with his patients, and he wasn't sure that was such a bad thing. In fact he felt more prepared to do the healing work of therapy than ever before (he certainly felt more capable of helping people as a therapist than he did as a monk). And his sense of readiness, he believed, had something to do with HIV.

He looked at himself faintly reflected in the glass case, then through the glass at the Christ-like face of Durer. Of all the portraits he had seen so far, this one appealed to him most, perhaps because it reminded him of his religious past. Or because it seemed somehow ironic—downright funny, even—though he wasn't entirely sure why. Sometimes he felt boorish in art museums. He could never take art history too seriously ("his greatest, most complex self-portrait," and all that self-important talk). And inevitably he got distracted by what was going on *in front of* the art objects. *That* was the real human drama! he thought. The people doing the looking. The drama depicted within the paintings, the drama which inspired them and went into their making so long ago—these were all part of the drama that included everything going on here and now *in front of* the paintings. It was all one shared human drama (thinking again of Nouwen's wounded healer). The same human condition. The same *mortal* human condition. Artist–subject–viewer: we exist in relation to each other, Bernard thought, forever and for all time.

The glass case now functioned as a portrait-sized window faintly mirroring what was going on behind him in the gallery. He watched the passing scene. A young couple, the guy's arm around the girl's waist, sauntered through the gallery, seemingly more interested in each other than the art on the walls. A middle-aged woman in a dark pantsuit with a flower at her lapel and an ID badge on a chain around her neck (a security guard) sat on a stool thumbing a paperback book. An old man leaning on an umbrella bent forward to read the label next to a painting, straightened his posture to look at the painting, and then looked up at something overhead, perhaps the cables from which the painting was suspended, strung from the cornice half way up the wall. The man had white hair. He wore a dark, full-length coat, even though it was mid-April. "Distinguished Gentleman" was the phrase that came to Bernard's mind. He thought of the photograph he kept on the bookshelf of his consulting room in which three well-dressed gentlemen, each wearing a fedora, one of them smoking a pipe, stood amid the rubble of a bombed-out library whose roof has fallen in. They appear to be leisurely browsing the still-intact shelves, as if it were an ordinary London afternoon and the time had come to take a break from the busy world, pay a visit to the local library, pull a book off the shelf, find a quiet corner, and sit down to read for an hour or two.

That photograph had become newly relevant ever since they started tearing down St. Ann's. It had always given him comfort to look out his window and see the steeple and long pitched roof of old St. Ann's and to know that, any day of the week, Mass was being said, confessions heard, prayers offered in the midst of this city so full of madness and suffering. It was a comfort to know that St. Ann's was there, a safe, warm hive of spiritual activity. He hadn't paid more than half a dozen visits since he'd moved to the neighborhood nine years ago, but now that it was being torn down (they started peeling off the wooden roof this morning; it was both wonderful and horrifying, he felt, to see the blue and gold interior, like the inside of a tender piece of fruit, violently exposed to view)—now that it was being torn down he was filled with... he looked at his reflection in the glass case... not sorrow, exactly. It was a feeling next door to sorrow, but it partook, in a strange way, of satisfaction. *Acceptance*—perhaps that's what he felt. He *accepted* the tearing down of St. Ann's. For the change was inevitable. One way or another, nothing stayed the same, not in a place like New York. Neighbors came and went. Buildings rose and fell. Shops closed, new ones opened up. A new crop of students flooded the neighborhood every September. Nothing lasted forever. Everything was only for now. St. Ann's had been a comfort, but perhaps it was a shallow comfort (he tried to remember what it was like *not* having to be so conscious of his health, before HIV). And anyway, it had been *his* decision to leave the Church. The Church wasn't home anymore. The consulting room, if anything, was home now. What he felt for St. Ann's was probably ninety percent nostalgia, and clinging to regret, he knew from experience, got him nowhere. It was better to welcome the changes and hope that something good, something totally unforeseen, might come of them. If nothing else, HIV had taught him that.

Inscribed prominently at eye-level to the left of the figure, Dürer's monogram is conjoined with the year 1500, suggesting a convergence between the artist's individual passage from youth to adulthood and the collective passage of the human race from one half-millennium to the next. Somehow Bernard couldn't quite focus on the information contained in the label. Instead he continued looking at the scene behind him, reflected in the case, and saw that the fine old gentleman had moved away, but in his place was a young man. He stood perfectly still before the self-portrait of Rembrandt dressed like a Renaissance dandy. Bernard himself had been looking at it only a few minutes ago, one in an impressive row of five that dominated the opposite wall of the gallery showing the artist aging from youth through old age. The young man struck Bernard as unusual because he wasn't accompanied by anyone, wasn't wearing headphones, wasn't carrying a backpack or shoulder bag (Bernard felt the weight of his own cumbersome shoulder bag and wished he had left it in the coat room), wasn't glued to a floor plan or poking at a cell phone. Wasn't making a statement with his wardrobe (he was dressed in a plain brown, long-sleeve shirt, jeans, and sneakers). Wasn't making a spectacle of himself in any way. He just stood there seemingly transfixed before the painting as if he had turned to stone. Or as if, perhaps, thoughts of Dorian Gray ran through his head. As soon as the words "Dorian Gray" crossed Bernard's mind, the young man turned around and looked in his direction. He wore glasses. He had a nice shape, Bernard thought, remembering how he pinched his waist this morning as he stepped out of the shower and decided he needed to exercise more often. But when did he have time to go to the gym? Dorian Gray, he thought and smiled. Why beat myself up about it? I'm a middle-aged man, after all.

Similarly, the Latin motto on the right, "Albertus Durerus Noricus ipsum me propriis sic effingebam coloribus aetatis anno XXVIII" (I, Albrecht Dürer

OF NUREMBERG, PAINTED MYSELF THUS WITH UNDYING COLORS AT THE AGE OF TWENTY-EIGHT YEARS), REINFORCES THE PORTRAIT'S AMBIGUOUS PARALLEL BETWEEN THE CREATIVE ARTIST AND THE CREATOR GOD. "Undying," Bernard thought with a smile; that's why this portrait is funny. Again he saw reflected in the glass the bustling space of the gallery behind him (the young man had turned back to the Rembrandts and was now standing before the one of the artist as an old man). What patients see, and what they say, when they look at themselves in the mirror or at photographs of themselves (focusing now upon his *own* face, faintly reflected in the glass and superimposed upon the face of Durer) revealed all sorts of things about self-esteem, certainly (Bernard thought that making peace with his spreading middle was a healthy sign of self-acceptance), but there was more to it than that. He thought of Todd. Only last week he had begun to look at family photos with Todd and to start the "mirror dialogue," as he now termed it, but already it seemed to have unsettled something important. Todd had brought a photograph of himself as a kid to his last session. Bernard asked him to look at the picture and say what he saw there. Todd said he didn't like what he saw.

"What do you see?" Bernard insisted.

Todd took a long time to answer. All he could say was, he didn't like the boy in the picture.

"Try to describe what you see without evaluating." Todd hesitated. "Just describe."

"He has a big grin on his face," Todd finally said. "I hate his grin."

"Try not to evaluate, *just describe*. You see that he has a grin on his face. What else?"

"He has buck teeth."

"OK, what else?"

"He has freckles, his eyes look Chinese. They're kind of puffy. It may have been early in the morning when the picture was taken. It was a school portrait. Probably seven or eight in the morning, because they used to take our pictures before the first period."

"And?"

"And I just don't understand why I look so happy. I mean, I really look *genuinely* happy. And I know that I wasn't happy. I was never happy in middle school. I hated my life and I hated myself and I hated my classmates and my parents. Nobody with buck teeth has any right to smile like that. It's like the whole world knows something about you that *you* don't know. It makes me look like an idiot."

Bernard was struck by his inability to describe without evaluating, to say nothing of the vehemence of his self-hatred. He decided to change tactics slightly. "Let's stay for a moment," he suggested, "with this idea that the whole world knows something that you don't know. Or that other people can see something about you that you yourself can't see. Can you say more about that?"

Todd sat for a long time thinking (it was one of the things Bernard loved about Todd; he thought before he spoke, though sometimes, clearly, he was busy censoring his thoughts). Eventually he said, "In seventh grade, I think it was, I belonged to a chess club at school, and I was playing with this girl in the club. She was a little older than me, and she was good at the game. I don't know why I joined this club because I knew nothing about chess, and it's a hard game to learn, and I don't think I was really all that interested in learning. I guess it was one of the few clubs that promised to be, I don't know, peaceful and quiet, not a bunch of boys running around screaming and acting like animals to blow off steam. Anyway, I was in this club and—I forget what we were talking about—it wasn't chess-related—but this girl was telling me how she would describe me to a person who didn't know me, as if they were supposed to meet me somewhere and she had to supply them with a description so they would know how to identify me, and she said something like, 'the kid with the blond hair and the buck teeth.' It was like being punched in the gut. It felt so insulting. And the worst part of it was that I *knew* I had a big overbite—I'm pretty sure by that time I was wearing braces, but even so, it took a couple of years to correct the problem—and I—of course I didn't like my overbite, but I think what upset me the most wasn't so much my overbite as the fact that *everyone else* seemed to have a problem with my overbite. Other people would comment on it, and it was embarrassing. I felt blamed for something I didn't choose, and it was visible all the time, so what could I do about it? And when she said that, she didn't say it with hostility. She said it as if it was just the simplest fact about me. My blond hair and my buck teeth. I think if she had said it aggressively, if she had intended it as an insult, I could have built up some kind of defense in my mind. I could have thought, I'm a victim, this is unfair, she's a bad person. But she wasn't saying it in a mean way. And *that's* what hurt. I wanted to cry, and I don't think I allowed myself to cry, because to cry over my buck teeth would have meant—it would have been like caving into despair, because there was nothing more I could do about it."

"So," Bernard asked, hoping to expose the contradiction he perceived at the heart of what Todd was saying, "were you unhappy with the way your teeth looked or with the things other people said about your teeth?"

Again Todd sat and thought. At last he said, "I don't know, I can't tell them apart."

"And now," Bernard asked, "when you look at a picture of yourself from that time, how do you see your teeth?"

"I already told you."

"Tell me again."

"I see a fucking buck-tooth idiot with a big smile on his face."

It was then that Bernard asked him if he might like to kiss the boy in the picture. Todd was horrified. "Why would I want to kiss a buck-tooth idiot?"

"Teeth out of place are very human."

"It may be human, but that doesn't mean I want to kiss him."

He suggested that Todd close his eyes during the kiss.

"It seems silly."

"I know," Bernard said gently.

But Todd refused. "It reminds me," he offered instead, "of the first time I ever kissed a man. Or rather, the first time I *didn't* kiss a man. I had this friend my senior year of college, and we had been flirting with each other for weeks. I didn't know if he was gay, and I still wasn't sure about myself, but it was obvious that something was going on between us, there was this tension, excitement, really thick in the air, every time we were together. So on my birthday some of my friends threw a party for me, and Todd—that was his name, which is funny. He was 'Todd' too, and there aren't so many Todd's in the world. Anyway, he was there at the party. Afterward we went back to our dormitory. He had saved his gift so he could give it to me when we were alone together. So we were in my room and it was late, and he gave me the gift, which was a large desk calendar from an Asian art museum in Washington, DC—you know, one of those calendars where on the right side they have the days of the week, and on the left side a reproduction of a painting or a sculpture. It was very beautiful. I never use calendars like that, and I ended up not using that one either. I still have it packed away in my parents' attic somewhere. Well, we were sitting next to each other on my bed, and we were very close, and little by little we allowed our bodies to get closer and closer and we let our legs and arms brush against each other, and at some point he just put his hand on my arm, and then he hugged me. Then he went in for a kiss, but I pulled away. He asked me what was wrong. 'Nothing,' I said, but I avoided his face. I couldn't kiss him. I wanted to touch him and embrace him, and all of that felt incredible, like a gift from Heaven, but I couldn't go the next step and kiss him. I couldn't kiss him because I had never seen two men kiss each other before. Or if I had, it was only for laughs, like on a sitcom where one man kisses another and the other one punches him in return and the audience roars with laughter. But I had never seen a serious, romantic kiss. I had never seen a lingering kiss between two men, so it didn't matter what I felt or what I wanted: if I hadn't seen someone else do it, I couldn't do it myself. It had to be validated, I guess, by the outside world for me to do it myself. That's what I think of when you ask me to kiss the photograph."

"Are you saying you can't help but see yourself in the picture through the eyes of people who disapproved of you?" Bernard suggested.

"I guess so."

"Can you image you might ever see the boy in the photograph differently?"

"I don't know."

That was where the session ended. What amazed Bernard was Todd's lucidity about his own behavior—behavior that Todd apparently knew was problematic—and at the same time his inability to change his behavior. It wasn't that Todd lacked insight into himself. In fact, he was exceptionally self-aware (another thing Bernard loved about him). No, the amazing thing, Bernard thought, looking at Durer's *Self-Portrait in Fur Cloak* but now seeing neither the painting nor the gallery reflected in the glass case but only Todd and himself sitting opposite each other in his consulting room—the amazing thing, Bernard thought, is that Todd knows a good deal about himself, but his knowledge is not enough to change his behavior. At least not yet. The face of Albrecht Durer came back into view. He wondered if, at their next session, it might be worth practicing the art of describing a face. He looked at Durer's long nose, manicured mustache, pillowy lips, eyes whose expression became harder to read the longer he scrutinized them. He might ask Todd to choose a reproduction of a favorite portrait and describe it. It might be easier, at this stage, than confronting a picture of himself.

The glass over the painting became a mirror once more, and Bernard saw, with a slight shock, that the young man with glasses now stood a few feet behind him, looking over his shoulder. Bernard concentrated his gaze more carefully to size him up. He seemed to be about the same height as Bernard and, as he appeared from across the room, nicely proportioned. His neck was rather long. Bernard liked that. He liked to see the breadth of a man's shoulders, not concealed by a mass of hair or complicated clothing (Durer's shoulders were completely covered by his long brown hair, and his torso was pretty much indefinable beneath the heavy brown cloak). His short hair, he could see if he looked carefully, was a mixture of brown and blond. He wondered if he colored his hair; it seemed everyone did nowadays (certainly most women did). His features were delicate, though his nose was unusually long, almost beak-like. In spite of his glasses, he could see there was something interesting about his eyes. At first he didn't know what. Then it appeared that, even with glasses, the young man was slightly cross-eyed. The glasses magnified his eyes, making them look extra large. His eyes together with his glasses (small, round "John Lennon" glasses) gave him a look of vulnerability. It was a look that appealed to Bernard. Had he come over to look at the Durer painting or to flirt with him? He wondered if the young man knew he was being looked at. It might be that when Bernard looked at him, reflected in the glass, he was looking right back at Bernard; it was hard to tell exactly where his eyes were focused.

Not wanting his attention to the young man to be perceived, he shifted his focus and looked at the painting instead. Durer's gaze too, Bernard thought, was hard to pin down. One eye—the left—seemed to look straight ahead at the viewer, while the other seemed to wander just slightly off to his right. It was a little disconcerting. The young man stepped from behind and stood over to Bernard's right to read the information label next to the painting. With that, Bernard stepped a foot to the left to give him more room but also to signal that he was aware of his presence. Bernard kept his eyes on Durer's eyes but then quickly and (he hoped) discreetly turned his head to look for a moment at the young man's profile. He had a well-shaped chin (Bernard was always self-conscious about not having much of a chin), his nose was indeed long and beak-like, and his glasses hugged close to his well-shaped head. Looking again into Durer's eyes, Bernard thought how Durer gave the viewer his full face but how the young man's face was fleeting, fugitive, turned to one side, turned away, not to be stared at, visible only from a distance or through layers of glass and mirror. We never get to see real faces very well, Bernard thought. Perhaps only when someone is asleep—asleep right next to us on the pillow. He thought of Chris (his ex). Or dead. He thought of Bill (the first of his patients to die while still in treatment), laid out in the coffin, his cheeks sunken and bronzed from so many years of HIV medication. Viewings were such ghastly rituals. One of Catholicism's many cruelties, he thought. (The young man was still studying the label, not looking at the painting.) Bernard wondered if his own face showed any sign of HIV. It was hard to see changes in one's own face, but now and then a set of wrinkles, or the never-before-noticed depression of an eyelid, would strike him as he looked in the mirror, and he would think, I am getting old, or, I am getting sick. He didn't mind, exactly, the thought that his face was changing, maybe even rapidly. It signaled his own lovability, he thought. How could you not love someone who is susceptible to the same things every other person on the planet is susceptible to? He looked at the handsome face of Durer. "Painted myself in undying colors," he thought and smiled, again, at Durer's hubris. *How* old was he when he painted this portrait? He stepped over to the right toward the label in order to double-check Durer's birth date.

Just as he leaned forward, his heavy shoulder bag swung away from his body. The exhibition brochure, which he had carelessly stuffed into a shallow, unzipped side pocket, slipped out of the bag and landed on the floor at the young man's feet. Bernard stooped to pick it up at the same time the young man bent down. Their heads collided.

"Oh forgive me, I'm such a clutz," Bernard said.

They both stood up straight again, but then both noticed the brochure still lying on the floor. With that, they both started to bend down to pick it up, but this time the young man stopped short and let Bernard accomplish the task.

"I got it," Bernard said, embarrassed that he'd come into direct physical contact with the young man in a manner so graceless. He stuffed the brochure into the large central compartment of his bag.

"It's OK," the young man murmured almost inaudibly, maintaining his position staunchly in front of the label.

For a moment Bernard wondered if he should seize the opportunity to engage him in conversation. Then he thought no, he'll figure I deliberately crashed into him in order to start chatting him up—but if he's at all interested or open he would probably welcome the overture—but he's given me no real indication that he's interested, except perhaps that he isn't moving away.

"Why do they make the print so small?" Bernard said finally, and pressing his bag against himself so as not to repeat the episode, he stooped a few inches and jerked his body forward once more in front of the young man to read Durer's birth date, then contracted his body and stood straight again. Like an owl the young man turned his head from the label to the painting but otherwise continued standing perfectly still.

Bernard suddenly felt like a hog, and he smiled at the thought of himself tramping about in front of the picture, spilling his bag, lasciviously (he exaggerated to himself) sizing up this young man and only pretending (more exaggeration) to take an interest in art while the young man just stood there quietly and politely off to the side, reading, looking, but otherwise keeping to himself. (Except, Bernard thought, he *did* seem to be looking at me a few minutes ago from across the room.)

Now it was the young man's turn to move. He stepped back from the label and walked behind Bernard over to the left of the picture. Their positions were now reversed. But starting to lose interest in this mild game of cruising, if that's what it was, Bernard sidled over to the right of the picture where the young man had been standing in front of the label and picked up where he'd left off reading. **FINALLY, THE FINGERS OF HIS LEFT HAND ARE ENGAGED NOT, AS MAY AT FIRST APPEAR, IN BESTOWING A CHRIST-LIKE BLESSING** For that was one of the things he liked least about gay male mores. So many gay men he met—and this was as true of the gay men he knew in the monastery as it was of the ones he met "on the outside," as he liked to say—so many gay men preferred the chase to having an actual relationship with the person they were chasing. They liked to flirt, to cruise, to look and look endlessly, but in so many ways they didn't want to touch. Not really. They didn't know *how* to touch. They didn't want to *be* touched. (Having sex with a man, Bernard believed, is not the same thing as "touching" him.) They were terrified of getting close, embarrassed by coming face to face. He thought of Todd not being able to kiss his boyfriend in college. He thought, too, of Chris and how wonderful it was when they first kissed, but then how guilty Chris felt later on, how he tried to push Bernard away by saying the Church forbade it, the Church had to come first, his first and only real love was the Church. He should have let that be his warning and cut off the affair, but he couldn't wait any longer. He was determined to have an intimate and fully sexual relationship with a man, and if it meant putting up with Chris's periodic panic attacks (and ignoring the real truth, which was that Chris was never going to leave the Church to become an openly gay man), then he would try. But men like Chris were impossible to crack, and the Church was full of them. They were stuck in place. At least Bernard knew himself well enough to know he had to move on. The Church had given him so many things, but it couldn't give him what he most needed to survive as a living, breathing, flawed human being. When he finally said goodbye to Chris, he also said goodbye to a decade in the Church. **BUT, RATHER, NERVOUSLY FINGERING A TUFT OF FUR FROM THE COLLAR OF HIS LUXURIOUS, BROWN CLOAK** But less than three months after moving to New York, and having just turned 32, **—ONE FURTHER INDICATION OF THIS PORTRAIT'S UNEASY POISE BETWEEN SACRED AND SECULAR VALUES.** he became HIV positive. He didn't blame his illness on his decision to lead an openly gay life, but it was hard to look back over the past ten years and not think that leaving the Church somehow put him at risk for HIV. That the Church, somehow, could have saved him. He knew better, of course, but the thought still occurred to him now and then, especially whenever he met a man he felt in some way attracted to. Like this young man now sharing the space with him in front of the portrait of Albrecht Durer. He stood in rapt contemplation of the painting in much the same way he had, earlier, seemed to be contemplating the Rembrandt self-portraits. The more Bernard felt his stillness and what, further, seemed an aura of heaviness about him, the more he felt the superficiality of his own physical attraction. He thought it best, then, to leave him alone and move away. Another room, perhaps. Yes, that would be best, since then he wouldn't be tempted to continue his spying game on this attractive young man, who was obviously content to stay in his own little world. And so with one last parting glance (he couldn't resist—just then he noticed he'd taken off his glasses—his eyes looked bloodshot and tired), and with one last look at the Christ-like face of

Durer, he left the self-portrait gallery and entered the next, a room full of portraits depicting the "Other."

"And I'm leaving Rome," he added. "I must bid you good-bye." Isabel, inconsequently enough, was now sorry to hear it. That was something she didn't get. Why was Isabel sorry to hear that Warburton was leaving her? After all, she had rejected his proposal of marriage on more than one occasion. It seemed that all she wanted was to be left alone, or at least to be left alone by him. So here he was on his way out the door, and all of a sudden she feels sorry! *She was on the point of naming her regret, but she checked herself and simply wished him a happy journey.* What would she have said she was sorry about? It was now the second time Dora was going over this mysteriously compelling scene. *They shook hands, and he left her alone in the glorious room, among the shining antique marbles. She sat down in the centre of the circle of these presences—*

She was jolted by a quick, sharp cry. She looked up and saw two people doubled over, as if they had just been struck. It was two men, one of whom was the young man with glasses. He and another man, who had a large black shoulder bag, were looking down at their feet. The young man rubbed his head, while the other stooped to pick something off the floor. For a second it sounded as if there had been some kind of assault. But now the two were silent as if nothing had happened, each absorbed in looking at the portrait underneath the bullet-proof glass—she forgot who it was, but it looked liked Jesus.

She flipped back through the novel until she found the scene she wanted, the one where Ralph was quizzing Isabel about her reasons for refusing Warburton. Every time he proposed a possible explanation, she maddeningly rejected it. You want to see life, he says. No, not the way young men want to see it, she says. You want to drain the cup of experience, he says. No, only to see for myself, she says. You want to see but not to feel, he says. One can't make the distinction, she says. The world interests you, he says. I never said that, she says—*I'm not in the least an adventurous spirit. Women are not like men.* But now Dora felt Isabel was retreating from the very thing that made her interesting—more than that, the thing that made her exciting. Isabel *was* an adventurous spirit as far as Dora was concerned. She wasn't ready to get married. She wanted to choose her fate, to see what life had to offer her. Why deny it? And that's exactly what Ralph was saying: *Don't repudiate it. It's so fine!* Instead, she was gravitating toward Osmond, who, as Madame Merle put it, had "no career, no name, no position, no fortune, no past, no future, no anything." No, no, no, Dora thought. It's all negation. Nothing positive. No positive embrace of anything, just rejection after rejection. As if Isabel were falling in love with rejection. As if that was the fate she was so eager to embrace! It suddenly made her so-called independence, Dora thought, seem empty—or worse, suicidal.

With that, she looked up and saw the young man with glasses and the man with the shoulder bag still standing silently as before, a few feet away from each other, in front of the painting in the bullet-proof case. But—unless her memory was playing a trick on her—she could have sworn they had now switched places.

Robin was taking a risk by coming to stand so near to this guy with the shoulder bag, but as soon as he had entered the room of self-portraits he became acutely aware of his presence. He seemed to have the gift—or was it the curse?—of being able to smell another person's presence even from many yards away. But maybe it wasn't so much his gift as other people's power to dominate a room, to take up space (like that sketch artist in the previous gallery), to attract attention to themselves. It was a power Robin usually felt lacking in himself, to the point where he often felt invisible, insubstantial, in the presence of other people. They might be thinking something else entirely while doing whatever it was they appeared to be doing, but the intensity of their thoughts somehow succeeded in broadcasting their innermost wishes and needs to those around them, or at least to those around them with the right antennae (he believed in the unconscious and often felt himself, for better and for worse, the object of other people's unconscious wishes). So that in spite of yourself, Robin thought, you can't take your eyes off them, you can't *not* pay attention to them. And you can't rest until they're gone. And it doesn't necessarily have anything to do with "physical attraction." This guy was a perfect example. There was nothing about him (was there?) that he found particularly appealing in a physical sense. Ordinary face, weak chin, average height, stocky build, square-cut pants, and that ridiculous, shapeless, oversized shoulder bag. Only his haircut, he thought, was at all flattering (long on top, short around the sides, and jet black, kind of a throwback to the '80s; from this angle he looked a little bit like the lead singer from The Cure—what was his name?). Maybe all that interested Robin was that, earlier, while looking at the Rembrandts, he had thought the guy was checking him out. But that wasn't usually enough to make him interested in return. On the contrary: often it was the sense of another man's attraction to him that made him flee in the opposite direction, especially when it was someone who didn't appeal to him physically. But now, standing less than three feet away, Robin had to admit the guy really wasn't unpleasant to look at, not at all, and he could certainly imagine *some* people finding him attractive (suddenly he wondered, looking at his broad shoulders, whether his shapeless clothing concealed a strong, muscular body underneath, and whether his body was hairy). He felt an inner turbulence, a kind of excitement, not unlike the excitement he felt at the sex club when pursuing someone he found attractive and who seemed attracted to him in return.

It was an emotional excitement mixed with an erotic thrill. At the same time, this was different. Well, obviously so. He was feeling the excitement in the aboveground world, not in "the underground," as he labeled his excursions two or three nights a week to the sex club. It was nice to feel even just hints of an attraction to another man in a place other than a sex club. Nowadays it seemed his entire erotic life was conducted in the underground. If he happened to meet a guy he fancied while passing on the street, he often joked with his friend Eric, it practically felt like an arranged marriage, it was so "legitimate" compared to the way he usually hooked up with guys. For it seemed nearly impossible to meet men anymore except in anonymous sexual situations. He had no patience for the bars, he'd outgrown the crowds and noise of the dance clubs, and the guys he met on the Internet, without exception, were unserious about getting to know him, much less entering into anything like a potentially intimate relationship. And then sometimes he wondered if he himself was really looking for anything more than quick sexual gratification. He had become cynical about ever finding someone to love, especially since Brian dumped him, and he could see how he'd arranged his life so that all he needed, now and then, was fast, clean, fun sex with no strings attached. But anonymous sex, though it was always fast, was often not fun, and it was rarely clean (he thought of the blood oozing from his penis last night). And on top of all that, it seemed he was doing it more and more frequently, not just "now and then." For instance: would he go back to the sex club tonight? He didn't want to think about it now.

Looking over the man's shoulder he tried to focus his attention upon the painting, but the glassy surface of the vitrine (he looked up) combined with the sun pouring through the skylight of the gallery made it hard to see anything except the reflection of the man himself. Just then it appeared the man was looking right back at him. Butterflies stirred in his stomach. Why? he wondered. I'm not really attracted to him. The light changed (clouds overhead, he figured), and the image of

Durer (wasn't it?) came into view. Conscious that any move he made would be keenly registered by the guy with the shoulder bag, and nervously enjoying the flirtation, he stepped over to read the label. **DURER WAS BORN IN THE COSMOPOLITAN CITY OF NUREMBERG, AN IMPORTANT CENTER OF HUMANISM AS WELL AS COMMERCE IN FIFTEENTH-CENTURY GERMANY. HE LEARNED TO DRAW WITH PRECISION WHILE APPRENTICING IN HIS FATHER'S GOLDSMITH WORKSHOP, FOLLOWED BY A THREE-YEAR STINT WITH THE PROMINENT NUREMBERG PAINTER MICHAEL WOLGEMUT.** The guy suddenly came very close and something dropped out of his bag onto the floor. Robin looked down and saw at their feet the exhibition brochure. Its title, "MOTIONS OF THE MIND: The Renaissance Portrait and Its Legacy," was printed across the portrait of a human figure stitched together from various details of paintings in the show: the eye of a Sargent, the mouth of a Botticelli, the hair of Durer, a bust of Velazquez, hands by Memling. He stooped to pick it up. Just then the guy lunged toward him and their heads collided. With that the guy let out a strange, sharp, high-sounding yelp and said, "Oh forgive me, I'm such a clutz."

Robin stood up, rumpled his hair over the spot where he had been hit, and smiled benevolently, both to show him that he wasn't really hurt but also (more obscurely) to exaggerate the effect of the collision so as to make the guy feel even more embarrassed than he apparently already did. He looked down and saw the brochure still lying on the floor. He bent to pick it up, but the guy hastily swiped it off the floor as if to say it was his mess and, so, his responsibility to clean up. There seemed something deferential about him. Robin was charmed.

Feeling it was now his job to calm the poor guy's nerves, but at the same time not wanting to give too much of himself away, Robin simply said, with all the sound of wealth, privilege, and serenity he could muster (for he knew at that moment he had the upper hand), "It's OK."

"Why do they make the print so small?" the guy said with a gentle laugh.

Robin froze inside. He didn't want to make friendly chit chat just now. Words always spoiled the perfect impression he had of other people. But rather than backing off or walking away, he decided to let him squirm a little. He trained his eyes on the label, stood firm, and gave no reply.

After a few seconds during which Robin could sense that he still wanted to read the label, the guy awkwardly leaned forward, squeezing his body between Robin and the wall, and peered at the label for a moment. He then stood straight. Robin continued reading. BUT IT WAS THE TWO LIFE-CHANGING TRIPS HE MADE TO ITALY, IN 1494-1495 AND AGAIN IN 1505-1507, THAT MOST INFLAMED HIS SENSE OF HIMSELF NOT ONLY AS A SKILLED CRAFTSMAN LIKE HIS FATHER BUT, AS PICO DELLA MIRANDOLA PUT IT IN HIS FAMOUS 1486 TREATISE, ON THE DIGNITY OF MAN, "AS THE VERY CENTER OF THE WORLD," "THE FREE AND PROUD SHAPER OF [HIS] OWN BEING," A MAN AND AN ARTIST ABLE TO "FASHION [HIMSELF] IN ANY FORM [HE] MAY PREFER." He mechanically turned his head toward the painting as if to confirm something in the image he had just read in the label, even though he hardly registered a word of what he'd read. The butterflies beat nervously inside him. THAT HIGH SENSE OF SELF-REGARD, BEST REFLECTED IN THE 1500 SELF-PORTRAIT, BECAME SOMETHING OF A SELF-FULFILLING PROPHECY: THE FIRST ARTIST IN HISTORY TO BE HONORED WITH HIS OWN MONUMENT, HE HAS BEEN COMMEMORATED WITH CENTENARY FESTIVALS EVER SINCE THE EARLY NINETEENTH CENTURY, HIS WORK APPROPRIATED FOR PURPOSES BOTH SHAMEFUL (SELF-PORTRAITS BY DURER APPEARED ON THE COVER OF THE NATIONAL SOCIALIST MAGAZINE PEOPLE AND RACE IN THE EARLY 1940S) AND REDEMPTIVE (A RECENT PHOTOGRAPH BY THE CONTEMPORARY GERMAN ARTIST THOMAS STRUTH, IN WHICH STRUTH HIMSELF STANDS BEFORE DURER'S 1500 SELF-PORTRAIT, REPRESENTS, IN STRUTH'S WORDS, "AN ARTICLE OF FAITH IN THE POWER OF ART, A KIND OF PERSONAL PEACE-FINDING MOVE WITH THE

GENERAL BACKGROUND OF GERMAN HERITAGE" [STRUTH'S PHOTOGRAPH HANGS IN THIS GALLERY TO THE RIGHT]). Robin turned his head and glanced momentarily at the large photograph next to the Durer painting—a photo of an anonymous-looking man in a blue suit (Mr. Struth, apparently), close to the camera, out of focus, seen only from the neck down, standing before Durer's *Self-Portrait in Fur Cloak*, which occupied the center of the photo. Yes, he remembered seeing it in the big Thomas Struth retrospective two years ago and thinking at the time that the photo was OK but what he really wanted was to see the Durer self-portrait in the flesh. And here it was.

He turned back to look at the face of Durer looking spookily right back at him. It was rare, he thought, ever to come face to face with another man. They turned their backs on you. They hid their faces. He thought of Joe last night at the club and how he probably just needed to get fucked. It wasn't really *me* he wanted, Robin thought; I could have been anyone. He suddenly realized that Joe bore a superficial resemblance to Albrecht Durer himself (all that long, wavy brown hair), though Joe was "cuter" than Durer, which made him, ironically, *less* beautiful than the man in the painting. Robin stepped back and walked behind the guy with the shoulder bag over to the opposite side of the painting, fancying that here, at least, was someone who wanted him. He felt oddly comfortable in his presence. He wondered why. For he had bristled, earlier, at the presence of the sketch artist, and that guy was better looking than this one. But this one was different. How, though? Was it his clumsiness? "We sought each other before we met" (the words from Montaigne's essay on friendship flitted through his brain). The guy with the shoulder bag moved away from Robin a few feet to the right. He leaned forward and read the label. Maybe he's not interested after all, Robin thought with a mild stab of disappointment. But why feel disappointment? It's not as if Robin was all that attracted to *him*! But taking an interest in a man was different from feeling attracted to him, or at least it was supposed to be. More and more he couldn't distinguish between the two. If he thought back on his friendships with boys and men—take Ricky, for instance—it seemed there was always, at some point in the relationship, the spark of an erotic connection. Usually for the friendship to last, the erotic component had to fade, or else there would be some awkward incident where one person's intentions were misunderstood, or understood too well, and the friendship would break off. With gay men especially, he thought, the line between friendship and romance was treacherous. (Come to think of it, Joe kind of resembled Ricky too. Joe, Ricky, Durer—they were all of one type. "My type?" he wondered.)

Unconsciously he took off his glasses. Everything was a blur. He thought about the club last night. He almost didn't go, he was so tired from working overtime. It would have been better if he'd just gone to sleep early and started today afresh. But something drove him to the club. And once he arrived and did his initial spin around the halls to see who was there, he realized he was in one of his picky moods. No one really appealed to him. He had to settle down for a long wait until the right person came along. His theory was that if he didn't find someone in the first half hour, it meant either the sexy guys were staying away that night or else he wasn't really in the mood for sex to begin with. When he felt like that he almost never found anyone attractive enough and was practically guaranteed to have a rotten night. He would keep waiting for someone better to appear, but inevitably that person never arrived. Which was one of the amazing things about last night. Joe appeared out of nowhere. He was the "11 o'clock number" that made the long, boring night suddenly worthwhile, as if that was his reward for suffering through hours of frustration and disappointment. Only it ended horribly (the blood coming out of his penis), as if that was his punishment for staying too long at the club or going there to begin with or fucking without a condom or going ahead with the sex even when he saw there was something not quite right about the guy. And he had gone all the way with him!

Sex was mystifying. He suspected his attractions to men had very little to do with what they actually looked like. He gazed at men through the fog of his emotions, but did he ever really see them? It wasn't a question of "seeing the person for who he really is," as if the problem lay in the contrast between the physical person and the person on the inside—his personality, his heart, his mind, his soul even (the guy standing to his right was probably a "very nice person," he thought sarcastically to himself, but I still wouldn't want to fuck him). In a way he seemed to be puzzling over a problem in optics. He thought of the passage from *Moby-Dick* on the whiteness of all creation, where "the sweet tinges of sunset skies and woods; yea, and the gilded velvets of butterflies, and the butterfly cheeks of young girls; all these are but subtile deceits, not actually inherent in substances, but only laid on from without." No, the problem he was puzzling over preceded the moral question of inner as opposed to outer beauty. The problem was, he couldn't trust his eyes. Couldn't trust his body. His body told him to do things, made him feel things, that had so little to do with reality. "I know but cannot tell," he thought and remembered the face of Homer Saint-Gaudens.

He wondered if other people were as baffled by their own motives and desires as he was. Stephen wasn't like that. He always knew what he wanted. He seemed to "know who he was," whatever it meant to put yourself in a package like that. "I am my own person," "I've got to be me," "I am what I am," "This is my life"—the catch phrases piled up in his head like debris. But what was he talking about? Stephen was dead! He destroyed his own life and nearly destroyed the lives of his wife and child along with him. To say nothing of the devastation his death caused in the lives of everyone else who cared about him. Brian was right: whenever Robin felt anxious or unhappy, he turned in his mind to Stephen, and the thought of Stephen magically made everything right. Stephen would have known what to do! If only Stephen were here to talk to! There's no one in this world like Stephen! No one but Stephen could have understood what I'm going through! Never mind that Stephen was an addict, lied to himself and to everyone around him, appeared and then disappeared from your life. You couldn't depend on him for anything. He used his charm and intelligence to lull you into thinking he had changed, but he hadn't. Ever since high school (ever since Dad died) he was set on a course there was no diverting him from. Fast, furious, self-destructive. And he's my great role model!

He felt the presence of the man standing next to him. What do I want from men? Robin asked himself. Is it only sex? Do I want more? There were moments with Brian when he felt he'd discovered what being in an intimate relationship was all about. He remembered their trip to Washington, DC. They arrived late after a long bus ride, tired and achy. They were bickering about something, he couldn't remember what. In the midst of the argument Brian said to him, "You know, Robin, I really love you." The words shocked him, especially when all along he was convinced the affair must be coming to an end. With Brian he discovered you could have an argument with someone and it didn't mean the relationship was over. Not like Stephen. If you had a fight with him, he turned away and didn't talk to you for days. It was almost a year, in fact, before Stephen would even speak to him after he came out on their 20th birthday, and even then it was still awkward for months. "You're just trying to get attention," Stephen would sneer. "You always want to be different! But guess what? You'll always be a twin, and you'll always be twenty minutes younger than me. Sorry, Little Squirt. You lose again." And that was the way it went with his family, and not just around gay issues. He envied families, couples, or even just friends who could squabble and then embrace afterward, refreshed in an odd way by the outbreak of hostilities, their commitment to each other renewed and strengthened. Arguments, sharp words, the release of anger—it always unnerved him. As a result he avoided conflict at all cost with friends, family, boyfriends, coworkers, everyone. But that meant he spent a lot of time feeling irritated by the people closest to him and not knowing what to do about it.

The guy with the shoulder bag was still reading the label intently. What am I trying to get from *this* person? Robin wondered. He suspected he was being a cock tease, flirting with someone he wasn't all that attracted to, just for the sport of it or because he wanted the good feeling of knowing that someone found him desirable. Do I want to chat with this guy, or not? Should I speak to him? Should I leave him alone? Is he waiting for me to make the next move? Is he only pretending to read the label? Should I speak to him now? But before Robin could decide, the guy exhaled, took one quick glance at the painting, and, without seeming at all aware of Robin's presence, headed for the entrance to the next room.

Robin felt abandoned. Rejected. He hadn't been terribly interested in the guy, but now that he was gone, Robin felt lost. Had he waited too long? Had he been too coy? He thought of a long corridor lined with closed doors on either side. Rejection hurt, and it came in all shapes and sizes. He looked at the face of Durer. So still, so poised, so perfectly balanced you got no inkling of his thoughts. The portrait inside the glass case looked like the door to a vault or a crawlspace hidden in the wall of an old mansion. One night you creep downstairs, hold up a candle to the painting, see the open eyes of the bearded man with wavy hair. The answer lies hidden within the vault. No time to lose. You place your hand on the frame—the face continues to stare impassively, a blank witness to your crime—and pull it toward you. The painting comes away from the wall and reveals a metal safe with a combination lock. You spin the lock. You pull the handle. But the door won't open. The wrong combination. You try the numbers again. You pull the handle, but in vain. You hear footsteps. The answer lies within. You've run out of time. Someone is coming. Quick! Replace the portrait, blow out the candle, and flee!

Robin shook himself as if from a dream. If he didn't get something to eat soon, he might faint. Instinctively he followed the guy with the shoulder bag into the next gallery.

DIEGO RODRIQUEZ DE SILVA Y VELAZQUEZ (1599-1660)
JUAN DE PAREJA, 1649-50
OIL ON CANVAS

DIEGO RODRIGUEZ DE SILVA Y VELAZQUEZ
JUAN DE PAREJA

An artist's studio in the Villa Medici, Rome. Early December, 1650. Evening. JUAN DE PAREJA stands with paintbrush and palette before an unfinished self-portrait. Attached to the canvas is a small mirror. To the left, the portrait of PAREJA by Velazquez. To the right, a table with several books piled on top. PAREJA examines the Velazquez portrait.

PAREJA. Flocky hair, round forehead, black eyes, squab nose,
   Broad face, blubber lips, weak chin, unkempt beard.
   All it wants are gold earrings and a toothy grin
   To finish the picture of the foolish African!
   And see how I am dressed. At first glance, I have
   The apparel appropriate to kings
   And great lords. I wear a splendid white lace
   Collar and a dashing cape. But
   Some of the buttons on my jerkin
   Are missing, and the elbow of my shirt
   Is frayed. If one looks carefully,

He sees my cape is made of coarse green cloth,

My sword strap merely serves to hold the cape

Secure, and my hand clutches the cape

Where the sword hilt ought to be. I am unarmed.

Unmanned. A servant aping a gentleman.

A slave mimicking his master. The portrait

Mocks me! When asked why does he not aspire

To paint more like that angel Raphael

But squanders his talent on so many

Pictures of kitchen maids, water sellers,

Embroiderers, and buffoons, Master

Replies, "I prefer being first in

Coarseness to second in delicacy."

Am I, then, just one more of his pathetic

Creatures? Brother to Calabezas the

Cross-eyed, Diego the dwarf, Francisco

The idiot? Not stunted or humpbacked

Or wrinkled, perhaps, but poor, black, and ugly?

The sun is going down. Soon it will be

Time to put away my palette and brushes,

Turn my canvas to the wall, and tidy up

The studio before Master returns.

True, he enjoys the sight of his faithful

Servant painting, especially, he says,

Here in Rome, where the air itself seems to

Inspire the creation of pictures.

But I prefer to paint while he is away.

When I am alone my thoughts are more

My own. Alas, I am rarely alone. As a result,

My work suffers from constant interruption.

I cannot paint for hours at a stretch

But must stop what I am doing as soon

As I am called to perform some servile

Task for Master: grinding the pigments, preparing

The varnishes, priming the canvases, fetching

The midday meal. Not that I mind so much.

I perform my duties with care, and I am

Amply rewarded for my diligence.

Just as he is the King's specially

Appointed *superintendente de*

Obras particulares, so I am

Master's personal serving man, his

Most trusted assistant. I am permitted

To stand by him during his audiences

With the King. Even the King knows my name!

How many in my position can say that?

But I must not delude myself. The

Chief point of wisdom, declares Erasmus, is

To know oneself. Does my Master's portrait,

In fact, mock me? No doubt it is

A wondrous bit of realism.

At the exhibition on the porch of

The Pantheon, it was applauded

By painters from around the world. They said

That all the other pictures on display

Were "mere paintings," but this alone was *truth*.

What truth does it tell? A long line

Of people, highborn and low, could be

Assembled who've been deceived by Master's

Skill. When the portrait of the Pope was finished

And placed within the antechamber of

The palace, the chamberlain of His

Holiness was about to enter.

Seeing the portrait in a dim light, he

Thought it was the Pope himself and turned to

Go out, telling various courtiers

He encountered on his way to speak

Quietly as His Holiness was in

The next room. Just so, one evening the King

Came to the workshop, as he often does,

To watch Master paint. A full-length portrait

Of one of his naval commanders stood

In shadow against the wall. Seeing it,

The King remarked, "What, are you still here?

Haven't I dismissed you already?"

At last, when the subject failed to reply,

His Majesty realized he had spoken

To a portrait, not a person. And when

Portraits at an Exhibition

I with Master's portrait of me

Accompanied Master around Rome

As he solicited criticism

From his friends, they professed themselves

Incapable of distinguishing

Between the portrait and the man himself,

Hardly knowing which one would answer to

The name Juan de Pareja.

See how I persist in calling Don Diego

"My Master," when, more than a week ago,

He granted me my freedom, "in view of the

Good and faithful service the slave has

Given me, and considering that

Nothing could be more pleasing to the slave

Than the gift of liberty." Nothing more

Pleasing, to me *and to him*. It is a

Pious act to free a slave, and with *my*

License of freedom he may secure the

Good opinion of the Pope, with whose

Support he hopes to win membership in

The Order of Santiago, thereby

Once and for all raising his status from

Mere craftsman to artist, from tradesman to

Courtier. A painter in Spain is considered

No better than a carpenter, stonecutter,

Innkeeper, or scribe, and painting is seen

As a base occupation—a form

Of manual, not intellectual

Labor. Becoming, at last, a Knight of

Santiago would surely dignify

His profession and establish

The Christian purity of his blood.

No Moors or Jews among his ancestors!

But what better proof of his piety

Than his great canvas, now hanging proudly

In the grand salon, showing the expulsion

Of the Moriscos, rightfully punished

For pretending to Christian obedience

While secretly practicing their

Mohammedan faith? At the center stands

King Phillip III, triumphant in armor,

Pointing to crowds of men, women, and

Children stricken with grief (I fancy

My parents among them) as they are led by

Soldiers toward ships at the coast from whence

They will leave Spain forever. To his right,

The figure of Spain in arms, and beneath her

The dedication: "To Philip III, most

Gracious of Kings, Catholic King of Spain,

The Netherlands, Germany, and Africa,

Fosterer of peace and justice, maintainer

Of the public order, in recognition

Of his successful expulsion of the Moors,
Philip IV, mighty in valour and in
Virtue, greatest of the great, with a spirit
Born for greater things on account of the
Antiquity of so great a lineage,
Moved by duty and reverence, erected
This monument, 1627,"
Signed "Diego Velazquez, Painter to
Philip IV, King of Spain, by whose command
He made this in the year 1627."
But Master's ambition may come to naught,
Since, contrary to the rules for membership,
He receives payment for his work, and the
Nobility of his ancestors is
Questionable. Don Diego, a
Nobleman? Ha! This evening he skulks
In the shadows of a street near the church
Of Santa Maria in Via with
The nurse Martha, grown suspiciously fat.
In exchange for my freedom, I have promised
To say nothing to his lawful wife and
Son when we return to Madrid. I am
Subordinate to him, but in so many
Ways he depends upon me.
A pair of sunflowers are we, bathing
In the warming rays of the sun!

But oh how easily self-examination

Becomes self-flattery. I am no

Equal to Don Diego! I am his

Inferior. My efforts at copying

His portrait are all the evidence I

Need of that. With dogged attention to

The original, I scumbled in the

Background. I reproduced the broad outlines

Of the figure (though I moved it a few

Inches to the right, seeing no reason

For Master's eccentric placement of

The figure off-center). I rendered the

Vestments just as he did (but mended them

As needed). I even managed to evoke

The texture of curly African hair.

But my powers of imitation fail

When it comes to my features. I cannot

Give the spark of life to my face. I draw

A blank where my face ought to be. I consult

My looking glass.

Peers into the mirror attached to the unfinished portrait.

Do I not see hair less clotted,

Forehead less bulging, a narrower face, longer

Nose, daintier nostrils, finer lips,

Trimmer beard? More Don Quixote than Sancho

Panza? In truth I do not. If ever I was wont

Portraits at an Exhibition

To see myself in the flattering light
Of my affections, I changed on the day
I saw Master's finished portrait of me.
Ever since, I have had to learn to live
With my face, this new shadow that goes
About the world under my name. I may
Pretend I do not recognize it, but
At my peril. Flocky hair, round forehead,
Black eyes, squab nose, broad face, blubber lips,
Weak chin, unkempt beard. I regret to say,
The portrait speaks the truth.
Only *my own* art lies
Within my power to change. It may
Improve with time and continued
Effort. Lead, if the philosophers are
Right, may turn to gold. All existence
Aspires heavenwards. No wonder the
Inventor of painting was Narcissus,
Who became a flower. Like painting itself,
He embraced the surface of the pool and
Was rewarded, through his death, with eternal
Life in an altered state.

Handles his palette.

    In these mounds of crushed stone—
    Lapis and ruby, emerald and pearl—
    Lies a secret. Mixed with oil, they

Become paint, and paint, when applied to

Canvas, can make a man, or a king, or

A god. Painting possesses a truly divine

Power, makes the absent present, restores

The dead to the living, and as it

Images forth the Father and Son binds

Us closer to our Maker and Redeemer.

I have risen thus far. I may rise further still!

Ah, my fancies confirm the folk

Wisdom, "He is more extravagantly

Conceited than a black." Master painted

My portrait *not* because of my intrinsic

Worth as a man, or because of our

Mutual dependence, or because of

My capacity for improvement, but

As a rehearsal for that greater work,

His portrait of the Pope. Even my *portrait*

Does service, is not an end in itself.

But if it were—if my face were

Looked upon as the face of a pope or

A king! But how foolish of me even

To dream. I know my place, and a black slave

May not dream. True, there was King Melchior,

Come from the East to pay homage to the

Christ child, dressed in costly silks and velvets,

Swirling headdress and jewel-encrusted cape,

Portraits at an Exhibition

His servants and hounds in attendance. But

The black king's pretensions meant nothing,

His gorgeous attire a foil for the

Greater dignity of the King of Kings,

Wrapped in coarse cloth, laid down amid the

Donkeys and pigs, the son of a carpenter.

My face, the face of a king? The face of

A *slave*, the son of a Morisco, given

To the Christian Brothers when my parents

Were forced to flee the country, apprenticed

To Don Pacheco because of my

Artistic inclinations and the

Likelihood I would prove useful in his

Workshop, given to Master as part

Of his wife's dowry. Passed from hand to hand

Like a piece of old furniture or

A filthy doubloon. In Italy, it is

Enough to be Spanish to be looked

Down upon. "*Spagnoli bassi*," they say

Behind our backs, apparently making

No other distinction between Master

And me. Low-class Spaniards. But if the Son

Of God shares His cradle with suckling pigs,

He might as well share it with

The slave who cleans the stables.

My face, the face of a king?

Consider King Philip's face.

Heavy, drooping eyelids; sensuous lips;

Clumsy, protuberant jaw. A hangdog face.

Rubens once observed during a visit

To Madrid that the King mistrusts himself

And so defers too much to other

People. Perhaps this is the quality

The King most prizes in Master's

Portraits of him, for if they are

Not handsome, they are penetrating, honest,

And true. Official portraits of the King

Are not intended to reveal the inner

Life of the sovereign but to glorify

His impersonal status as ruler,

And yet Master's portraits of the King

Quietly acknowledge the invisible

Character of the human being

Beneath the robes and crown. The King may

Secretly thank him for revealing His

Majesty's truth. Has Master done me a

Similar service? And might I, like the King,

Pay him thanks for his honest portrayal,

His power of insight? Has he pried open

My crusted shell to reveal the milky

Pearl of my true character underneath?

Black men are famous for their supposed

Merriment, and that merriment is taken

As the sign of their defective brains.

Master has portrayed me without a smile.

I would not simply call my expression

"Serious," although there is a serious

Element in it. If it is not the face

Of a gentleman, much less the face of

A king, neither is it the face of a fool.

Picks up a small volume on the table, opens it, and reads.

"Know yourself. There are mirrors for the face

But none for the mind. Let careful thought

About yourself serve as a substitute."

Father Gracian advises me well.

And yet I know not how to think about myself

Without the snares of self-delusion.

"Keep your imagination under

Control. The imagination can

Tyrannize, not being content with

Looking on, but influences and

Even often dominates our life."

"Look into the interior of things.

They are generally other than they seem,

And ignorance that never looks beneath

The rind is disillusioned when you show

The kernel." "Do not make mistakes about

Character. In dealing with people,

More than with other things, it is necessary
To look within. To know people is different
From knowing things. People must be studied
As deeply as books." "Self-knowledge is the
Beginning of self-improvement."
If one day I am to become
The master of my own workshop,
I must learn everything I can from
Don Diego. I must persist in my
Efforts to copy his works,
Including this portrait of me.
"Grace in everything. It is a
Shortcut to accomplishment
And an easy escape from embarrassment."

Again, looking at the Velazquez portrait.

With my arm across my paunch, I appear
To be on guard. "Nature scarcely ever gives us the
Very best—for that we must have recourse
To art." The expression in my eyes lacks
Confidence. "We are born barbarians
And only raise ourselves above the beast
By culture." I am uncertain.
"Simplicity flourished in the golden
Age, cunning in these days of iron."
Cautious. "Do and be seen doing. Things do
Not pass for what they are but for what they

Seem. What is not seen is as if it was

Not. Even the right does not receive

Proper consideration if it does

Not seem right. Deceit rules—things are judged by

Their jackets, and many things

Are other than they seem."

The Art of Worldly Wisdom.

A Jesuit has written this!

"What all say is so, or will be so."

Closes the book and replaces it on the table.

Here in Rome

Master copies the frescoes of Raphael

And Michelangelo and learns from their

Genius as well as their mistakes.

He benefits all he can from these great

Teachers and then surpasses them,

Doing things with paint that no one else has

Ever done. With only his eye and

His fancy to guide him, he reinvents

The art of painting. I must trust his vision,

At least so long as it takes to copy

His portrait of me and discover the

Differences, for it may be that therein lies

The secret of his work,

And the secret of my life.

I am a free man, though I am committed

To serving Master for five more years at least.

I still have much to learn from him. In his

Service, I do not diminish but increase.

He taught me to paint: for that alone I

Must be grateful. But I am not and have

Never been Master's dog. Though I tend

His horses and sleep on trunks, though I stretch

His canvases and clean his studio,

He has taken me for his student. I

Am a man, but in teaching me to paint

He has made me more than a man. He has

Granted me my freedom, and it may be

That teaching me to paint is the greater

Gift, for as an artist I am more than

Free. I create, and creation is god-like.

Juan de Pareja, a god among men!

Who knows but some lowly worm or

Pathetic plant may speak a divine

Language and maintain itself in silent

Meditation on the perfection of

Its creator, its prayer more pleasing to

God than the words and deeds of the most

Outwardly pious priest. Whatever share

I have of imperfection, I may grow

(Lord, keep me from self-delusion),

And change, and prove myself, one day, a better

Man. My life may revolve still further, as

All things in nature grow and change and die,

And revive once more.

Like the moon, our dark, silent mother.

There she is, outside the window.

Not enough light in the sky now

For painting. The air is pure. I see the

Garden with its statues and its curious,

Ensnaring labyrinth. Beyond it, the

Rooftops of Rome, with the dome of St. Peter

Rising above the rest like a shapely,

Transcendent idea. Farther still, the

Soft, beautiful Roman countryside,

Where every step one takes is an ecstasy,

Every view an inspiration. Rome fills me

With a desire to expand, to perfect myself.

It is the homeland of the arts.

Turns to his unfinished copy of the Velazquez portrait.

Portraiture is among the lowliest

Of genres, history painting

The highest. No handsome, homely,

Or misshapen face, however true to life,

But it must take its place in the

Historical pageant. Classical

Or Christian, painting must tell a story.

What have I been called to do? What story

Was I born to tell? Not Gracian,

But a higher authority shall guide me.

Picks up the Bible, opens it, and reads.

"As He moved on, Jesus saw a man named

Matthew at his post where taxes were

Collected. He said to him, 'Follow me.'

Matthew got up and followed Him. Now it

Happened that, while Jesus was at table

In Matthew's home, many tax collectors

And those known as sinners came to join

Jesus and His disciples at dinner.

The Pharisees saw this and complained to

His disciples, 'What reason can the Teacher

Have for eating with tax collectors and

Those who disregard the law?' Overhearing

The remark, He said, 'People who are in

Good health do not need a doctor; sick

People do. Go and learn the meaning of

The words, "it is mercy I desire and

Not sacrifice." I have come to call

Not the self-righteous, but sinners.'"

I have found it!

If, as Master insists, to be

An artist means to conceive of

A composition, not merely to execute it

With one's hands; to design, not simply

Portraits at an Exhibition

To imitate; to invent, not merely

To copy—then I have set my standards

Too low. I must learn all I can from

Don Diego, but I must surpass him,

Just as he learns from Raphael and

Michelangelo and surpasses them!

If my talents prove unequal to my

Ambition, at least I will have navigated

The coastline of my being. One day I

Will paint my Lord and Savior Jesus Christ

As He gathers together His disciples.

He took the lowest of the low—the hated

Tax collector, the spat-upon sinner,

The broken-hearted prostitute,

The denigrated slave.

He said, "Follow Me, be my friend."

I see a table, draped in a

Heavy, Oriental carpet, laden

With bags of coins, account books and writing

Instruments. Matthew and his fellow tax

Collectors, richly dressed, seated at the

Table, are interrupted in their labor

As Jesus and His disciples enter

The room. Placing his hand over his heart,

Matthew looks with reverence toward his Savior,

Standing before him with opens arms:

"I have come to call not the self-righteous, but
Sinners." At the opposite end of the
Composition stands an African with
Flocky hair but fine-trimmed beard, dark almond
Eyes, sensitive lips, and handsome, though not
Immodest, courtier's clothing. Disciple,
Sinner, or both? He looks the viewer
Calmly and confidently in the eye.
In his right hand, a piece of paper.
On the paper, an inscription: "Juan de Pareja,"
And the year of our Lord, "16__."

AN ACCOMPLISHED ARTIST IN HIS OWN RIGHT, JUAN DE PAREJA (C. 1610-1670) NEVERTHELESS WORKED HIS ENTIRE LIFE IN THE SERVICE OF OTHERS, MOST NOTABLY AS AN ASSISTANT IN VELAZQUEZ'S STUDIO AND, UNTIL SHORTLY AFTER THIS PORTRAIT WAS PAINTED, IN HIS CAPACITY AS VELAZQUEZ'S SLAVE. Bernard was shocked by what he had just read. He looked again at the gorgeous and imposing figure of the black man, with his expansive white collar and sweeping cape. Velazquez's slave. He would have thought him an African prince or some heroic warrior. There was something vulgar, he felt, about the painting in light of this information, but he didn't stop to reflect on his reaction. IN JANUARY 1649, PAREJA ACCOMPANIED VELAZQUEZ ON A TOUR OF ITALY TO COLLECT PAINTINGS, SCULPTURES, AND OTHER OBJECTS OF ART FOR THE DECORATION OF KING PHILIP IV'S PALACE IN MADRID. UNOFFICIALLY IT WAS VELAZQUEZ'S AMBITION TO WIN THE SUPPORT OF POPE INNOCENT X IN HIS BID FOR INDUCTION INTO THE ORDER OF

Santiago, one of Spain's oldest and most prestigious orders of knighthood. The young man he'd collided with in the previous gallery was now standing beside him, less than three feet away. Clearly something was up with this guy. He'd had an aura of "don't look at me, don't touch me, don't talk to me" a few minutes ago, but here he was again, ready for more... flirtation? intrigue? What was the word gay guys used nowadays for cruising? But this wasn't cruising exactly. This was more cat-like than that (more cat-like even than cruising! he laughed to himself). Bernard felt the same force field enveloping the young man as he stood looking at the painting. He wanted to flee but felt he shouldn't be chased around the exhibition by some stranger who appeared to want nothing so much as attention. Besides, this painting interested him, and he wanted to stay with it. At the same time, he felt imposed upon. He read on with a rising resentment. **His portrait of Innocent X (see right)** He looked at the tiny reproduction of the Pope's portrait beside the text. Innocent X, he thought; what an outrageous name for a Pope! He looks like he could be the meanest, most corrupt old bastard in the history of Catholicism. **is one of Velazquez's finest works and one of the great portraits of Western culture.** Damn this guy. He continued to stand there, crowding his space, not moving a muscle, like a statue. "S&M," he remembered his friend Dan once saying—"I'm taking you to an S&M bar. You know, Stand and Model." **To prepare himself for that important and demanding work, Velazquez painted Pareja's portrait. This portrait, too, won great acclaim when it was exhibited on the portico of the Pantheon in March 1650.** Should he engage the young man in conversation? **Although the precise reasons for the timing are not known, Velazquez signed a notarial act granting Pareja's freedom in Rome on November 23, 1650, "in view of the good and faithful service the slave has given me, and considering that nothing could be more pleasing to the slave than the gift of liberty."** By breaking down and initiating a conversation, was he acting like a therapist? He sensed that the guy needed to be spoken to, and when confronted with a patient's need this palpable he usually responded accordingly. **PAREJA NEVERTHELESS CONTINUED IN VELAZQUEZ'S SERVICE UNTIL THE LATTER'S DEATH, AFTER WHICH HE SERVED IN THE HOUSEHOLD AND WORKSHOP OF VELAZQUEZ'S SON-IN-LAW, THE ARTIST JUAN DE MAZO.** Hardly conscious of what he had just read, he looked into the fathomless black eyes of Juan de Pareja. Large and wet, he thought, like the eyes of an abused child. How had Velazquez managed to convey such humanity in a pair of black spots? Then he thought, Hell, it might be interesting to find out who this guy is and what he wants.

"So what do you think of him?" Bernard said abruptly.

Robin jumped at the invitation to speak, for as soon as he heard the man's voice he had the strange sensation that they knew each other, had always known each other, and so most of the formalities of approaching a stranger could be dropped.

"Oh," he responded with a sigh of admiration, as if they were already deep into a conversation about the painting and he'd already tried unsuccessfully to articulate his feeling of awe at Velazquez's accomplishment, "you know, I... " He decided it was safe to come out to this man, sensing that their shared sexuality was already a given. "I feel some kind of attraction to him, but he's not..." And then he decided it was even safe to express an aversion that might, under other circumstances, be considered politically incorrect (big, frizzy hair, bulging forehead, mushroom-shaped nose, blubbery lips, saggy chin, scraggly beard: in the most superficial sense, it was an almost comic litany of the things he *didn't* look for in a man). "He's not my type, you know?"

"Not your type?" Bernard replied, struck by the unearned intimacy with which he answered the question but also struck by the sound of his voice. It had a "bedroom" quality, he thought and felt a zing of butterflies in his stomach. He knew he was being flirted with.

For the first time since he'd entered the exhibition, Robin summoned all his reactions so far and realized he'd been scrutinizing only the portraits of men and relating to them in somewhat the same way he related to strangers on the street or in the sex club. "To be honest," he said, "I'm really thinking about which of these people I'd like to take home with me, and this guy isn't one of them."

Bernard thought it wasn't quite an appropriate thing to say to someone you'd just met. But people did it all the time; they smelled the therapist and let loose. He thought it amazing how he gave off a therapist vibe with even the simplest of questions.

The young man continued talking. "What I mean is, I look at this painting and feel something seductive, but it isn't erotic seduction, and I'm trying to figure out what other kinds of seduction there can be if it's a picture of a human being you're talking about."

Bernard looked puzzled.

"I'm sorry," the young man said, "you probably just meant to ask a straightforward question—"

"No, no," Bernard encouraged, for suddenly the young man's discourse had taken a turn that interested him. "But I'm not sure I'm following you."

"I think I'm trying to understand what happens when you look at a picture of another person... " As he continued, a light seemed to be leading him through a tunnel of thought. "... and how that's different, if it's different at all, from looking at a real human being."

He's talking about my research project, Bernard thought. He hung on the young man's words.

"Because," Robin went on, feeling a bit too much like a precocious graduate student trying to engage his favorite professor in conversation, but letting himself go anyway (there was something about this man that seemed to breathe permission to let oneself go), "it's like all these pictures allow you to look, as if they're actual *people* who've come to stand here and allow you to look at them. They don't avert their eyes, you know, the way strangers do if you catch their eye on the subway, and I guess I really love that about portraits. I mean, I've seen portraits all my life, but I never really thought until now about what it's like to look at them."

Bernard was bemused. He decided to risk it and go back to the question of Juan de Pareja not being the young man's "type."

"So why wouldn't you want to take this guy home with you?" He laughed warmly, but there was an edge of suspicion in his laugh, for he was trying to guard against the seductions of his interlocutor.

The young man turned from Bernard to the canvas. He looked for a moment... and another moment... and another... as if he felt so comfortable in Bernard's presence that he could allow silence to reign between them. It was the kind of thing Todd would often do when Bernard asked a question. Bernard was charmed whenever he did it, but also suspicious (it seemed deliberately seductive).

"When I look at this man," Robin said, and now he was choosing his words with extreme care, as if he wanted to get as close to articulating his thought as possible, "I feel warded off."

Bernard was fascinated. "Have you read the label? Do you know who this is?"

"I have no idea. I've been avoiding doing that thing that everyone does, you know: they look at the painting for two seconds, read the label to find out who it is, look again for another second, and walk away." He laughed. "I'm trying not to let the information about the sitters—"

"Just read the first sentence of the description."

Robin leaned in front of Bernard and read the label. "Wow. Velazquez's slave... "

"Yeah, it's incredible."

They stood together, silently, looking at the portrait.

But now Bernard, still intrigued by the thoughtfulness of the young man's comments about the portrait and about portraits in general, felt compelled to ask him some more questions, but this time not about his reaction to the paintings, but about himself.

"You seem to have thought a lot about art. Are you an artist?" Somehow he didn't think he was, but asking "So what do you do?" would sound (he feared) like too much of a come-on, and he was trying not to come on to him.

"No, I'm not an artist. I'm just..." Robin wondered how to finish the sentence. His living room, with its few, inexpensive furnishings, flashed before him. "...interested in art," he fudged, then decided to tell more of the truth. "I used to be an art historian." No, that sounded too grandiose. "Well, I was studying for my PhD in art history and..." He trailed off, not wanting to give away the sorry conclusion. But the way the other man paid attention to him made it impossible not to take the final step. "...I never finished it."

"I can tell you have a background in art history."

Robin groaned.

"Is that a bad thing? The question you're asking is kind of interesting. Actually, an art historian probably wouldn't ask that question. What you're saying seems very personal. Almost *post* art history."

"Oh, well that's good, because I am definitely post art history!"

They both laughed, though neither one knew exactly what he was laughing at. The laughter seemed a mutual signal that it was safe to proceed with the conversation and that it need not stay confined to matters at hand.

Bernard, as usual, found it easy to ask questions. "Did you study a particular period or movement?"

Robin drank in Bernard's attention. "You mean in graduate school? Yeah. Well, not exactly. I thought I was interested in the Renaissance, but—I mean I *was*. Most of the courses I took were in the Renaissance. But then I became interested in the critical discourse on the Renaissance, and I started thinking about how weird it is, in a way, what art historians do, which is, you know, they use language—words—to apprehend a visual medium." As he said this, Robin looked almost challengingly at Bernard to see whether his interest was genuine. Clearly it was. "So I started getting really involved with certain modern critics of the Renaissance, but it also went beyond the Renaissance to other periods. Basically, it came down to a few art historians whose work interested me, and then a whole other set of issues came up which had to do with depictions of masculinity and male friendship and ideas about homosexuality and brotherhood…" When the list of things that had interested but ultimately stymied him reached the point of brotherhood, Robin stopped himself and laughed. "It just got out of hand." He realized he was explaining to a man he'd only just met how it was he ended up never finishing even one chapter of his dissertation. And then Stephen flashed across his mind, and he felt untrue both to himself and to Stephen for making it sound as if his research had undone him because it was too complex or too ambitious. But the man was listening with intent. Robin continued hesitantly, "And then there were other things that interfered with the dissertation."

"Like what?"

Robin looked as if he were facing an oncoming car.

Bernard preempted him. "I'm sorry, what's your name? I'm Bernard."

"Robin." (He remembered saying "Stephen" last night when he met Joe. But this was different.)

"Nice to meet you," Bernard said with the kind of gently patronizing warmth that he reserved for prospective patients whose only-half-understood reasons for seeking therapy he was about to hear. "So: other things."

"Yeah. My brother died, and that pretty much put an end to the dissertation."

Bernard regretted pushing him to this point, for now there was no escaping the role of therapist. "Oh, I'm sorry," he said. His empathy was genuine, but also professional. He felt an impulse to encourage Robin to say more about his brother, then doubted the impulse (I'd be taking advantage of him, he thought; I have no intention of pursuing him beyond this conversation), then gave into it. "That must have been really hard."

"It was," Robin said, feeling awkward now even broaching the subject of Stephen's death. Either I talk about it honestly, he felt, or I don't talk about it at all. But he makes me want to tell him *everything*. He thought of the blood coming out of his penis last night. "It was difficult, and…" He started thinking about all the ways in which his life had changed since Stephen's death. He thought about his nights at the sex club. "He was my twin."

"Oh, wow. Identical?"

"Uh huh." Robin now felt passive, waiting for Bernard to ask him anything he wanted but hoping he would pursue the topic of Stephen. Opportunities to speak openly and honestly about his brother, it seemed, came rarely these days, and when they did he was made conscious of how much he needed them.

But instead Bernard decided to change the subject, as if he were window-shopping with no intention to buy. Now he felt he could ask the question that only moments before he worried would sound like too much of a come-on. He sensed that Robin had given control of the conversation over to him. This was how it always went with new patients once they started feeling the power of an empathic listener. "And what do you do now?"

"I work in a gallery."

"Nice. What do you do there?"

"I'm the girl at the front desk," Robin laughed, but seeing that Bernard's serious, attentive expression wasn't ruffled by the self-deprecating joke, he tried to recover himself. "I do a lot of different things. Sometimes I help to write the catalogues. I write press releases. I handle bookings for the artists, travel arrangements." He sighed as he pushed his way through the job description. "I answer the phones, set up for parties. It's a small gallery. I like it because it gives me time to write my own stuff. And I get to read a lot of novels when my boss isn't around."

"You're a writer?"

Robin thought that saying "yes" would be pompous. He'd only had one short piece published in an online journal, and it was so transparently autobiographical it hardly even qualified as fiction. "Well, I'm *trying* to write fiction. I'm not getting too far, but it's something I like doing." As he listened to himself, his life sounded like a failure. He felt embarrassed. Maybe he'd said too much. Now it was his turn to change the subject. "What do *you* do?"

Bernard wondered what made him suddenly deflect attention away from himself. Dead twin, unfinished PhD, "not getting too far" writing fiction—I guess he's had enough confession for one afternoon, he thought. He was enjoying the relative anonymity of being the one to ask the questions, and as usual he enjoyed listening to someone tell his story while hunting for other strains that were less explicit. Now he would have to disclose something about himself. Could he at least delay announcing that he was a therapist?

"It's funny you should talk about how to look at a portrait, or what it means to look at the image of a person, because that's actually very much related to the research I'm doing right now." He didn't want to be mysterious because he felt that doing so would only be another form of flirting, and he wasn't interested in flirting with this guy. "I'm a psychotherapist."

"Really?" Of course, Robin thought; no wonder I've been spilling my guts. Still, he didn't mind the fact.

Not wanting to give Robin any opportunity to express discomfort (as soon as you say you're a therapist, they start getting all weird on you, he thought), Bernard pressed on, "I'm writing an article on self-image. I'm working with mirrors, trying to get patients to look at themselves in the mirror and talk about what they see. It's sort of along the lines of Louise Hay; I don't know if you're familiar with her work, but she encourages her patients to say nice things about themselves out loud while looking into a mirror." He laughed. "It's sort of hokey, and I'm not doing *that*, exactly, with my patients, but it *is* revealing when a patient talks about what he sees in the mirror. I've also begun using portraits... "

"... uh huh... " Robin's curiosity was piqued.

"... having a patient describe what he sees when he looks at a portrait as an indirect way of prodding him to see—to begin to understand how he sees himself. It's still pretty unformulated."

Robin wondered what it would be like to be Bernard's patient. He was silent for a moment. Bernard felt his silence and wondered what it meant. Was he bored? Was he baffled? Did he want to get back to talking about himself? But so what if he does? Bernard thought. I'm not working; he's not my patient. I don't need to cater to him. He decided to say more, conscious of pushing himself to do something that didn't come naturally when talking with a stranger—though he felt Robin wasn't a stranger, somehow. He often felt this with gay men who were more or less his age.

Meeting gay men and feeling that almost instant connection was still a novelty for him, even though it was now almost ten years since he'd left the monastery and come to New York. But there was a barrier, he could tell, with Robin. He felt the familiar tug, but at the same time an aversion, and he suspected it came from his sense that here was a person whose self-esteem was fundamentally damaged, so much so that it poisoned every move he made, every word he said, every reaction he had to the world and the people around him. Bernard didn't want to get roped into it, but a little further conversation, he thought, wouldn't hurt either of them. And for all the sudden intimacy of their conversation, he felt something oddly impersonal about it, something—the word emerged almost visually in his brain—*anonymous*.

"I don't know much about art, not formally, anyway," Bernard ventured, "but I *do* know what I like." Robin smiled. "I bet everyone who knows nothing about art says that," Bernard added, also with a smile.

"They do, actually," Robin said with a soft laugh, feeling himself at that moment immensely attractive and loving the idea, which had never occurred to him before, of getting a therapist to talk about himself.

"OK, so, I don't know much about art, but I love museums."

"Really? Why?"

"They're quiet. They're clean. They exist… " He thought of St. Ann's being torn down outside his living room window. "… so that, in a way, people can come to worship the objects inside."

"Worship?" Robin said, knitting his brow. The idea seemed freakish.

"I feel like I'm in church when I'm in a museum." Anticipating that Robin, like so many educated gay men, would automatically recoil at the mere mention of church, he added, "I mean that in a good way." But now he stood at another precipice. He wondered if he dared to reveal more. Robin seemed glued to what he was saying. He decided to take the dive, and as he prepared himself to do so, he remarked at his own willingness, today, here with Robin, to talk about himself. He had been wanting, ever since he'd become HIV positive, to reveal more of himself to his patients. Let Robin be a test case, he thought. "I used to be a monk."

Robin gave him a challenging, almost adversarial look. "For how long?" he asked.

"Ten years."

"That's a long time. Where?"

"South Carolina."

"So why did you leave..." He groped for the right word. "...monkhood, monkdom?" He laughed. "Sorry."

Bernard laughed too. "It's OK. The monastery."

"Monastery, of course!"

"Monastic life, religious life. The shining path."

"Isn't that a terrorist organization?"

"There are many paths to God." Bernard enjoyed being able to exchange irreverent banter about religious life with a friendly stranger. "I left... " Again he hesitated. Yet another precipice. But he kept going. "I left because I couldn't be a self-respecting gay man and stay in the Church. I mean, the institutional Church. The real Church is just people, and it's much bigger than the official one."

As Robin listened, a feeling of warmth gradually spread through his body. He wondered if it might be a fever coming on and if perhaps he ought to sit down. He was hungry and his mouth was dry, but he was too involved with what Bernard was saying to make a move. He wondered if what he was feeling was some kind of genuine attraction to Bernard. A hundred questions clamored in his head, but he quickly summed them up into just one. "What was it like being a gay monk?"

Bernard decided not to go any further. He felt the enormity of the question.

Into his mind crowded images and thoughts of Chris, of his narrow bed at the monastery, of the intensity of feeling his presence at Vespers, of their walks around the farm, of Chris's refusal to let Bernard touch him in public, of the long night Chris said goodbye and Bernard's tears and anger, of his weekends in the city and the guys he picked up, of the night he had unprotected sex with the musician from Toronto and his panic afterward, of his terrifying visit to the doctor a month later and taking the test and going for the test results the next week and the impenetrable look on the doctor's face when he ushered him into the examination room and the way he stood there in his long white coat holding his chart and talking about other things besides the one thing Bernard needed to know—about lipids and cholesterol, and he was negative for gonorrhea, syphilis, and chlamydia, and then he said, almost as an aside, "The test does show some traces of HIV in the blood, but there's another test we should do for confirmation because this one only shows evidence of *some* HIV in the blood, but it doesn't tell us how much, and in any case with a test like this we *have* to repeat it because sometimes the test comes out to a false positive," and the doctor's words blurred and became meaningless sound as what Bernard had just been told pounded into his being, some traces of HIV in the blood, HIV in the blood, HIV positive, *you are now HIV positive—*

What was it like being a gay monk? All he could say was, "You'll have to find out for yourself." And both Robin and Bernard laughed, and their laughter was brittle, for together they realized they had come to the end of at least this particular avenue of conversation.

Robin tried another approach. "So you think being in a museum is like being in church?"

"Did I say that? A little while ago I was thinking it was like a train station, actually. But *church* is like a train station sometimes!" He could see that Robin wanted to know more about him. He tried not to be evasive. "I guess I just meant something about the quiet. It's rare nowadays to find any kind of public space where you don't hear Top 40 music playing. At least not in New York."

"That's so true," Robin said. He thought of the sex club and the thumping dance music they always played there.

"Here it seems at least some people are content to be alone with their thoughts. I like that about museums. And maybe it's not like church in the sense that church is often where you go for community. Looking at art objects is more like prayer—private prayer—or the Latin Mass, where you stand alone before God, as we say in the monastery."

Bernard rolled his eyes as he said "as we say in the monastery" because he still didn't trust that Robin's apparent interest in his religious life wasn't laced with scorn. He wasn't ready to speak in all sincerity about matters that remained, ten years after he'd left professional religious life, enormously important to him.

But Robin wasn't feeling scorn. The idea that there could be a religious dimension to looking at art, or at least a resemblance between a person's behavior in a museum and his conduct in a religious setting, only made him take his passing thought about the music in the sex club more seriously, and it now occurred to him that a museum was not unlike a sex club in that both involved a kind of idolatrous looking at objects, or people, or people as objects. At the sex club, at least when pursuing a guy down corridors, up steps, into the showers, and on and on, nobody said a word. It was a silent game of looking, stalking, pursuing, pulling away. Maybe that's one of the reasons why, Robin thought with a sparkle of insight, I love looking at portraits.

"I guess the difference between prayer and looking at a painting," Bernard went on, seeing the sparkle in Robin's eye and thinking it was a direct response to what he was saying about prayer, "is that when you pray... Well, there are different kinds of prayer. There's prayer with words, but then there's another level of prayer that goes beyond words. And to get to that level, you have to empty your mind of all thoughts and images."

"How do you do that?" Robin asked, still thinking about the sex club and its affinities with the museum—and, for that matter, its affinities with church.

"It's not something you do by force of will. It takes time as you gradually withdraw your attention from things outside yourself to... " Here Bernard wanted to say "the kingdom of your own heart," remembering the words of St. Makarios, whose homilies he'd read as a novice ("Within the heart are unfathomable depths. There are reception rooms and bedchambers in it, doors and porches, and many offices and passages... The heart is Christ's palace"). But of course he couldn't say anything like that to someone he'd just met, and especially not to Robin, whom he didn't quite trust. So he simply said, "the things within." He rolled his eyes. "It's not easy to talk about prayer. I could never get to that level of prayer. I think I was always too worldly; I love the flesh too much. That's why when I look at certain paintings of Jesus all I can think is how sexy he is. I don't *want* to get beyond the image. Pale skin, long dark hair, flat stomach—what more could you want?" he laughed, and remembered his last conversation with his spiritual director, who told him that some men were not cut out for rigorous feats of self-denial, that complete isolation was probably not good for him. He felt like a failure, but he knew Bruce was right. Chris may not have been the right man for him in the end, but their relationship revealed how much need he had of a man, both physical and emotional, and how, if he were being honest with himself, the institutional Church would never be the place to fulfill that need. He thought again of St. Ann's, with its roof peeled off and the tender blue of its inner walls exposed to the harsh sunlight and the dirt and noise of downtown Manhattan.

Suddenly he felt he'd said enough. It was time to leave. He had a patient coming at 7:30, he told himself, and needed to get back to his office to review his notes.

"Hey, I don't mean to be rude," he started, "but I think I should be going. I have a patient this evening, and..." He stopped, deciding there was no reason to apologize.

Robin was relieved. For just when Bernard mentioned Jesus' "flat stomach," he glanced for a split second at Bernard's waist and noticed that he had a belly, and suddenly the feeling of warmth, which had arisen when Bernard was talking about his life as a monk, began to cool. I'm not attracted to him, he said to himself, at least not physically. He wasn't even sure he was attracted in any other way. Something about his reference to the body of Jesus made Robin uncomfortable. He worried that Bernard might be on the verge of asking him out on a date, and he didn't like to be put in the position of having to turn someone down. It made him feel like a jerk, and he hated it when guys made him feel like a jerk. At the same time, he was angry with himself for not finding Bernard more appealing. Bernard was intelligent, not bad looking, not in terrible shape; he was sensitive, seemed stable, had an interesting past. Why couldn't Robin fall for guys like this? Why was it always some piece of ass he'd met at the sex club? Why prefer anonymous and dangerous sexual encounters to an encounter like this?

"No, that's fine, I need to get going myself," he said, feeling the need to make it look as if it was his idea to end the conversation as much as Bernard's. "I'm just gonna take a spin through the last room, and then I need to get home," he added, in case Bernard should see that he wasn't in a hurry to leave and conclude that he had nothing else to do, nowhere else to go, no one waiting for him. He might have added, "because I haven't eaten all day," but that might quickly lead to a disclosure of what he did last night, and though he wanted to tell someone like Bernard what happened, he couldn't. For now, he would have to keep it to himself. He thought he probably ought to see a therapist, maybe one like Bernard—a kind, intelligent, gay therapist—and a feeling of panic swept over him as he saw Bernard reaching out to shake his hand.

"Well, it was nice to meet you, Robin."

"Same here." But not wanting to let him go without some hope of a reunion, Robin said, "Hey, let me give you my email address. Let's continue the conversation some time." He took the pad and pen from his back pocket, jotted the address, tore out the page, and handed it to Bernard.

Bernard suspected that Robin needed a therapist, not a friend. But he wasn't interested in any further exchange. "OK," he said simply. "Thanks. Enjoy the rest of your day." And he walked into the next room.

Robin returned to the label. **VELAZQUEZ'S PORTRAIT OF JUAN DE PAREJA IS UNIQUE IN THE ANNALS OF RENAISSANCE DEPICTIONS OF BLACK AFRICANS.** He felt like such a fool. "Enjoy the rest of your day," he repeated to himself. He hated the expression. It meant "we can and will share no more." **PAREJA IS SHOWN WITHOUT ANY OBVIOUS ATTRIBUTES SIGNALING HIS IDENTITY, THUS ENCOURAGING THE VIEWER TO SEE HIM SIMPLY AS A HUMAN BEING.** What have I done? Robin wondered. Why did I offer my email address like that? And why didn't he offer me his in return? **HIS EXPRESSION IS SERIOUS AND HIS BODY IMPOSING, AN EFFECT HEIGHTENED BY THE PLACEMENT OF THE FIGURE TO THE LEFT OF CENTER,** Why did he end the conversation so abruptly? **WHICH TENDS TO ENERGIZE THE SPACE AROUND HIM.**

Robin was tired and hungry. He felt a slight chill. But he would finish studying the Velazquez painting. At least he would do that. **ON CLOSER INSPECTION, HOWEVER, VELAZQUEZ'S INTENTIONS WITH REGARD TO HIS SUBJECT BECOME LESS CLEAR. PAREJA IS SHOWN IN THE COARSE, DRAB-COLORED CLOTHES OF THE WORKING MAN; THE PLAINNESS OF HIS GARB IS, IRONICALLY, EMPHASIZED BY THE INCONGRUOUS GRANDEUR OF HIS WHITE**

Portraits at an Exhibition   169

LACE COLLAR. ADDITIONALLY, VELAZQUEZ HAS CAREFULLY PAINTED A HOLE IN PAREJA'S SLEEVE AND LEFT SEVERAL BUTTONS MISSING FROM HIS JERKIN, SUGGESTING, PERHAPS, A JAB AT PAREJA'S GENTLEMANLY PRETENSIONS. If he was such a valued servant, Robin wondered, and if Velazquez believed the greatest gift he could give him was the gift of freedom, why risk even an ambiguous statement in his depiction of Pareja? He felt a rising irritation. All that rhetoric about the "gift of freedom" may have been just that—rhetoric. And anyway, what did it mean that freedom was a "gift" you could bestow on another person, as if it was a material object you either possessed or didn't possess, transferable from one to another, like an antique vase or a valuable painting? Whatever else you might say, a portrait was an object. Looking at a portrait may have something to do with looking at a real human being, he thought, but when you looked at a portrait you were looking at an object. He thought of the sex club, of all the hours he spent there, week after week, looking at guys. The whole business of looking started to feel slightly corrupt. FINALLY, PAREJA WEARS A SWORD STRAP, BUT HE CARRIES NO SWORD. A SLAVE IN 17TH-CENTURY SPAIN WAS FORBIDDEN TO CARRY ARMS EXCEPT WHEN TRAVELING IN HIS MASTER'S RETINUE. Pareja is unarmed, Robin thought with indignation. He had been so impressed with Velazquez's realistic technique, but it was beginning to seem that, far from being "realistic," the painting was an elaborate, even wasteful joke at the slave's expense. All that was needed to complete the insult was a gap-toothed grin or a slew of cheap, glittery rings on his pudgy fingers! Fucking asshole.

ONLY A HANDFUL OF PAREJA'S OWN WORKS SURVIVE, THE GREATEST OF WHICH, *THE CALLING OF SAINT MATTHEW* (1661), HANGS IN THE PRADO IN MADRID (SEE RIGHT). THIS PAINTING IS OF SPECIAL INTEREST BECAUSE IT CONTAINS, AMONG A CROWD OF ONLOOKERS, PAREJA'S OWN SELF-PORTRAIT. Robin glanced at the figure of Juan de Pareja at the far left of the tiny image. The face was narrower than in the Velazquez painting, the facial hair more manicured. The expression was haughty, even blase. **PAREJA'S IMAGE OF HIMSELF DIFFERS STRIKINGLY FROM VELAZQUEZ'S DEPICTION.** Robin looked again at the Velazquez portrait. The face seemed weathered, molded by at least forty years of experience. The white highlights on the face conveyed the impression of sweat. **PAREJA GIVES HIMSELF MORE ARYAN FEATURES,** There appeared to be circles under the eyes, **A MORE FASHIONABLE BEARD,** a weak chin hardly concealed by the goatee, **AND AN APPEARANCE AT LEAST AS YOUTHFUL AS VELAZQUEZ'S DEPICTION OVER A DECADE EARLIER.** and a feeling of heaviness in the face that was echoed, it now occurred to Robin, in the roundness of the torso, the plumpness of the right hand, and the downward curve of the cloak. He glanced at the reproduction of *The Calling of Saint Matthew*. Pareja depicted himself as a "finer" gentleman, but the rendering was shallow and uninteresting as art. But so what? What good was an artist's talent if he had nothing to say, or worse, if what he had to say was bullshit? **JUST AS CURIOUS, THOUGH HE UNDOUBTEDLY LEARNED TO PAINT IN VELAZQUEZ'S EMPLOY, PAREJA'S STYLE SHOWS LITTLE TRACE OF HIS MASTER'S INFLUENCE; HIS AFFINITIES AS AN ARTIST TEND MORE TOWARDS THE ITALIAN BAROQUE.** The look in the eyes that Pareja painted for himself inspired no thoughts of any kind in the viewer, Robin felt, whereas Velazquez managed to capture in the eyes of his slave—Robin focused his gaze now on the mysterious black depths of Pareja's eyes—a look of wariness. That is the quality that appealed to me from the beginning, he thought. He looks cautious, hesitant, even slightly afraid. And if you take into consideration the way Velazquez dressed him (but who's to say Pareja didn't choose the clothing himself?), the hole at the sleeve, the missing buttons, the missing sword (a kind of castration, Robin thought)—if you add it all up, you could argue that Velazquez's portrait is the ultimate compliment. For it is Pareja's vulnerable humanity, in spite of the failed trappings of respectability (failed not only, perhaps, because his master could never fully recognize his humanity, but because, even if

Velazquez was a better, kinder, more well-meaning master than most, he was still the master, Pareja was still the slave: theirs was a slave society)—it is Pareja's humanity, Robin finally decided, that emerges in this portrait. He felt the sting of tears.

But why should I be so moved? he asked himself as the tears came to the verge and then retreated. He thought of the photograph he kept on his bedside table of Stephen with Catherine and Elizabeth on Elizabeth's third birthday. Stephen is seated with Catherine in his lap, and she, in turn, struggles to hold Elizabeth as she springs out of the frame, reaching for their dog, Zoogpup, whose tail alone is visible among the fallen birthday balloons and discarded wrapping paper. The photo wasn't his "style" in the sense that he didn't go for that kind of sentimental family photo (in fact, its saving grace, he felt, was that it was taken at the "wrong" moment, when Elizabeth was squirming out of the picture altogether), and he tried not to clutter up his home and workspace with stock photos of his "significant others." He hated that expression. Who are my significant others anyway? he silently asked the portrait of Juan de Pareja. I have none, unless you consider a dead man your significant other. He thought of Bernard. He imagined him dressed as a monk, standing in a cotton field in South Carolina. Then he saw him wearing civilian clothes, sitting in a book-lined office opposite a couch. He saw himself lying on the couch. What would he say to Bernard if he were his therapist? First he would talk about last night. What was he going to do if he was HIV positive? He should get tested. But the thought of going for the test and the agony of waiting for the results was unbearable. He couldn't do it. He *wouldn't* do it. And what was so wrong with Bernard that he couldn't see him as a potential romantic partner? Was it all because of Bernard's physical flaws? Was he so superficial?

Robin looked at the face of Juan de Pareja. The most astonishing thing about him, he thought, is the fact that he was an artist. But it isn't his *self*-portrait that gets the praise; it's someone *else's* view of him. But Juan de Pareja, at least, had Diego Velazquez to teach him to paint. He thought of Stephen, his "role model." There must be consolations even in the most degraded of lives. But why assume Juan de Pareja's life was degraded? What did it mean to him to be a slave? What did it mean to be free? How did he regard his master? What were his aspirations? The figure of Juan de Pareja assumed massive proportions in Robin's eyes, and he looked and looked at the face of the black man who stared back at him like a lion and was so lifelike he seemed to move a fraction of an inch. He would never understand Juan de Pareja. He would never know the meaning of the look in his eyes. Pride? Cunning? Suffering? Sorrow? Did Velazquez intend to say anything at all about him, or did he just record what he saw and then let the portrait speak for itself? If he could speak, Robin wondered, what would Juan de Pareja say? *I, Juan de Pareja, was born...* No, it was a silly schoolroom exercise. Juan de Pareja, as far as he was concerned, was nothing more than paint. Oil on canvas. All the rest—the sensation of reality, the depiction of "character," the tracing of the motions of the mind, the plumbing of the inner life through the representation of physiognomy—it wasn't that none of that mattered, but it was always someone else's hypothesis, someone else's fantasy of who the sitter was and what he was thinking. And the artist? He might have been preoccupied with a thousand things other than the task at hand, even if skill guided his brush, controlled his instincts, and dictated his method. Artist-subject-viewer: we exist in isolation from each other, Robin thought, forever and for all time.

Just then he saw Bernard in the next gallery. He thought Bernard had said he was leaving to see a patient. He lied to me, Robin realized. He didn't need to rush off to a session; he just wanted to get away from me. Robin stood before the portrait of Juan de Pareja but peered at Bernard through the entrance to the last gallery of the exhibition. Bernard stopped in front of a small painting, then walked away outside his line of sight. Robin stepped a few feet to the right in order to see if he had gone to look at another painting in the same gallery or if he had left the exhibition altogether. He couldn't see Bernard anywhere. Probably gone for good.

Now it was safe to go into the next room. The worst thing imaginable, he thought, would be to cross paths with him after they'd already said goodbye, after he'd given him his email address. For then they would have to pretend not to see each other, or they would look at each other without acknowledging they were no longer strangers. Or they would have to say goodbye all over again. If there was one thing Robin couldn't stand, it was a goodbye.

The gallery was thinning out. Only half an hour left. She looked forward to spending a couple of hours after work reading—that is, if she wasn't too tired. She might not even answer the phone, which she was sure would be ringing off the hook. People were so predictable: calling to wish you happy birthday on your birthday! Sometimes she thought she should have been a Jehovah's Witness. They didn't believe in birthdays, and when she found out why, she thought it made so much sense: you didn't make yourself, God did, so why do you have to be going around proclaiming your big day?

She saw the young man with glasses walk into the last room of the exhibition. Why had she kept her eyes on him? Dozens of visitors had come to the exhibition today, but there was something about him that caught her attention, that called out to her. He seemed naked, somehow. Other people gave the impression of passing through, of being on their way to somewhere else. Most people, she would say, had come in pairs or small groups. True, there were a few by themselves, but this young man seemed truly lonely—maybe that's what caught her attention. Even when he was talking with that other guy, as she had observed a little while ago (they had bumped into each other in the self-portrait gallery, and then, when she started working in this room, she noticed the two of them standing and talking in front of the Velazquez portrait)—even then, she got the distinct impression that he was an isolated person. He had no crutch to hold him up; he might be standing on his own two legs, but he didn't look strong. The more she thought about him, the more she found herself touched by something in him. She didn't often get this feeling about people, but the sensation came upon her with increasing frequency, she had begun to notice, ever since she entered graduate school. More and more she regarded strangers, white people especially, with a kind of curiosity she didn't used to feel. She thought it might be the result of all the reading she was doing. Reading opened up the world to her in a new way. Now when she looked at a stranger, her first thought was of how little she understood, how many possibilities existed, how that person could turn out to be almost anything in the world. In a weird way, it made people seem both more remote and more likeable. Loveable, even. But what kind of love depended on distance?

She opened her book. *"You're in a great hurry to get rid of me," said his lordship quite dismally.*

"Not in the least. But I hate paintings"—hate paintings? But Isabel—oh—*partings* (she had misread the word). *"I hate partings."*

Hate partings. I hate partings...

She was stuck on something in this scene. Isabel hated partings but was sending Warburton away. She wants to be alone, Dora said to herself, but she hates to be *left* alone. *They shook hands, and he left her alone in the glorious room, among the shining antique marbles. She sat down in the centre of the circle of these presences, regarding them vaguely, resting her eyes on their beautiful blank faces; listening, as it were, to their eternal silence. It was as if the company of statues was more congenial to her than the company of real* people. Why? she wondered. Perhaps with their blank faces she could fill them in as she liked. *Isabel sat there a long time, under the charm of their motionless grace, wondering to what, of their experience, their absent eyes were open, and how, to our ears, their alien lips would sound.* Maybe the fascination of wondering, Dora thought, makes the company of statues the best. Their "absent eyes," she thought, their "alien lips." *People* were aliens, and that meant you had to keep your distance from them. Keeping your distance meant you could appreciate them. Up close, you had to smell them, talk to them, listen to them, feel for them, but at a safe distance you could treat them—she looked around her at the walls lined with portraits—like works of art.

She wanted to stretch her legs. She walked over to the portrait of the black man by Velazquez. She had heard a docent giving a tour of the exhibition the other day, and he had stopped in front of this one and talked for a long time about Velazquez and his relationship to his servant, his workshop assistant who was also his slave. Dora pretended not to be listening because the docent and everyone in the group were white, and she felt exposed when they were discussing the painting, as if they were talking about her. As soon as they left, however, she hurried over to the painting and read the label. She hadn't looked at him yet today, so she decided to pay the brother a visit. He had the big, wet eyes of a newborn baby. The whites of his eyes looked a little pink, as if he'd been crying. There was an innocence in his eyes that hadn't struck her before. She looked at the label to the right of the painting, at the little reproduction of—what was his name? Pareja?—of Pareja's painting, *The Calling of Saint Matthew*, and the detail showing his self-portrait. She would like to see the actual painting, not just some tiny reproduction. But even in reproduction she found the image fascinating. She wasn't surprised that the way he portrayed himself differed from the way Velazquez saw him. What was the line Isabel gave Warburton the first time she rejected his marriage proposal? "We see our lives from our own point of view; that is the privilege of the weakest and humblest of us." She remembered one of the people in the group asking the docent why art historians assume Velazquez's portrayal is more trustworthy than Pareja's. That was a good question. Probably because Velazquez is a universally acknowledged master, whereas Pareja, if he is known at all, is considered third-rate. But she didn't feel she could judge what made one painter great and another mediocre. She looked more closely at the reproduction of *The Calling of Saint Matthew*. She didn't know who was who. Well, it was obvious that was Jesus standing on the right, although she noticed His features didn't have the delicacy artists usually gave them. Actually, He looked Jewish, she thought. The man with the turban sitting at the end of the table—perhaps he was Saint Matthew? She tried to make out the white spot over his head—a halo? Then she saw a small, dark head just above Saint Matthew's head, peeking out from around the pillar behind him. It was the head of a little black boy. His skin wasn't just dark; it was ebony. And unless you were looking carefully (what was that series of picture books for kids? *Where's Waldo?* They were Louis's favorite)—unless you were searching for him, you could easily miss him. But there he was. Funny, Dora thought. Juan paints himself, let's say, lighter than he really was, but in the same painting he puts a little ebony-colored boy hiding behind a pillar. It started to seem like some kind of sly commentary. She looked again at the face of Juan de Pareja in the Velazquez portrait. There he sat with his impressive cape, his posture erect, his fancy white collar. She looked at his eyes. She thought of her friend Patrice. She was the kind of person who made you laugh just from looking at her. It probably wasn't anything in particular she did with her face, just the effect of knowing her and the kinds of things that came out of her mouth. Outrageous things! Patrice was, no question, the funniest person she knew. She looked into the big, black, wet, babyish eyes of Juan de Pareja and thought, I don't know what's behind those eyes. I only know what *I* put there. That's what I see when I look in your eyes. She turned away, not with a sense of defeat but with a feeling that Juan was an ally. The truth *was* in his face, but it wasn't a truth about skin color.

She leaned against the threshold between this and the last room of the exhibition. She saw the young man with glasses peering closely at a little portrait of an old man. It was getting late. She thought she ought to tell him not to get too close, but she had already said that to him this afternoon. She preferred, for the moment, just to watch him. Now he turned and walked to the center of the room and sat down on the circular sofa. He slumped a little bit. He looked tired, almost like he was going to faint. Should she approach him? She thought of Isabel Archer, sitting in the middle of the Capitoline Museum, surrounded by statues. She opened the book. *At the end of half an hour Gilbert Osmond reappeared, apparently in advance of his companions. He strolled toward her slowly, with his hands behind him and his usual enquiring, yet not quite appealing smile.* "*I'm surprised to find you alone, I thought you had company.*"

"*So I have—the best.*"

She felt her cell phone vibrate in her pocket. She pulled it out and saw there was a text message from Marion. "happy bday mommy! we love u! if u change ur mind we will come after dinner. with cake. louis wants 2 sing 4 u." Her heart leapt. Of course she wouldn't refuse her daughter and her grandson. It meant she probably wouldn't get any reading done tonight. She looked at her watch. In ten minutes she would start making the announcement. The young man with glasses was now leaning his head back on the sofa, like he was asleep, even though his eyes were open. Maybe she should be true to her original plan to spend the evening alone. Marion and Louis could come over tomorrow night, or she could go to Jersey City for the weekend. Well, she didn't have to decide this minute. She looked at the young man, slumped on the couch, his eyes wide open, staring up at the ceiling. She felt the strongest impulse to walk over and speak to him. But what would she say? She didn't want to disturb him. More than anything—and the thought sent an unaccountable surge of warmth through her body—she wanted to know what he was thinking.

HANS MEMLING (C.1435-1494)
PORTRAIT OF AN OLD MAN, 1475-80
OIL ON WOOD

Hans Memling
Portrait of an Old Man

Out of the depths I cry to You, O Lord. Hear my voice! Let Your ears be attentive to my pleading.

Lord, I yearn to withdraw from the comfort of creatures and find sweet consolation in You. But I do not find it at once, nor without sorrow, toil, and effort. Old habits stand in my way, and I despair of overcoming them.

If it is dreadful to die, it is more dangerous to live long. I grow foolish and forget my mortality. Every day I become less mindful that the road I travel is leading towards death.

The desires of my senses call me to roam abroad, but when their hour is spent I bring back nothing but a burdened conscience and a distracted heart. My inner life is greatly hindered by the appetites of my body.

I have not prepared my heart sufficiently, Lord, so that You may come and dwell within me. I have not loved You enough. I have not kept Your word.

I have made my home here on Earth rather than in Heaven. I have put my trust in the perishable things of this world. I have become entangled with transitory things, though I do not know them at their true worth, only as they are said or reputed to be. My knowledge comes from man, not from You, Lord.

I am unduly influenced by outward things. Prayer does not come easily to me. My outward occupations and needful tasks distract me, and my inner life is disordered. I am troubled by the strange and perverse ways of others. They hinder and distract me.

I pay too much attention to what men say of me, for I do not take heed to what I am within. I cling to other creatures and fall with them when they fall. I put my trust in windblown reeds. I ride fortune's wheel.

I open the doors to the desires of my senses. I put aside the things of eternity and seek the things of time. I listen more willingly to the world than to You, Lord, and prefer the desires of my body to Your holy pleasures. I serve the world with great eagerness in hopes of reaping its benefits, while my heart is indifferent to Your rich and eternal rewards.

I rely overmuch on my own quenchless desires without asking Your counsel, Lord. Hence I grow displeased with what first pleased me and for which I was eager. I act upon every feeling that seems good. I immediately reject every feeling that runs contrary to my inclinations.

My mind wanders, and my lack of discipline causes offence to others. I am confused and upset by the opposition of others.

I give in to my sensual appetites, indulging what my body likes and dislikes. My flesh is unruly, uncorrected, and disobedient. It takes no pleasure in simple things and is discontent with little. At every hardship, my body complains. I subdue my spirit to my flesh.

Lord, I find no rest in You, but only in created things: in a fur cloak, a good fire on the hearth, a soft bed, a glass of wine. How I enjoy all the rare and beautiful things of this golden world of Bruges: oranges and lemons from Castile, fruit and wine from Greece, fabrics and spices from Alexandria, furs from the Black Sea, rosaries made of amber and African ivory!

I hate the cheap and clumsy. I take no pleasure in simple and humble things. Instead I prize lovely houses and streets, fine churches and monasteries, excellent inns. I despise the rough. I refuse to wear old and ragged clothes. I take pleasure in the world's wealth, am angered by a slighting remark, grieve at every loss. I ignore things eternal; I am attached to the temporal. The loss of worldly goods moves me. Hard words anger me. I lay up my treasure and joy here on Earth, where everything can be lost.

I am neither comforted nor content that Your holy will and the good pleasure of Your eternal purpose should be accomplished in me. I prefer to be accounted the greatest of men. I find peace only in first place; I am willing to be honored and exalted only among the great. I shun the outcast, the leper, the beggar, the nameless, the man of low reputation. Your will and the honor of Your name come last with me. I take greater comfort and enjoy richer pleasure in all other benefits.

I give nothing of myself to You and keep back everything from You. My love is tainted, adulterated, and wayward. I am the slave of things. I hanker after things I may not rightly have and seek to possess things that hinder my spiritual progress, that rob me of inward freedom. I am unwilling to trust myself to You with all my heart, together with all I desire and enjoy.

I exhaust myself with useless grief. I burden myself with needless anxiety. I want this thing or that only to satisfy my convenience and pleasure. I am never at rest nor free from care. There is always something that does not please me, and everywhere I find someone who opposes my wishes.

I see my advantage in winning and accumulating possessions. I love riches, honors, and vain praise. I am obsessed by self-interest and self-love, the plaything of my desires. I am greedy and inquisitive. I spend myself in pleasure but never in Your service, Lord. My whole interest is in passing affairs.

I exchange what You hold in high esteem for what men consider desirable and honorable. Having an exalted opinion of myself, I seek recognition from the world. I disregard true heavenly wisdom. Too often it seems useless and unimportant. I give lip service to it, but it plays no part in my life.

I fear mortal man, though he is here today, gone tomorrow. He injures me, and he appears to escape Your judgment, Lord. I judge by outward appearances rather than asking Your guidance. I take little refuge in prayer to support me amidst the dangers and wickedness of men. I take little refuge in the depths of my heart. I neglect to pray for Your help.

I am always more ready to slip back than to go forward. I never remain the same. I am discouraged if I see others given honors and advancement while I am overlooked and humiliated. The contempt of men troubles me.

I am subject to weariness and sadness of heart. My body is a burden and hinders me from giving myself wholly to the life of the spirit and to divine contemplation.

I make pilgrimages to various places to visit the relics of the saints, wondering at the stories of their lives and the splendor of their shrines. I view and venerate their bones covered with silk and gold. When visiting such places, I am moved by mere curiosity and the urge for sightseeing, and seldom does any amendment of my life result, especially as my thoughts and conversation are trivial and lack true contrition. Only levity, curiosity, and sentimentality draw me, not firm faith, devout hope, or sincere love.

I revel in the company of my friends and relations. I boast of noble rank and high birth. I make myself agreeable to the powerful, flatter the rich, and acclaim those who are like me. I do not love my enemies, I take pride in the number of my friends, and I think much of high birth even when it is allied with low virtue. I favor the rich rather than the poor. I have more in common with the powerful than with the honorable. I admire the deceiver, not the honest man. I constantly encourage men to labor for earthly gifts in order to become more like me and less like You. I am curious to know secrets and to hear news. I love to be seen in public and enjoy sensations. I relish the torment inflicted upon others.

I am unholy and impure. My heart is corrupt and unfit for You to dwell in. My heart is unprepared and unclean. The world and its sinful clamor have crowded into my heart.

I cling to the consolations of this fallen world. I crave human companionship. I prefer the comforts of other men to Your will. Though I know we must all be parted from one another at last, still I grieve over the death of my wife. And yet it is less the absence of my dear one I bemoan than the inevitability of my own death.

I dread the thought of having to pass through the gates of death. Even more, I fear the endless torment that awaits me there. Last night I dreamt of a mountain of sand as large as the universe. Every 100,000 years a grain would be taken from it. I knew the mountain would disappear at last, but my suffering would be no nearer its end than when the first grain was removed. I awoke in terror!

This morning I sit alone like a sparrow on a rooftop and consider my sinfulness and bitterness of soul. Though now I endeavor to prepare the best and fairest room for You, Lord, and in so doing attempt to show You my love, I know that even my best efforts cannot make a worthy preparation for You, even if I were to prepare for a whole year and do nothing else besides. For it is of Your mercy and grace alone that I am allowed to approach Your table, as though a beggar were invited to a rich man's supper and could offer no return for his kindness save humble gratitude.

Lord, though I do not burn with so ardent a desire as those who are supremely devoted to You, still I long to feel that great and burning desire. I beg and pray that I may have a part with all Your true lovers and be numbered in their holy company.

Grant me, most dear and loving Jesus, to rest in You above created things: above all beauty and health, above all glory and honor, above all power and dignity, above all knowledge and skill, above all fame and praise, above all sweetness and consolation, above all hope and promise, above all merit and desire, above all gifts and favors that You can bestow and shower upon us, above all joy and jubilation that the mind can conceive and know, above angels and archangels and all the hosts of Heaven, above all things visible and invisible, above everything that is not You Yourself, O my God.

Strengthen me, Lord God, by the grace of Your Holy Spirit. Grant me inward power and strength, and empty my heart of all profitless anxiety and care. Let me never be drawn away from You by desire for anything else, whether noble or base. Help me never to forget that all things are passing, including myself. For nothing in this world is lasting. Everything is uncertain.

How wise is the man who knows these truths! Though I pronounce them, I do not live by them. Grant me heavenly wisdom, Lord, that above all else I may learn to search for and discover You, to know and love You, and to see all things as they really are, as You in Your wisdom have ordered them. May I prudently avoid those who flatter me and deal patiently with those who oppose me. True wisdom cannot be swayed by every wordy argument and pays no regard to the cunning flatteries of evil men. Only thus shall I go forward steadily on the road on which I have set out.

May You grant in one short moment, Lord, what You have withheld for a lifetime.

Alas, my Lord, there are many fires, but the flames never ascend unaccompanied by smoke. Though now I burn for heavenly things, I am not yet free from the lusts of the flesh. I do not act solely for Your glory when I make such earnest requests of You. I do not place myself entirely in Your hands. I do not submit to Your correction. I dodge the blows You administer. My wayward stubbornness does not yield to Your will. I fear my very confession this morning is corrupt, insincere.

I say to myself, "Rise and begin this very moment! Now is the time to be up and doing! Now is the time to fight! Now is the time to amend!" But things go badly. I am in trouble. I put off my good resolutions.

How great is my frailty, Lord, ever prone to evil. Today I confess my sins, but tomorrow I commit the very sins I have confessed. Now I resolve to guard against them, but within the hour I act as though I had never made any such resolution.

It is vanity to give thought only to this present life and to care nothing for the life to come, to love things that so swiftly pass away and not hasten onwards to that place where everlasting joy abides. Yet my eye is too satisfied with seeing, my ear too filled with hearing.

I deceive myself by my inordinate love of the body. I live in enjoyment of all honors and pleasures, but how will these profit me when I die? Surely all is vanity except to love and serve You, Lord, and yet my love for You is selfish, my service half-hearted.

I forget my purpose and do not keep before me the likeness of Christ crucified. I do not try to conform myself to You. I seek other models besides You.

I see how they behave who live strictly under the monastic discipline. They seldom go out, live retired, eat the poorest food, work hard, talk little, keep long watches, rise early, spend much time in prayer, study much, and always guard themselves with discipline. They praise You, Lord, without ceasing, and they give themselves wholly to spiritual things. They seem much happier than I, who am compelled to serve the needs of my body.

I fear to take up the Cross. In the Cross is salvation, life, protection against my enemies, infusion of heavenly sweetness, strength of mind, joy of spirit, excellence of virtue, perfection of holiness. There is no salvation of soul, no hope of eternal life, save in the Cross. You have gone before me bearing the Cross. You died for me on the Cross that I also may bear the Cross and desire to die on the Cross with You. For if I die with You, I will also live with You. And if I share Your sufferings I will also share Your glory. But I seek to arrange all things according to my own ideas and wishes, and so I find suffering. I find bodily pain and anguish of mind and spirit. I find the Cross. But I flee from it.

I do not love to dwell within Your sacred wounds. I have not sought the precious marks of Your passion.

It is true that I do not enjoy the pleasures of this life without bitterness, weariness, and fear, for the very things from which I derive pleasure carry with them the seeds of sorrow. Having sought and followed my pleasures to excess, I do not enjoy them without shame and bitterness. Ah, how short-lived and false, how disorderly and base, are all these pleasures! Yet so besotted and blind am I that, like a dumb beast, I persist in pursuing them and so bring death to my soul for the trivial enjoyments of this corruptible life!

I cannot rest in You, Lord. My heart does not find its peace in You alone. If You are the heart's true peace, then my heart is restless and broken, for I am not ready to suffer in You. I only wish to be carefree. I am unwilling to be needy and poor. I want only wealth and plenty.

Too often I forget, Lord, that whatever powers of soul and body I still possess, outwardly or inwardly, natural or supernatural, they are Your gifts and they proclaim Your love and bounty. I, who have received abundant gifts, boast of my merits, exalt myself above my fellows, and despise any who are less richly endowed. I hold myself in high esteem and judge myself most worthy.

I abandon truth for illusion, the spirit for the flesh, the Creator for created things, eternity for things of time, light uncreated for light created. My lower nature is strong within me. It is not yet wholly crucified, nor is it entirely dead. It still fights strongly against the spirit, stirring up conflicts within me, and will not allow the kingdom of the soul to remain at peace.

Lord, I wish to hold fast to heavenly things, but worldly affairs and desires that I cannot master hold me down. I wish my mind to rise freely above all these things, but my body holds me captive. Thus I struggle unhappily with myself. I am a burden to myself, for while my spirit longs to mount toward Heaven, my body wishes to remain below. I long for close communion with You but cannot attain to it.

I slide backwards with corrupt, doubting faith. I come to the Sacrament with pride and cravenly hide from You all that I do not understand. I am deceived, for I put too much trust in myself. Yesterday as I passed by the Hospital of St. John, I saw a beggar in the street. He smiled and wished me good day. I looked him in the eye but continued on my way, giving him neither a penny nor even a kind word. His conviviality, I thought with disgust, was a mere show, a mockery of the kindness he asked of me. I was burdened with my own cares and anxieties. What did I have to offer him? Had I remembered You in that moment, dear Lord, I might have seen You in the face of that filthy beggar. For You walk with the simple, reveal Yourself to the humble, give understanding to children, disclose Your secrets to pure minds, and conceal Your grace from the conceited and curious. You grant healing and comfort to those in distress. You raise up to Your divinity those who acknowledge their weakness and make their confession.

"Blessed are you when they insult you and persecute you and utter every kind of slander against you because of Me. How blessed are the poor in spirit: the reign of God is theirs. Blessed too are the sorrowing; they shall be consoled. Blessed are the lowly; they shall inherit the land. Blessed are they who hunger and thirst for holiness; they shall have their fill. Blessed are those persecuted for holiness' sake; the reign of God is theirs." I speak the words of Your holy sermon, Lord, but they do not penetrate my heart.

Lord, I fear You are far away from me. I fear the battle is almost lost. Things do not turn out according to my plans. I allow the feelings of the moment to obscure my judgments. I yield to depression as though all hope of recovery were lost. I feel utterly forsaken. Yet rather than struggle against difficulties, I persist in my selfish desires.

I know that I need Your grace in fullest measure, Lord, to subdue that nature which always inclines to evil from youth up. For it fell through Adam, the first of men, and was tainted by sin, the penalty of Adam's fault descending upon all mankind. Thus the nature that You created good and upright has now become old, crooked, and corrupt.

The little strength that remains in me is only a spark, buried beneath ashes. Yet this same natural reason, though hidden in profound darkness, retains the power to know good and evil and to discern truth and falsehood. But it is powerless to act upon what it knows to be good. It enjoys neither the full light of truth nor its former healthy affection.

Thus, O Lord my God, it comes about that while I may at times inwardly delight in Your law and know Your commands to be good, just, and holy, both for the condemnation of all evil and the avoidance of sin, yet in my body I serve the law of sin and obey my senses before my reason. While I may possess the will to good, I find myself powerless to follow it. In this way I make many good resolutions, but, through lack of grace to support my weakness, any small obstacle causes discouragement and failure.

Thus, too, I know the way of perfection and see clearly what I ought to do, but I am weighed down by the burden of my corruption and advance no nearer to perfection.

My life has lost its foundations. I am weak and see no way to amend my life. When the opportunity for self-surrender arises, I do not seize it.

And yet... how can You O Lord expect me to remain always in a state of virtue when this was not possible even for an Angel of Heaven or the first man in the Garden?

For I am not an Angel, but a man. I am not God, but only human.

I understand nothing.

Robin entered the last gallery of the exhibition with a distracting wish to know where Bernard had gone, though he didn't understand why. There was the exit, through which he could see some of the displays of the gift shop. Could he be there? Against his better judgment he walked swiftly to the exit. No sign of Bernard in the shop. So he must have left the museum after all, like he said. Maybe something about that particular painting caught his eye and he couldn't help but stop to look at it on his way out. He turned around and saw the tiny portrait, a picture of an old man. It was hung in the center of the wall with only one portrait on either side of it. Surrounded by so much white wall space, it looked from a distance like a dark, precious object. He walked toward the painting, and the closer he got the more he realized he needed to get closer still in order to really see it. For the portrait was the size of a closed book. Even a foot away from it seemed too far. He wanted to press his nose against it. He turned and saw the guard, who seemed to have followed him in from the previous gallery. She must have thought his movements—rushing toward the exit, then turning back and making a beeline for the painting—a little strange. Well, never mind; let her think what she wanted. He was too preoccupied to care what anyone else thought.

He stationed himself in front of the portrait, but his thoughts followed Bernard out of the exhibition. Where had he gone? Was he still somewhere in the museum? Did he go to the men's room? And why did he care? He had decided he wasn't interested in him, but then at the last minute he gave away his email address. Bernard, in turn, offered nothing except a polite goodbye. Robin felt he was owed something more, as if he had given Bernard a valuable gift and gotten a piece of coal in exchange. But what had he given that was so valuable?

He applied himself to the label. **THIS DEEPLY SYMPATHETIC PORTRAIT OF AN ELDERLY GENTLEMAN IS A MIRACLE OF NATURALISTIC OBSERVATION AND PAINTERLY VIRTUOSITY.** He read the words, but they competed with thoughts of his conversation with Bernard. **MEMLING EXACTINGLY RENDERS** What had they talked about? Religious life. Being a gay monk. **THE JOWLS ON EITHER SIDE OF THE MOUTH,** Robin had said something silly about working in the gallery—no, it was worse than silly, it was self-denigrating. **THE SPIDER'S WEB OF TINY WRINKLES ABOUT THE EYES,** The phrase "spider's web" caught his attention, and he looked at the old man's eyes. He noticed the rims of red flesh on the inside of the lower eyelids—red, wet, trembling flesh. Suddenly it looked as if the old man's eyes were wet with tears. **INDIVIDUAL STRANDS OF SILVERY HAIR,** He looks like a monk, Robin thought, seeing the painting through the screen of his preoccupation with Bernard. It was something about his hair, the way it was combed, scrubbed clean, perhaps, utterly lacking in vanity. He thought of Bernard's belly, and he remembered what it was he said that instantly flipped the switch from intrigue to revulsion. Bernard had said how hot he was for images of the naked Christ—long hair, hard abs. For some reason he didn't want such intimate knowledge of what turned Bernard on. It was intimacy, he supposed, that he didn't want. Not *that* kind of intimacy, anyway. The waist, he thought, was one of the first places to show signs of aging on both men and women. A vulnerable strip of flesh, like the inner eyelid. After a certain point, he guessed, you couldn't keep it in any longer. You had to let it out, let it go. As soon as Bernard said that thing about guys with flat stomachs, Robin's eyes flashed to his midsection, and that's when he noticed he didn't have such a narrow waist. BITS OF GRAY STUBBLE UPON CHIN AND CHEEK, Was it frivolous to be turned off by a man with a belly? He remembered Eric once saying that Catholics turned into apples when they got old, whereas Jews turned into pears. He wasn't sure which was worse. He and Bernard would turn into apples. Oh God, never, he thought, and realized anew, as if he'd had his eyes closed all this time, that he was looking at the picture of an old man.

He started the sentence over again. MEMLING EXACTINGLY RENDERS THE JOWLS ON EITHER SIDE OF THE MOUTH, THE SPIDER'S WEB OF TINY WRINKLES ABOUT THE EYES, INDIVIDUAL STRANDS OF SILVERY HAIR, BITS OF GRAY STUBBLE UPON CHIN AND CHEEK, LINES IN THE SKIN ACROSS THE KNUCKLES, AND THE PERFECT FIT OF FINGERNAILS INTO FLESH. You could appreciate these kinds of things in a painting, he thought ("a miracle of naturalistic observation and painterly virtuosity"), but it was altogether different, he added, if they were the things that confronted you every time you looked in the mirror. He took a step back. He wanted to pry himself away from the examination of details and see the old man as a whole person; he had started from the wrong end of the telescope. There he was. The old man. His head was turned slightly to the side and tilted down a bit. His eyes looked... it was hard to tell whether they looked at something in particular or at nothing. Was he caught in the act of observing, or was this the image of a man thinking? Was his gaze turned outward or inward? He thought it was incredible on the part of Memling that a painted face could be made to look as though it were actively thinking ("Motions of the Mind," he remembered) as opposed to looking at something outside of itself. Perhaps still more amazing, he thought, was the fact that the expression on the face was open to interpretation, unless we as humans so strongly identify with the image of the human face—it could be the merest cartoon, a mere yellow smiley face with black dots for eyes and the letter U for a mouth—that we project onto it all kinds of shades and colors that are not really there. **THE PORTRAIT, HOWEVER, IS MORE THAN A BRILLIANTLY REALISTIC STILL LIFE OF THE HUMAN FACE AND HANDS.** The words of the label seemed to keep pace with his thoughts rather than the other way around. Now the old man seemed to erect himself a fraction of an inch, the result, Robin figured, of seeing just now for the first time the whole outline of the figure and feeling the contrast between the warm, yellowish skin tones and the dark blue-green background. Indeed, the old man seemed to thrust himself forward toward the viewer, almost as if he were peering out of the darkness of a room, through a window, which was the picture frame, with his hands perched on the window ledge, peering into the viewer's own space. It was disturbingly lifelike.

Robin swallowed and felt the dryness in his throat. He reached into his pocket in hopes of finding a lozenge or piece of gum. Nothing. He wanted a drink of water. Too much trouble, though, to go in search of a water fountain. He'd be finished soon. He could buy a bottle of water from one of those street vendors at the entrance to the museum. Probably charge three dollars—for a lousy bottle of water! Maybe he could survive until he got home. But that wouldn't be for another hour at least.

Mixed with the dryness in his throat and the fatigue in his limbs was another nagging discomfort. Something he'd said to Bernard was bothering him. It wasn't the self-deprecating remark about being a shop girl, or the banter about monastic life—all the flirty things one says when meeting a possibly eligible man for the first time. No, it was something else. He ran through the conversation more carefully. They had talked about art history. He was describing his dissertation, his interest in the Renaissance. He said something about not finishing his dissertation. He was explaining *why* he hadn't finished it, was that it? Telling all his problems to a therapist he'd just met—what a cliché! But Bernard's reply seemed equally scripted: "I'm sorry." What was he sorry about? That he hadn't finished his dissertation?

Stephen! He had mentioned Stephen. He said he had a brother who died. And Bernard said, "I'm sorry." But he couldn't know what to be sorry about; it was just one of those things that therapists say, that people in general say when you tell them about a death in the family. He'd spoken about Stephen. He wished he hadn't done that. Not to this guy. But why? Was it because he was a therapist? Was that why he felt guilty for having mentioned Stephen? But why *not* mention Stephen? And who *better* to mention him to than a therapist? As soon as they started talking he felt he could trust him, felt in some way he already knew him, knew him well enough to mention Stephen. God knows he felt comfortable enough telling him he wasn't attracted to the painting of the black man! But Stephen... It was one thing to make a fool of himself; it was another to make a fool of Stephen. *Had* he made a fool of Stephen? All he'd said was that he had a brother who died. But he was explaining why he never finished his dissertation. He was using Stephen's death to explain something else, to explain a failure of his own, and to do that, he thought, was to cheapen Stephen's death. To make it the means to some other end rather than the end in itself. To subordinate it to something rather than to subordinate everything else to it. To *use* it, rather than—the image of a golden calf burning on a pyre came into his mind—rather than to worship it. Stephen's death was sacred. It was not to be tampered with. It was to be worshiped or not to be spoken of at all.

"The sorrow for the dead is the only sorrow," he thought, "from which we refuse to be divorced" (he remembered the words from Washington Irving's *Sketch Book*). "Every other wound we seek to heal, every other affliction to forget; but this wound we consider it a duty to keep open; this affliction we cherish and brood over in solitude." He had given his email address to Bernard, but Bernard hadn't offered his in return. He had spoken about his dead brother to a perfect stranger, whom he would probably never see or hear from again. He had been unfaithful to Stephen, and his reward for being unfaithful was... nothing at all. He looked around the gallery, as if Stephen had been let out of hiding and was now wandering the world on his own. He might be found standing before a painting on the opposite wall. Robin scanned the room. There stood the guard. A few others meandered about: a woman pushing a baby stroller, and that young couple he'd seen at the entrance to the exhibition, still arm in arm. It must be getting late. He looked at his watch. Four-thirty. Soon they would start kicking people out.

He felt compelled to finish reading the label, even though he probably wouldn't have walked up to this particular portrait if it hadn't been for Bernard. He had seen Bernard looking at it, and so he had to look at it too. Bernard probably thought this old man was as marvelous as any other portrait in the exhibition. Good for him, since he's a therapist. He imagined that, as a therapist, you were always having to "take people where they're at," as his boss, Leonore, liked to say. She'd been in therapy all her life, or at least since her twenties. She would never finish therapy, it had become so much a part of her daily life. He could appreciate the skill of a portrait like this, but it didn't captivate him as some other portraits had, like the one of the little boy and his mother, or the Botticelli portrait of the young man. Those paintings excited some kind of desire in him, he thought, whereas this one... He looked again at the red rims beneath the old man's eyes. I am attracted to the portraits of beautiful young men, he said to himself and thought wearily of *The Picture* of *Dorian Gray*. He had begun rereading it over the weekend. That book, he thought, will follow me until the day I die. He remembered the blood coming out of his penis, and a chill shot through his body. It was easy to dismiss the flouncy characters and melodramatic plot, but he had to admit that Wilde was on to something. **WITHOUT EVER QUITE PROBING THE SITTER'S CHARACTER** He recalled that long chapter where Dorian goes in mad pursuit of all kinds of antiques—priests' vestments, exotic jewels, Renaissance tapestries, Medieval manuscripts—and starts collecting one thing after another, bouncing from one obsession to another. You get the sense that Dorian doesn't really know what he's doing, doesn't really understand his own urges, but his urges overtake him and fill the pages completely. He remembered discussing the book in a graduate seminar, and he was the only one in the class who hadn't skimmed over that chapter of the book, "the aptly named Chapter Eleven" the professor wryly called it. He had felt somehow, at least at that point in his life (he was writing his dissertation, Stephen seemed to have stopped drinking for good this time, and they were getting reacquainted with each other, warily, now that he had come out as gay)—he had felt that Dorian's appetites made perfect sense. It was, he remembered confessing to the class, perhaps naively, his favorite part of the book, the *only* part, he said, where Dorian seemed a recognizable human being. As soon as he said it, the entire class burst out laughing. He felt at the time as though he'd triumphed by making them laugh, but now he wondered if there wasn't an element of derision in their laughter.

(INDEED, THE IMAGE SEEMS TO CONCEAL RATHER THAN TO REVEAL THE OLD MAN'S THOUGHTS), He was interested in this idea of the sitter whose thoughts are concealed, of the portrait that first makes us wonder what the sitter is thinking, then makes us feel as though the sitter's thoughts are off limits. He thought about the sex club and how hard it was to tell just from looking at a guy what he was thinking. He remembered the first time he ever went to the sex club with his friend Michael. He was nervous and self-conscious, dressed only in a white towel around his waist. He felt all his imperfections were on display. He walked around and around the maze of hallways and saw plenty of guys who appealed to him, but he didn't know whom to approach or even how to make an approach. Michael, meanwhile, had hooked up with someone and was nowhere to be found. Then he spotted a slender, olive-skinned, dark-haired guy with glasses. He had a pretty face. He sat on his bed in his room, leafing, oddly enough, through a comic book. Robin stopped outside his door. The guy glanced up from his book and smiled. Others walked by, but the dark-haired, dark-eyed, sweet-faced guy remained fixed on his comic book, only now and then glancing up to see if Robin was still there. Robin figured he must be somewhat attracted to me, otherwise why would he keep on looking up? On the other hand, he wasn't making any moves that clearly indicated he wanted Robin to come into the room. Finally Robin stepped across the threshold, and as soon as he did so the guy firmly shook his head "no." Robin turned on his heel and fled, feeling as if he'd just received a blow. He was embarrassed. He decided it was time to leave. Without even waiting to find Michael to say goodbye, he got dressed and went home. It was another year before he got up the courage to try his luck again. For that's what it seemed to be all about—luck. After all, he asked himself, why is it someone like Michael, who's not especially good looking (at least not by conventional standards—kind of overweight, never works out, hair thinning on top)—why is it *he* finds guys to have sex with at the club, and sometimes even hot guys, but not me? It seemed like a meaningless game of roulette. He didn't know how to read the faces of the men he found there. He couldn't tell what they were thinking, what they wanted. And gay men were notoriously good, he thought, at hiding their feelings. They wore the mask.

MEMLING NONETHELESS MANAGES TO CONVEY A SENSE OF INNER STRENGTH DERIVED FROM YEARS OF EXPERIENCE, But it wasn't just other men whose desires mystified Robin. Looking at the old man and going over in his mind the conversation with Bernard, he had to admit that often he didn't know what *he himself* wanted, didn't even know sometimes (how strange not to know something presumably so basic) whether or not he was attracted to a person. Bernard said he didn't know much about art but he knew what he liked, and he was smart enough to suspect everyone said that kind of thing. It was ignorance, of course, that motivated a statement like that. The response Robin always made silently in his head was, "No, you *don't* know what you like. You have opinions, mere opinions. But an opinion is something based on nothing." **AN ATTITUDE OF GENTLE FORBEARANCE,** He was proud of the fact that if he didn't know something about a topic, he kept his mouth shut. **AN AIR OF CONTEMPLATIVE CALM,** But that meant he was often left waiting for someone else to show him the way, to explain how to think and feel. Or else he was in the position of reacting to someone else, to what other people said or wanted, rather than speaking and acting for himself. He didn't like it in other people, but the ability to just throw out an opinion—to say, "I like this, I don't like that, I want this, I don't want that, here's who I am, this is what I do, take it or leave it"—there was some kind of idiotic power in that ability to speak up for oneself. To know yourself, if "knowing" yourself was indeed what it was all about. You could get through life like that, **A STATE OF SPIRITUAL REPOSE** or at least get through the day. **—IN SHORT, AN IMPRESSION OF THE OLD MAN'S DIGNITY AND THE DIGNITY OF OLD AGE IN GENERAL.**

"Ladies and gentlemen, the museum will be closing in 15 minutes."

He turned around to look at the guard who had just made the announcement, but when he looked at her she stood stock still, silently looking back at him from across the room as if to pretend it wasn't she who had spoken. Their eyes met for what seemed to Robin an eternity (it might have been two full seconds). He thought there was a challenge in her expression. He averted his gaze. **MEMLING'S COMMISSIONS CAME LARGELY FROM WEALTHY BURGHERS, COURT FUNCTIONARIES, AND MEMBERS OF THE ITALIAN BANKING COMMUNITY OF BRUGES. THE ITALIANS IN PARTICULAR FAVORED PORTRAITS WITH LANDSCAPE BACKGROUNDS (AN INNOVATION IN THE GENRE OF PORTRAITURE PIONEERED BY MEMLING), WHILE LOCAL PATRONS FAVORED NEUTRAL BACKGROUNDS IN KEEPING WITH THEIR MORE CONSERVATIVE TASTES. THE OLD MAN, THEN, MAY WELL HAVE BEEN A LOCAL COURT FUNCTIONARY OR MERCHANT.** He shifted the weight of his body from one leg to the other. He felt he couldn't stand much longer. Just as well the museum was closing soon. His fatigue seemed to grow heavier by the minute. **THE PORTRAIT IS CLOSELY RELATED IN DIMENSION, STYLE, AND OVERALL APPEARANCE TO MEMLING'S *PORTRAIT OF AN OLD WOMAN* IN HOUSTON'S MUSEUM OF FINE ARTS (SEE RIGHT), LEADING SCHOLARS TO SPECULATE THAT THE TWO PORTRAITS ONCE FORMED A DIPTYCH IN CELEBRATION OF A LONG AND SUCCESSFUL MARRIAGE.** Now that he was about to leave, his hunger and thirst felt more powerful than ever. What would he do about dinner tonight? There was a piece of leftover chicken in the refrigerator. But he hated leftovers; he wanted something fresh. He felt he owed it to himself to have a big, delicious dinner, to somehow make up for everything that was missing from his day. He felt like going out to dinner, but he didn't like dining alone in public. It would be nice to have someone to go out with, of course, but on such short notice and on a Tuesday night there was no one he could think of to call. That meant staying home and ordering in. Maybe Indian food, always good for comfort when he needed it. He realized, as he thought about what he might eat for dinner, that he wanted comfort. But not just comfort *food*. He wanted to *feel comforted*. He'd had a similar craving last night as he sat home alone, going back and forth in his mind, should I go to the sex club, should I not? It wasn't horniness that sent him out onto the street at 11pm to find a taxi ("Manhattan—14th Street and Eighth Avenue," he said to the driver, wondering if somehow the driver knew what he was going there for, could see right through him) when any rational person, tired at the end of the day, would have stayed in, curled up with a book or watched TV until falling asleep, which, if he'd allowed himself, probably would have happened by midnight. No, it wasn't horniness, exactly. It was a desire for closeness. Maybe I'll meet the man of my dreams, he had thought. Maybe I'll meet a beautiful young man who will sweep me off my feet and make me feel...

LESS CONCLUSIVE HAVE BEEN ATTEMPTS AT DATING THE PORTRAITS. THE PORTRAIT OF AN OLD MAN CANNOT BE DATED DENDROCHRONOLOGICALLY (THAT IS, BY STUDYING THE GROWTH RINGS OF THE WOOD ON WHICH IT IS PAINTED) BECAUSE THE PANEL IS SET INTO ANOTHER PANEL AND SHOWS NO ORIGINAL EDGES. DENDROCHRONOLOGY OF THE HOUSTON PORTRAIT, MEANWHILE, IS OPEN TO INTERPRETATION. THE EARLIEST POSSIBLE FELLING DATE OF THE TREE IS 1470; WITH A MINIMUM OF TWO YEARS' DRYING AND STORAGE TIME FOR THE SMALL PIECE OF WOOD, ANY DATE BETWEEN 1472 AND 1480 IS POSSIBLE.
He saw the tall, thin tree shake its leaves, dislodge itself from the surrounding trees, and come crashing to the forest floor. The image appealed to him. Somewhere in the trunk of that tree, he thought, is the wood upon which the face of this old man would one day be painted. He fancied the face of the old man impressed on the trunk of the tree even as it stood in the forest. One night a traveler, lost in the woods, might happen upon that spot in the forest, see a mysterious, glowing rectangle in the trunk of the tree, hasten toward it, and kneel down in awe before the face miraculously emanating from the side of the tree. He might pour forth in confession before the tree, *Out of the depths I cry to You, O Lord. I yearn to withdraw from the comfort of creatures and find sweet consolation in You, but old habits stand in my way and I despair of overcoming them.*

Hans Memling (c. 1435-1494) was the most successful portraitist of his generation in the Burgundian Netherlands. Employed as a young man in Rogier van der Weyden's Brussels workshop, the German-born Memling became a citizen of Bruges in 1465, the year of Rogier's death. By 1483 he was married. His wife died no later than 1487, leaving him with three children. He thought of Elizabeth. She was only four when Stephen died. **Little else is known about his personal life.** What would my biography say? Robin asked himself ruefully. Born September 7, 1971, Westfield, NJ, twenty minutes after a twin brother, Stephen. Branded a faggot by classmates on first day of first grade, 1979. Compensated by getting straight A's. Father died of alcohol-related heart failure, 1986. Came out as gay freshman year, Columbia College, 1991. BA in English, summa cum laude,1994. Started PhD in art history, Harvard, 1995. Brother died of drug overdose, 2000. PhD dissertation abandoned, 2002. Moved to East Williamsburg, Brooklyn, 2002. Works on staff in Manhattan art gallery, 2002 to present. Spends free time reading books, writing fiction (not for publication), serially dating, and having risky, anonymous sex. The end.

What was happening at work tomorrow? He couldn't remember if the Jack Pierson press release was due Friday or next Monday. He tried to visualize his date book for the rest of the week. Anything happening in the evenings? Not until Monday, when Catherine comes to town. It was the fifth anniversary of Stephen's death. Their odd, yearly ritual. He had to remember to make a dinner reservation somewhere. Too bad she wasn't bringing Elizabeth this time; he always enjoyed Catherine more in the company of his niece. Which reminded him, he needed to clean the apartment this weekend. His heart sank at the thought. There goes half the weekend. But what else would he be doing if not that? He was more than halfway through *Dorian Gray*, which he would easily finish before Catherine arrived. Then he wouldn't mind their long conversations in the evening, the ones that circled around and around but somehow always managed to avoid the topic of Stephen's death. (Why was it so hard to talk about Stephen? He was their reason for getting together in the first place!) At least he would feel as if he'd done something productive. But tonight? Right now he wanted to go home and lie down, take a nap. But he didn't want the day to end like that. He didn't want to go back to work tomorrow either. He wanted... The face of Joe from last night appeared to him. He wanted to meet someone like Joe, someone who would kiss him and hold him and make him feel...

He looked at the portrait of the old man. He thought he detected a look of disapproval in his eyes. It seemed to be the effect of the angle of his eyebrows, sternly slanting down towards the bridge of the nose, but also the line of the mouth. It went straight across, with a slight downturn at each end. The jowls increased the sense of that part of the face falling, as if in a grimace. He looked tight-lipped, as if he were repressing a disapproving remark or bravely holding out against some injustice or scandal he could see before his very eyes. He seemed heart-sunk at the sight of it, whatever it was—"the depravity of the world" was the phrase that came to Robin's mind. But the more he looked into the old man's eyes, the more he lost the sense of reproach he saw there. The lines in the forehead, the knitted brow, the sagging cheeks, the grim, down-turned mouth—they were all simply the marks of old age. He remembered a group of school kids visiting the gallery one day a couple of weeks ago, and their teacher had asked them to describe their reaction to a photograph of an old woman on display. "She looks angry," a number of them agreed. The remark seemed cruel, not only because young people's ignorance of the feelings and concerns of their elders seemed to him cruel by definition but also because, on some level, he felt they must be right. Being old, growing old, seeing your powers diminish, seeing the body decay, finding your freedom more and more restricted, having to accept the end of youth, health, and beauty, the end of your life closing in upon you—it must, on some level, maybe entirely unconscious, make you angry. The divide between the old and the young: he wondered if it wasn't the most basic human divide there is (certainly it was a fault line running right through the gay community). For I, he started to say to himself, and again thought of Dorian Gray, for I feel the years slipping away. In September I will be 34. I alone. Stephen was dead. He would never be older than 28, his father never older than (he did the calculation—born July 1952, died June 1986)—my God! he said to himself. In September I will have surpassed the age of my father when he died. I will have outlived them all. He didn't know if it was cause for celebration or weeping. He looked at the old man's hooded eyes. They seemed softer, more sympathetic ("This deeply sympathetic portrait of an old man... "). They were red-rimmed, as if tears might well up at any moment. He may still be gazing, Robin thought, upon the sins of the world, but the world's iniquity, suffering, and pain have pressed themselves into his face, like carving in the bark of a tree. He looks with sorrow, not reproach, at the fallen world. There is nothing he can do but turn to God for help. His hands are folded. There is nothing else he can do, nothing but look and bear witness.

MODERN ASSESSMENTS OF MEMLING'S WORK HAVE RANGED FROM THE DERISIVE— ERWIN PANOFSKY FAMOUSLY DISMISSED HIM IN 1953 AS "THAT VERY MODEL OF A MAJOR MINOR MASTER... WE FEEL INCLINED TO COMPARE HIM TO A COMPOSER SUCH AS FELIX MENDELSSOHN: HE OCCASIONALLY ENCHANTS, NEVER OFFENDS AND NEVER OVERWHELMS"— But now he really did need to sit down. He turned his head and again locked eyes with the guard. Disturbed by what he felt was her censorious presence, he hesitated to make a move, but decided, finally, his need for a moment's rest outweighed his discomfort at being watched. **TO THE SOMEWHAT BEGRUDGINGLY RESPECTFUL—A RECENT BIOGRAPHER CALLS HIM "ONE OF THE KEY PAINTERS OF FIFTEENTH-CENTURY BRUGES—**

ALONGSIDE JAN VAN EYCK, PETRUS CHRISTUS AND GERARD DAVID." He retreated to the settee in the center of the room, sat down, and looked at the portrait of the old man. From this distance it looked like nothing more than a dark rectangle amid vast stretches of white. He wished he could lie down, he felt so utterly exhausted. What was the matter with him? He'd heard of seroconversion accompanied by a flu-like syndrome, but if he'd contracted HIV last night the effects couldn't have come so soon. Could he have gotten infected some time before last night? He leaned as far back as possible, coming to rest in a slouching position. He folded his hands across his chest and tried taking long, deep breaths. He thought of Bergotte in *Remembrance of Things Past*. Reclusive, bored with a thing once he attained it, addicted to love as long as it enhanced his ability to write (it did so by evaporating his interest in society and just about everything else except the motions of his own mind and heart, hence its ability to spur his creativity), he suffered from insomnia and, when he did manage to steal a moment of sleep, from feverish dreams in which old women tried to suffocate him with damp rags and lunatic cabmen chewed his fingers like wild animals. Doctors and drugs proved ineffectual. He took his last breath in front of Vermeer's *View of Delft*. Moved by an art critic's assertion that one passage of the painting in particular, "a little patch of yellow wall... was so well painted that it was, if one looked at it by itself, like some priceless specimen of Chinese art, of a beauty that was sufficient in itself," he went to the gallery where the painting was on view to see it for himself. Thanks to the critic's words, his appreciation of the painting expanded. He saw things in the painting he never saw before—"some small figures in blue, that the sand was pink, and, finally, the precious substance of the tiny patch of yellow wall." He fixed his gaze on the patch of yellow wall. He felt dizzy. "That's how I ought to have written," he said to himself. "My last books are too dry, I ought to have gone over them with a few layers of colour, made my language precious in itself, like this little patch of yellow wall." Then "in a celestial pair of scales there appeared to him, weighing down one of the pans, his own life, while the other contained the little patch of wall so beautifully painted in yellow. He felt that he had rashly sacrificed the former for the latter." He chanted, "Little patch of yellow wall, with a sloping roof, little patch of yellow wall." He sank down onto a settee, rolled to the floor, and died. What am I, Robin asked himself, as if he lacked even the tiny dignity of Bergotte, and thinking of his nights at the sex club, barebacking, putting himself at risk for reasons he couldn't understand—what am I sacrificing my life for? And the white wall upon which was hung the tiny portrait of the old man, with a portrait to the left and a portrait to the right, turned black, and the portraits became rectangles of bright white. Then the edges of the rectangles blurred, he heard the clip clop of horses' hooves, a strange odor like glue filled his nostrils, daggers on fire came shooting down from the heavens, an old man begged for water but his voice was the sound of an infant crying, screaming so violently the cry of pain scattered a flock of birds beating their wings madly until the room was empty, and a voice woke the dead, the museum will be closing in ten minutes.

"The museum will be closing in ten minutes."

He raised himself a few inches on the settee and turned to look at the guard who had just made the announcement. There she stood, within arm's reach. She looked at him and spoke again, only now in a kind, personable voice, directed at him alone, even though there were three or four others still in the room. "We'll be closing in ten minutes," she said, smiling gently.

"Thank you," he answered, looking back at her and noticing, again, the purple flower at her lapel. A feeling of warmth spread through his body. His anxieties seemed to fall away. Grateful for a moment of simple, kind communication with a fellow human being, he stood up. He gained his balance with ease.

He walked up to the label next to the portrait of the old man. **BUT PERHAPS ONLY A LATE-ROMANTIC LIKE THE FRENCH PAINTER AND CRITIC EUGENE FROMENTIN COULD FULLY APPRECIATE MEMLING'S GALLERY OF SITTERS, ABOUT WHOM HE WROTE IN 1875, "THERE IS IN THEM AN INDESCRIBABLE AIR OF GRAVITY AND OF TRIAL UNDERGONE THAT MAKES THEM LOOK AS IF THEY HAD GONE THROUGH LIFE SUFFERING AND WERE MEDITATING UPON IT NOW."** I wonder if Bernard will send me an email tonight, he thought. Maybe when I get home I'll find a message waiting for me. **ON THE INTANGIBLE SPIRITUAL QUALITY OF MEMLING'S WORK,** He saw the icon of the mailbox with the little red flag raised. **"IMAGINE," HE WROTE,** The red flag which meant, you are not alone, someone wants you. **"IN THE MIDST OF THE HORRORS OF THE CENTURY, A PRIVILEGED SPOT, A SORT OF ANGELICAL RETREAT IDEALLY SILENT AND ENCLOSED,** A retreat, he thought. That's what I need. Not just a "personal day" or a weekend off, but a real retreat, a real escape to a place I've never been. I want to escape to a time and a place, he said to the old man, **WHERE PASSIONS ARE QUIETED**

"Where passions are quieted," he began to read aloud. He murmured the words of the label like a prayer:

AND TROUBLES CEASE,

"And troubles cease,"

WHERE PEOPLE PRAY AND ADORE,

"Where people pray and adore,"

WHERE EVERYTHING IS TRANSFIGURED,

"Everything is transfigured,"

PHYSICAL UGLINESS AND MORAL UGLINESS,

"Physical ugliness and moral ugliness,"

WHERE NEW FEELINGS ARISE,

"New feelings arise,"

WHERE SIMPLICITY,

"Simplicity,"

GENTLENESS,

"Gentleness,"

AND SUPERNATURAL MILDNESS

"Supernatural mildness"

GROW,

"Grow,"

LIKE LILIES—

"Like lilies—"

AND YOU WILL HAVE AN IDEA OF THE UNIQUE SOUL OF MEMLING, AND THE MIRACLE HE WORKS IN HIS PICTURES."

"The miracle he works... "

He looked at the old man one more time as if to say goodbye. He tried to see the entire picture at once, as if in so doing he could take it with him. Then he wouldn't feel torn from the object of his desire but would carry it with him always and everywhere.

He turned and approached the exit. On the wall just outside the gift shop hung a mirror about the size of the portrait he'd been looking at. He walked up to the mirror. He hesitated. Feeling a little foolish, he nevertheless forced himself to look at his reflection. Might as well play along, he thought. He regarded himself silently for a few seconds. His eyes darted around his face. They rested on a knot above the bridge of his nose. His brow was furrowed, which he hadn't realized. To him, his face felt at ease, normal, but looking in the mirror he saw that he was actually wearing a scowl. How long had he been doing that? he wondered. All day? He tried to relax the muscles in his face. Strange, it took more effort *not* to frown. He remembered how his father would always say to him, out of the blue, interrupting whatever he was doing or saying at that moment, "Robin, stand up straight!" and he was always surprised (apart from feeling mildly humiliated, for no one ever said that kind of thing to Stephen)—he was surprised he *hadn't* been standing straight. It meant that he never quite appeared to others as he thought he appeared, that the Robin others knew him to be was not exactly the Robin he understood himself to be. And which was the real Robin? He noticed the round shape of his head, more obvious now since he had cut his hair short. He observed the way his small, round glasses hugged his temples. He saw the magnification of his features through the distorting lenses. He saw his lazy eye. Brian once said his face had the asymmetrical beauty of a portrait by Picasso. What a liar. Then he noticed at the corner of his left eye a network of lines in the skin that he'd never seen before. "A spider's web of tiny wrinkles about the eyes," he remembered. He would turn 34 in September. He alone. That's still six years away from being 40, he thought. As for tonight—he pictured the living room of his apartment, the sofa and chair facing each other with no one there, the phone silent in its cradle, the street outside his windows empty of traffic and pedestrians, cars parked along the curb. He wanted a drink of water. He felt a powerful hunger. Yes, he said to himself, I'll go home, rest, make some dinner, shower, then go to the sex club. Maybe he would find Joe there again tonight. Maybe the blood meant nothing. He knew of guys who had lots of unsafe sex and never got HIV, and he knew of guys who were careful and used condoms and still got infected. Anyway, it was supposed to be less risky for the one on top. He thought of Joe and the feeling of holding him in his arms and the incredible sensation of sticking his hard dick up his ass (Joe hardly looked at him when they fucked—maybe it was just shyness), and he thought: you never know, tonight I may meet the man of my dreams, a beautiful young man who will sweep me off my feet and make me feel... real. At least for an hour or two. It could happen.

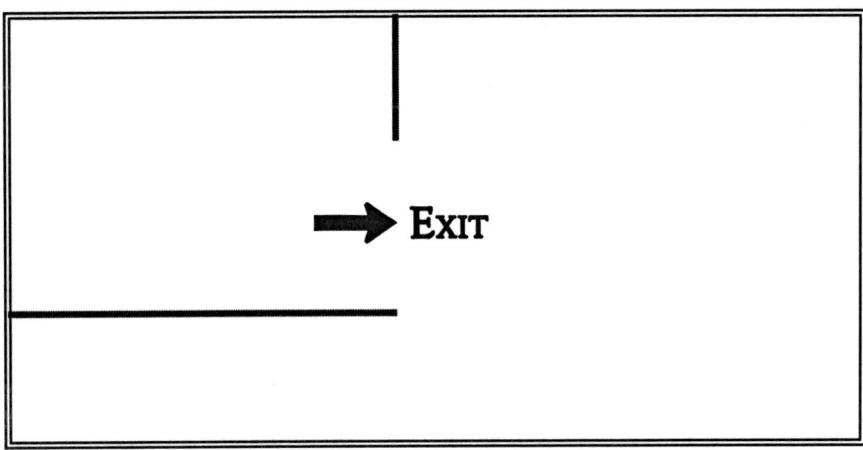

Leaving the mirror, he passed through the gift shop without, as was his custom, looking for a souvenir post card. For he had a purpose now. There was someplace he had to go tonight. He wended his way through one gallery after another towards the main exit. He walked, then ran, down the grand staircase and across the main lobby, prying loose his museum pin from the collar of his shirt and dropping it into the bin as he passed through the double doors. He stepped outside onto the landing, took a full breath of fresh, evening air, and tripped down the front steps of the museum. He stood at the curb's edge waiting for the light to change. He turned around and looked at the facade of the Metropolitan Museum of Art. People spilling out from the museum onto the sidewalk accumulated around him, all waiting to cross the street. He saw the enormous red banner hanging down the facade of the building, heaving in the wind. "MOTIONS OF THE MIND: The Renaissance Portrait and Its Legacy."

The light changed. Now the little group around him moved as one to cross the street. He moved with them, felt caged, then picked up his pace to get ahead. After a few vigorous strides he had the sidewalk to himself. Alone again, he thought with relief. Right now he was so hungry he could eat anything.

ACKNOWLEDGMENTS AND NOTES ON SOURCES

Portraits at an Exhibition is fiction. It takes place in New York City's Metropolitan Museum of Art in April 2005, at an imaginary exhibition featuring portraits that actually exist. Each chapter begins with a reproduction of a particular portrait in the exhibition along with a "flashback" to some other time and place associated with the history of that portrait. What follows is an accounting of the sources used in the making of those flashbacks and of the attendant wall text and labels that the contemporary characters read throughout the exhibition.

John Singer Sargent, *Portrait of a Boy*. The scene in which Sargent paints Augusta and Homer Saint Gaudens is indebted to several biographies: *John Sargent* by Evan Charteris, *John Singer Sargent: His Portrait* by Stanley Olson, *The Life and Works of Augustus Saint Gaudens* by Burke Wilkinson, and *Clover* by Otto Friedrich. Sargent's thoughts about his Boston mural project are inspired by *Painting Religion in Public: John Singer Sargent's Triumph of Religion at the Boston Public Library* by Sally M. Promey. The label associated with the Sargent portrait draws upon the three volumes of the *Complete Paintings* of Sargent by Richard Ormond and Elaine Kilmurray, *John Singer Sargent: The Sensualist* by Trevor Fairbrother, and *Great Expectations: John Singer Sargent Painting Children* by Barbara Dayer Gallati.

Image credit: John Singer Sargent, 1856-1925; Portrait of a Boy, *1890, oil on canvas, H: 59 ¾ in. x W: 56 in. (151.76 x 142.20 cm); Carnegie Museum of Art, Pittsburgh: Patrons Art Fund, 32.1.*

Sandro Botticelli, *Portrait of a Young Man*. The narrative of Yukio Yashiro's visit to London's National Gallery is inspired by Yashiro's 1925 monograph, *Sandro Botticelli and the Florentine Renaissance*, especially the preface to the

1929 revised edition in which the author responds to Roger Fry's criticism of the book. Additional support for my characterization of this art historian is provided by Yashiro's September 6, 1936 *New York Times Magazine* review of an exhibition of Japanese art in Boston; his essays for the *Bulletin of Eastern Art*, in particular his September 1940 tribute to Arthur Waley; and his introduction to *Art Treasures of Japan* (1960), a book which he also edited. Further sources on Yashiro and his milieu include "The Career of Professor Yukio Yashiro" by John A. Pope and Yashiro's address accepting the Charles Lang Freer Medal, published together in a 1965 memorial pamphlet by the Smithsonian Institution; *Being Bernard Berenson* by Meryle Secrest; *The Drawings of the Florentine Painters* by Berenson; *Roger Fry* by Virginia Woolf; and a pair of memoirs by Kenneth Clark, *Another Part of the Wood* and *The Other Half*. Information on Botticelli is drawn from Vasari's *Lives of the Artists* and *Botticelli: Life and Work* by Ronald Lightbown. Savonarola's speech is adapted from George Eliot's *Romola*. Jessica Collins of the National Gallery in London gave me access to the museum's files on the Botticelli portrait. The character of Luke is inspired by the artist Jeff Woodger.

Image credit: Sandro Botticelli, 1444-1510; Portrait of a Young Man, c. 1480-85, tempera and oil on wood, 37.5 x 28.3 cm; bought 1859 (NG626); National Gallery, London, Great Britain; image copyright: National Gallery, London / Art Resource, NY.

Albrecht Durer, *Self-Portrait in Fur Cloak*. The interior monologue of the contemporary German photographer Thomas Struth, while flying from New York to Dusseldorf at the dawn of the new millennium, is loosely inspired by Struth's life and work as discussed in catalog essays, especially "The Space of History" by Maria Morris Hambourg and Douglas Eklund, which accompanied the retrospective exhibition *Thomas Struth: 1977-2002* organized by the Dallas Museum of Art.

Further sources on Struth include *Portraits* from the 1990 show at the Marian Goodman Gallery in New York, *Thomas Struth: Portraits* from the 1997-98 show at the Sprengel Museum Hannover, *Thomas Struth: New Pictures from Paradise* from the 2002 show at the University of Salamanca and the Staatliche Kunstsammlungen Dresden, and Peter Craven's October 29, 2012 interview with Struth as part of Deutsche Welle's "Talking Germany" TV program. Information on Durer is drawn from *Albrecht Durer: A Biography* by Jane Campbell Hutchinson, *The Moment of Self-Portraiture in German Renaissance Art* by Joseph Leo Koerner, *The Life and Art of Albrecht Durer* by Erwin Panofsky, *The Hidden Durer* by Peter Strieder, and *Durer* by Stefano Zuffi. The character of Bernard is partly inspired by Gilbert Cole's *Infecting the Treatment: Being an HIV-Positive Analyst.*

Image credit: Albrecht Durer, 1471-1528; Self-Portrait in Fur Cloak, 1500, oil on board, 48.9 x 67.1 cm; inv. no. 537; Alte Pinakothek, Bayerische Staatsgemaeldesammlungen, Munich, Germany; photo credit: bpk, Berlin / Alte Pinakothek / Art Resource, NY.

Diego Rodriguez de Silva y Velazquez, *Juan de Pareja.* Pareja's soliloquy is partly inspired by Jennifer Montagu's November 1983 *Burlington Magazine* article, "Velazquez Marginalia: His Slave Juan de Pareja and His Illegitimate Son Antonio." Further information about Pareja and Velazquez comes from *Velazquez* by R.A.M. Stevenson; *I, Juan de Pareja* by Elizabeth Barton de Trevino; *The Metropolitan Museum of Art Bulletin* 29 (1971), which is devoted entirely to Velazquez's portrait of Pareja; *Velazquez* by Enriqueta Harris; and *Velazquez: Painter and Courtier* by Jonathan Brown. Ideas about slavery and Africans in Renaissance Spain come from various sources, including *Muslims in Spain, 1500-1614* by L.P. Harvey, *Black Africans in Renaissance Europe* edited by T.F. Earle and K.J.P. Lowe, *Aristocrats and Traders: Sevillian Society in the Sixteenth Century* by Ruth Pike, *The Golden*

Age of Spain, 1516-1659 by Antonio Dominguez Ortiz, *Slavery from Roman Times to the Early Atlantic Trade* by William D. Phillips, Jr., *The Making of New World Slavery: From the Baroque to the Modern, 1492-1800* by Robin Blackburn, and *Black Slaves and Freedmen in Portugal, 1441-1555* by A.C. de C.M. Saunders. I am especially grateful to Javier Portus, curator of seventeenth-century Spanish painting at the Prado, for allowing me to see Pareja's *The Calling of Saint Matthew* and for discussing it with me; to Marcus B. Burke, curator of paintings at The Hispanic Society of America, for showing and discussing with me the Hispanic Society's copy of Velazquez's portrait of Pareja; and to the staff of the Metropolitan Museum of Art's Central Catalogue for giving me access to the Met's files on Velazquez's portrait of Pareja.

Image credit: Diego Rodriguez de Silva y Velazquez, 1599-1660; Juan de Pareja, 1650, oil on canvas, 32 x 27 ½ in. (81.3 x 69.9 cm); Purchase, Fletcher and Rogers Funds, and Bequest of Miss Adelaide Milton de Groot (1876-1967), by exchange, supplemented by gifts from friends of the Museum, 1971 (1971.86); photo: Malcolm Varon; The Metropolitan Museum of Art, New York, NY, USA; image copyright: The Metropolitan Museum of Art; image source: Art Resource, NY.

Hans Memling, *Portrait of an Old Man*. The old man's prayer is based on passages from *The Imitation of Christ* by Thomas à Kempis. Sources on Memling and fifteenth-century Netherlandish painting include *Memling's Portraits* by Till-Holger Borchert; *The Mirror of the Artist: Northern Renaissance Art in its Historical Context* by Craig Harbison; the spring 1986 *Metropolitan Museum of Art Bulletin* by Guy Bauman; *The Age of Van Eyck: The Mediterranean World and Early Netherlandish Painting, 1430-1530* edited by Till-Holger Borchert; *From Van Eyck to Breugel: Early Netherlandish Painting in The Metropolitan Museum of Art* edited by Maryan W. Ainsworth and Keith Christiansen; and *Bruges and Europe* edited by Valentin Vermeersch. Sources on old age during the Middle Ages include *History of Old Age from Antiquity to the Renaissance* by Georges Minois and *A History of Old Age* edited by Pat Thane. Sources on medieval spiritual practices include *The Waning of the Middle Ages* by Johan Huizinga and *The Art of Devotion in the Late Middle Ages in Europe, 1300-1500* by Herik van Os. Roger S. Wieck, curator of Medieval and Renaissance manuscripts at the Morgan Library, gave me access to some of the Morgan's books of Hours and was kind enough to talk with me about them. His monographs, *Painted Prayers* and *Time Sanctified: The Book of Hours in Medieval Art and Life*, were also of assistance. Betsy Bing and the staff of the Metropolitan Museum of Art's Central Catalogue shared with me their files on the Memling portrait.

Image credit: Hans Memling, 1425/40-1494; Portrait of an Old Man, c. 1475, oil on wood, overall 10 3/8 x 7 5/8 in. (26.4 x 19.4 cm); painted surface 10 x 7 ¼ in. (25.4 x 18.4 cm); bequest of Benjamin Altman, 1913 (14.40.648); The Metropolitan Museum of Art, New York, NY, USA; image copyright: The Metropolitan Museum of Art; image source: Art Resource, NY.

Many thanks to Malaga Baldi, Sara Campbell, Elaine Freedgood, Marcy Arlin, William Burgos, Seymour Kleinberg, Michael Mallick, and Amy Pratt for their feedback on the manuscript; to Steve Berman, Riley MacLeod, and the staff of Lethe Press for their commitment to the book; to Matt Cresswell for his handsome design; and especially to Eduardo Leanez for his generosity of mind and heart every step of the way. Eduardo gives me courage to be an artist, and I dedicate this book to him.

Works Directly Quoted in Text

Abbot, Willis J. *Blue Jackets of 1812: A History of the Naval Battles of the Second War with Great Britain.* New York: Dodd, Mead, and Company, 1887.

Cervantes Saavedra, Miguel de. *Don Quixote*. 1604-1614. Trans. John Rutherford. Middlesex: Penguin, 2003.

Chariton, Igumen of Valamo, comp. *The Art of Prayer: An Orthodox Anthology*. London: Faber and Faber, 1977. [quote from St. Makarios in introduction by Timothy Ware]

Eliot, T.S. "The Love Song of J. Alfred Prufrock." 1915. *The Norton Anthology of English Literature*, 8th edition, Vol. 2. Ed. Stephen Greenblatt et al. New York: W.W. Norton, 2006. 2289-2293.

Fromentin, Eugene. *The Masters of Past Time: Dutch and Flemish Painting from Van Eyck to Rembrandt*. 1876. Trans. Andrew Boyle. London: Phaidon Press, 1948.

Fry, Roger. "Sandro Botticelli." Rev. of *Sandro Botticelli and the Florentine Renaissance*, by Yukio Yashiro. *Burlington Magazine* April 1926: 196-200.

Gracian, Balthasar. *The Art of Worldly Wisdom*. 1637. Trans. Joseph Jacobs. Boston: Shambhala, 1993.

Irving, Washington. "Rural Funerals." *The Sketch Book of Geoffrey Crayon, Gent.* 1820. *Washington Irving: History, Tales and Sketches*. New York: Library of America, 1983. 865-876.

James, Henry. *The Portrait of a Lady*. 1881. London: Penguin, 1984.

"Japanese Critic on Botticelli." Rev. of *Sandro Botticelli and the Florentine Renaissance*, by Yukio Yashiro. *Times Literary Supplement* 12 Nov. 1925: 745-746.

Melville, Herman. *Moby-Dick: or, The Whale*. 1851. London: Penguin, 1987.

Mirandola, Pico della. *Oration on the Dignity of Man*. 1486. Trans. A. Robert Caponigri. Washington, DC: Gateway Editions, 1999.

Montaigne, Michel Eyquem de. "Of Friendship." 1580. *The Complete Essays of Montaigne*. Trans. Donald M. Frame. Stanford: Stanford University Press, 1958. 135-144.

Nouwen, Henri J.M. *The Wounded Healer: Ministry in Contemporary Society*. 1972. New York: Image Books, 1990.

Panofsky, Erwin. *Early Netherlandish Painting: Its Origin and Character*. 1953. New York: Harper & Row, 1971.

Panofsky, Erwin. *The Life and Art of Albrecht Durer*. 1943. Princeton, NJ: Princeton

University Press, 1995.

Pater, Walter. *The Renaissance: Studies in Art and Poetry*. 1873. Mineola, NY: Dover Publications, 2005.

Proust, Marcel. *Remembrance of Things Past*. 1913-1927. Trans. C.K. Scott Moncrieff and Terence Kilmartin. New York: Vintage, 1982.

Saint-Gaudens, Homer. *The American Artist and His Times*. New York: Dodd, Mead, and Company, 1941.

Smith, Logan Pearsall. "Altamura." 1898. *Reperusals and Re-Collections*. New York: Harcourt, Brace, 1937. 76-84.

Author Photo: Robert Ordonez

Patrick E. Horrigan was born and raised in Reading, Pennsylvania. He earned a BA from The Catholic University of America and a PhD from Columbia University. He is the author of the memoir *Widescreen Dreams: Growing Up Gay at the Movies*, the play *Messages for Gary: A Drama in Voicemail*, and (with Eduardo Leanez) the solo show *You Are Confused!* He is Associate Professor of English at the Brooklyn campus of Long Island University and lives in Manhattan.

www.patrickehorrigan.com

CPSIA information can be obtained
at www.ICGtesting.com
Printed in the USA
FSOW02n1533031016
25682FS